Tennessee Murder Ballad

Heather Jones

Tennessee Murder Ballad

Copyright © 2023 Heather Jones.

Design: Heather Jones; Elizabeth Herrmann

Paperback: **979-8-9876864-0-9**

Ebook: **979-8-9876884-1-6**

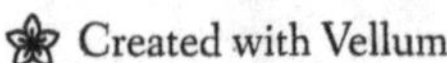 Created with Vellum

Tennessee Murder Ballad

Acknowledgments

I could not have written this book without Friday morning breakfasts with my writing buddy, Julie Armstrong. Thanks also to the rest of the prose posse, Tom Hallock and Anda Peterson, and to the staff at the Archives of Appalachia, Eastern Tennessee State University. My thanks and appreciation go to the many people who read, performed, and responded as this book developed from one-act play, to full-length play, to novel, especially to Jill Kelly Koren and Martin Billheimer, who generously read everything I write.

vii

The True Story of Ellen Bridges and How the Children Came to Be Cursed

In the year 1798, Ellen Calhoun was born in the mountains of East Tennessee. As she grew, Ellen's parents taught her what she needed to know: how to hunt, how to make medicine from plants, how to midwife babies, and how to bury them too, as her mother bore child after child, many going directly from the warmth of their mother's womb into the cold forest ground.

Though none in her family sang much but hymns at Christmas, Ellen hummed tunes before she could crawl or speak. No matter the family sorrows, or perhaps because of them, Ellen grew more musical each day. Because no song she knew told the way she knew the world, young Ellen began to compose her own. The summer she turned seven years old, she sang this song to her mother:

> *O the wintertime come to the mountain*
> *O the snows grew deep*
> *Young Ellen looked up at the mountain,*
> *and she heard the mountain speak*
>
> *Up she spoke to the mountain*
> *When she heard his whispered words*
> *Please don't take my loved ones from me, pray,*
> *Don't take my loved ones away.*
>
> *The mountain looked down at small Ellen,*
> *He offered not a word*
> *Poor Ellen looked up at the mountain*
> *And the snows came on like a wall*

Young Ellen went out to the mountain
In her weak sweet voice she called,
Please don't take my loved ones from me, pray
Don't take my loved ones away.

But snow flowed over the mountain
So cold she had to sleep
And when Ellen finally woke
It had buried her family deep

Her loved ones were lost in the snow, pray
Her family was dead in the snow.

When Ellen finished her song, her mother sent her into the woods to choose a switch. Fearfully, Ellen went out, returning dutifully with a vine that would bend but not break. Her mother stripped its leaves before beating her daughter until they both wept. After the final blow, Ellen ran to the woods. She climbed the side of the mountain, all the while begging it to send snow down its sides to swallow her mother. When at last she had climbed and cursed for as long as she could, she crouched on the ground to rest. Her breath came slow and deep; the cold wind from the mountaintop burned her lungs. To her surprise, she longed for the warmth of home, so she turned, now silent, to make her way back down. When Ellen entered the cabin, she found that her mother, filled with regret for beating her child, had made Ellen's favorite quail soup. Exhausted and hungry, the girl sat down to eat, forgetting the song, the whipping, and her own angry wish.

Seven winters came and went, until came the winter when more snow fell on the mountain than anyone could remember. It seemed not a day nor night went by when snow didn't hide the world. The family huddled inside their cabin, worried about the dwindling firewood. On the third frigid, moonless night, the snow began to crawl down the mountain. As it crept, the snow gathered weight and speed, until finally it suffocated the Calhoun cabin. Ellen awoke in the morning, cold and darkness all around her. She dug her way from the snow to find her mother, her father, her brothers and sisters, all frozen dead. She knelt in the snow, weeping with sorrow and remorse, her tears freezing before they fell like icy pearls.

When finally she stood, Ellen looked into the sky to see the sun blazing white-yellow, sending shafts of light to somewhere down the mountain. After kissing the frozen, bloodless cheeks of her family, Ellen followed the sun toward the valley, where lay the town of Babbling Springs, so called because of the springs bubbling up on the east end of town. Some said it was the sound of the water itself that gave the spring its name; others said it had more to do with the women who went there to collect water.

As she neared the town, she encountered a man hunting in the forest; this was Lemuel Bridges. When he saw Ellen, her nightdress thick with frost, her eyes like blue ice, Lem at first thought a fairy had come down off the mountain. But when she reached out her blue frozen hand and he took it, their hands, then their bodies, warmed. Ellen and Lemuel fell in love.

Within a year, Ellen gave birth to a baby boy. Having helped her mother bring so many babies into the world, she chose to give birth to him alone, with only her singing for comfort while she labored. They named their son James, after Lem's father. Now a family, they moved to a little house on the eastern edge of town near the spring, and while Lem worked in the sawmill, Ellen stayed at home with little James.

In fair weather Ellen would take James into the woods to play. Each time they went they stayed a little longer, Ellen sitting under a tree singing to her child as he played among the moss and pine needles or hid in the laurel. One day they stayed so long Lem returned from work to find his family away and no supper prepared. By the time mother and child returned, coated in mountain dirt and burrs, Lem's rage and hunger drove him to beat his wife while his son trembled beneath the table.

That night, instead of singing her usual lullaby to James, who was no longer a baby but a strapping young boy, Ellen sang:

Hush, hush little baby
Mama gon' be all right
Hush little baby hush

The wounds will heal to scars O,
the bruises fade away O
hush hush baby hush.

Don't you cry little baby
Mama gon' be all right

When bad men go down to the saws, child
When bad men go down to the saws,
Their hands they catch in the blades, child
And their red, red blood does flow

Sleep, O sleep little baby
We gon' be all right

Your mama knows how to hunt, child
She knows how to plant and sow
O hush baby sleep and dream

The next day Lem went to the sawmill in the pouring rain. It rained so hard wet moss grew across the floor, causing him to slip and fall toward the spinning saw, cutting his thigh on the blade. Lem tried to wrap a rag around his leg, but the saw had sliced clear through to the bone; before the sun had set, he bled to death on the sawmill floor. No one found him until the next morning.

When young James learned of his father's death, rather than feeling relief from his father's rages, he blamed his mother and her song for killing his pa. Ellen sorrowed that while trying to save her son from violence, she had turned him angry and sullen. She vowed she would never sing again. So nights in their home turned silent, with only her son's anger and her own regret in the air.

Not many months after her husband's death, Ellen went to Slacom's store in town, and there on the wall hung an odd instrument made from a stick, and a gourd strung with catgut. Mr. Slacom told her its name: Banjo. He told her one of the free Colored folks who had settled a little village on the west end of town had exchanged it for food. Slacom didn't know what good the instrument was, but thought someone might want it for a curiosity. Ellen traded some raccoon meat for some seeds and went home. But she couldn't stop thinking about the banjo.

That night in her sleep she saw the brown hands of the banjo's maker. While his fingers pressed the strings on the stick, his hand picked and banged where the strings crossed the gourd. In her dream, she sang with the twang of the instrument, and her magic returned. In thrall of the music, rivers rose up in their banks, corn grew ten feet high, animals lay down for slaughter. The next day, awake, she heard music in her home, in the garden, in the forest. She could not help but go back to Slacom's store, carrying a fat possum she had killed. There, she traded the possum for the banjo. By the end of the evening, relying on the memory of the hands in her dream, Ellen could play the banjo as if it had always been hers.

Soon she found herself singing, so she told herself that God had sent the banjo so she would sing again. Ellen was so delighted by the melodies she invented that she sang her garden into a jumble of vegetables; she sang the hearth fire into lighting itself; she sang colorful fish into the river, and she sang the spring into digging deep into the ground until its waters flowed like never before. The next day she made a wall around the new deep water, building one of the first wells to be found in those mountains. This well became the place for all in the town of Babbling Springs to fetch fresh water and share gossip.

Ellen sang health into the sick (secretly), and even life into the nearly dead (another secret), but no matter how she tried, she could not sing the violence out of her boy. As he neared manhood, he continued to trample angrily through the world, and she feared for his future. Therefore, Ellen was as surprised as she was pleased when on the cusp of his twentieth birthday, James fell in love with a red-haired girl from town who returned his feelings.

While courting, James seemed a different man. He helped Ellen do chores without complaint before he left for the new marble quarry in the mornings, and he went to visit his sweetheart Margaret before he came home in the evenings, always stopping at Slacom's store on the way to buy her a sweet. Ellen sang many songs about the love between James and Margaret, until finally James appeared to lose his violence inside his love. After the wedding, he brought his bride to live in the little house with Ellen, and Ellen was happy. Mostly.

In secret, Ellen sang a song about a fair baby with red hair and magic in his blood, and in no time Margaret's belly began to grow. Ellen's joy grew too, as she watched the young woman cooking or sewing, a sweet smile on her face and new life in her womb. Ellen was so filled with happiness, she didn't at first notice her son no longer showed interest or pleasure in his wife, even seeming contemptuous of his coming child. More and more often, James returned from the quarry to hurl insults at poor Margaret, afterwards tramping off to the tavern, where he'd stay until Margaret and Ellen were asleep.

As the time of the baby's expected arrival neared, James began to knock down furniture and throw whatever came to hand whenever he was home. He became the same anger-filled boy he had been before he met Margaret. Ellen sang until her voice cracked, but to no avail; her son still burned with inexplicable fury. On the day James pushed Margaret to the floor, Ellen told him to leave her house. To her terror, rather than storming out alone, he grabbed Margaret by the arm, dragging her with him. The two moved into the boarding house in town run by old Hirum McGill and his daughter Nora.

In secret, Ellen visited Margaret after James left for the quarry each day. The young woman grew increasingly pale and sad, but her belly swelled as it should, and her baby boy came into the world healthy, with a shock of red hair. Ellen acted as midwife while her son sat drinking whiskey in The Hammer and The Axe. Margaret named the baby by herself. She called him Carter, after a boy she had known when she was a child, before anything disappointing happened in her life.

Soon after Carter's birth, though, Margaret began to leave him with Nora while she joined her husband at the tavern in the evenings, becoming one of the first women in Babbling Springs to openly drink spirits. In the mornings, exhausted from drinking, fighting, and making love to her husband, Margaret hid her face under a pillow while her child cried. Ellen took to going to the boarding house early in the mornings. She fed goat's milk to the baby, then rocked him while singing songs about safety, love, and magic.

When Carter began talking, he often spoke of things no one else could see. At first his visions seemed childish imaginings, but as time wore on, it became apparent that what the child saw had a bearing on the future. For instance, one day as Ellen left the boarding house, little Carter told her she should fix her shoe before she went out. After showing him her shoes were in perfect condition, Ellen left for home, chuckling at such an odd concern for a child. On her path, however, the sole came clear off her shoe, and she had to make her way wearing just one.

In particular, Carter saw things about and around his mother. One day he saw her covered with mud, and sure enough, Margaret slipped and fell on the muddy road while returning from The Hammer and The Axe after fighting with her husband. One morning Margaret woke to the boy screaming about hair all over the floor. She whipped him and sent him outside without breakfast. That night, drunk and violent, James used a knife to cut off Margaret's thick red braid.

Carter terrified Margaret; yet she loved him enough to refrain from telling his father about the visions.

One afternoon Ellen arrived at the boarding house to

find three-year-old Carter sitting alone outside on the steps. When she asked why he wouldn't go in, he said, Pa ain't safe and Ma sent me out.

Concerned, Ellen rushed into the rooms only to find Margaret sitting in a chair, staring at the wall. James was nowhere to be seen.

Please take that child, said Margaret, I don't know what to do with him.

Without asking questions, Ellen turned on her heel. Outside she held out her hand as she passed Carter on the step. The child took her hand and together they walked to the little house just past the east end of town.

That night Margaret slipped out with a man she had met in The Hammer and The Axe. When James learned of the affair, he drank whiskey until his rage consumed him. He tracked the lovers down, cut their throats, and tossed them into the river. When he woke up sober the next day, he quickly realized the trouble he was in. He stole a horse and rode over the mountain and into the wilderness. No one in Babbling Springs ever heard from James Bridges again.

Carter and Ellen lived a congenial life together. The little boy never asked where his parents had gone, and Ellen never spoke of them. She paid close attention to Carter's visions, and they both learned to respect them. Ellen sang to the boy every day, mostly old ballads. She only sang songs that influenced the future when they were absolutely needed, like during the spring with no rain, or the winter that froze even the clouds. Before long, the joy Ellen took in her grandson overshadowed the sorrowful memories of her husband and son. In this way, three years passed.

Then, in 1847 a preacher rode into Babbling Springs. He rode bareback on a splay-legged mule that appeared as if any moment its hooves would slide in all four directions, causing the animal to land on its belly in the dirt. The preacher's name was Paul Crane. He came from upstate New York, a place where God was presently slamming down into the souls of farmers and others of ordinary and lowly professions, forcing them to spill his word onto paper and into the world. Crane had been a stonemason when God first spoke to him. He went to the Methodists, who while they found him ill-mannered and unqualified to lead a church, thought him uniquely suited to ride into the wilderness to spread the word of God.

Crane rode south. Out of New York, through Pennsylvania and Virginia, into North Carolina, and west to Tennessee. From the Alleghenies to the Blue Ridge to the Smokies, the mountains merged one into the next, slipping into valleys, darkening in the woods. The mountains cast spells on all who traversed their ridges, their hollows, their forests. Magic threaded through them, spring to stream, stream to river, river to river. Reverend Crane noted the magic and said to himself that all it lacked was the word of God to give it voice.

That is how Reverend Paul Crane, dirty, stinking, full of what he took to be the spirit of the Lord, came to ride his mule into Babbling Springs, Tennessee. When he reached the center of town, he dismounted his wobbly-legged mule and stood in the empty dimness of early morning. Crane was a passionate man, but he was also a patient man. The sun and his congregation would come to him.

As always, the sun rose. People began to go about their business, and as they did, they became curious about the dirty man standing quiet next to his ancient mule in the center of their town. Some stopped to observe him.

Reverend Crane waited. He waited until he felt enough had gathered, then he said, God is waiting for you to listen.

An old man spit on the ground. No one spoke. Crane sensed that some listener, perhaps the most important listener, had not arrived. So, he waited, ignoring the growing tension of the crowd. No one left. Crane watched the townspeople, and the townspeople watched him.

Finally, she arrived. A woman not young, but not old either. With her was a redheaded child.

Paul Crane looked into the eyes of Ellen Bridges. And she looked back into his. They recognized each other immediately.

A year from today, I will preach in Babbling Springs, Tennessee, and nothing will be the same again, he said.

Cold ran through Ellen's veins. With a trembling hand, she clasped Carter's shoulder.

The child closed his mind against the premonitions her grasp evoked.

The preacher mounted his ancient mule and rode away. The crowd dispersed. Ellen and Carter went back home, forgetting the errands they meant to do in town that day.

Nearly a year passed, and the preacher was forgotten.

❋ ❋ ❋

Returning to her house from the garden one morning, Ellen stopped to watch Carter work with a stick at the dirt in the yard. When she looked over his shoulder, she saw he had drawn people, seemingly a mob of them.

Who are these, she asked.

The children I saw in the yard, Carter replied, The ones you're going to sing to our house to be my friends.

Ellen was both delighted and mortified. The boy had

just turned eight years old. How was it she had never considered that the child might be in need of friends? Certainly, he would be in school before very long, but Ellen had neglected to prepare him for even that. (She had brought the boy up to think of magic as a common thing, like praying at night or washing his face in the morning.) Ellen had forgotten to consider what might happen to Carter when he went among other children if he had never met any.

That evening, when she and Carter sat together before evening prayers, she took her banjo and strummed out this song:

> *Once a lad sat in a yard*
> *O so alone so alone O*
> *He left oncet but din't get far*
> *O so alone so alone O*
>
> *He ain't got no Pa*
> *He ain't got no Ma*
> *O so alone so alone O*
>
> *He ain't got no brother*
> *He ain't got no sister*
> *O so alone so alone O*
>
> *But this child he got him a gran*
> *And this child's gran got a song*
> *Call all the children*
> *O the children*
> *Call all the children home O*

The next morning Carter went outside to draw children

in the dirt, but no real children appeared. He assured his grandmother that they were coming, but just to be sure, she sang the song again that night.

The morning after that, Carter again went outside. This morning two boys stood in the yard. Ellen recognized them as Charles and Davis MacAllister, both a few years older than Carter. The two boys were the sons of the man who now ran the general store after marrying old Slacom's daughter. They had a ball with them, and the three boys played all day.

The following morning it truly seemed a mob had appeared. Not only did the two MacAllister boys return, but also all the Harpe children came down from the farm on the north mountainside. Led by the eldest, Tommy, there were also sisters Ethie and Cora, and their shy brother Frank. Their younger brother Johnny ran about like a wild animal, squawking while chasing the chickens. Little Lucy Harpe gripped tight to her sister Ethie's hand. Tommy stepped forward, saying, We just felt of a sudden we shouldn't be unneighborly to those who live far from us.

The next day, more children arrived. To Ellen's surprise, the Adair girls, Emily and Polly, strutted around her dirt yard in their fancy dresses. Willie Reed, one of the poorest children in town, hung at the edge of the group. Little Lucy Harpe let go of her sister's hand to go and hold onto Willie's. Soon enough, though, Carter had coaxed Willie into wrestling with the boys, and Ethie took Lucy to play with the girls.

On the fourth day, carrying his baby sister Alva on his hip, Edmond Calloway came out of the woods where his family lived in a cabin by the turnpike. Ellen took the baby from him so he could play with the other children.

The fifth day it seemed all the children of Babbling

Springs played in Ellen's yard. They ran about throwing balls, fighting with sticks, racing beetles. Polly Adair had abandoned the gentle games of the girls, taking up a stick and showing up some of the boys with her agility and fierceness. Polly's sister Emily had befriended Ethie and Cora, and they sat with little Lucy among the wildflowers at the edge of the yard. Ellen kept baby Alva with her, though Edmond always had one eye on his sister, and would rush over if she seemed to fuss.

At midmorning, just after Ellen handed out apples to the children, she glanced up toward the woods to see a small dark face duck behind a tree. Ellen called Carter to her and sent him out to fetch the hiding child. He came back holding the hand of a Black girl just about his age, who said her name was Delia.

No sooner had Delia introduced herself, than a Black boy of the same age ran out of the woods to join her. He said his name, Elijah, and announced that his papa was a preacher and a teacher. Immediately the MacAllister boys began shouting words Ellen didn't think children knew. She grabbed her broom and chased the offenders, administering swats until they apologized.

Something called me here, Ellen heard Delia tell Carter. And where I go, Elijah goes too.

Though Ellen had never seen Delia before, she guessed the girl might be the daughter of the free Black man and woman who lived out in the woods to themselves instead of in the Colored village at the western edge of town. Ellen had heard rumors that the girl's mother knew more about roots and mountain magic than Ellen herself, that she and the Harpe children's mother had studied magic together with the old witch who used to live in a cave far out in the forest. Ellen had never met the woods witch; having learned all she needed to know from her own mother, she never sought any other instruction. Now she thought she would like to meet both the Harpe children's mother and Delia's mother. Seeing her grandson with friends made her notice she had never had any herself.

This was April of 1848, one year to the day since Reverend Paul Crane had stood in the center of Babbling Springs announcing he would return to preach. Everyone had forgotten him until that afternoon when he returned on the same old mule, or a different one that looked just like it. Word spread from one person to another, and soon, the townspeople swarmed around him.

Reverend Crane preached a fiery sermon about all the ways the devil lurked in the wilderness, all the ways God could protect his children or not, as he saw fit. And though the preacher meant every word, and though with one eye he met every eye that fell upon him as he preached, his other eye searched for the one he had come to meet. She wasn't there. His one wandering eye made him appear all the fiercer; the townspeople stood transfixed. When he finished his sermon, Crane fell into what looked to them that watched to be a holy trance. He did in fact feel holy, for a voice that must be God whispered inside him, telling him where to meet his destiny.

Ellen Bridges knew the preacher had returned. In the afternoon, as the children played, she felt the Reverend Paul Crane like a shadow creeping over the mountains. Though she couldn't hear his voice as he preached in town, the ground beneath her feet vibrated with his hellfire and damnation. She knew when his sermon ended, felt him make his way toward her, knew that he knew where to find her. Carter sensed the preacher but couldn't conjure any vision of him. This frightened the boy, and afraid for his grandmother, he clung to her all that day.

The preacher arrived at the well just as Ellen had come to fetch water for supper.

I came to rid the world of those who hate the Christ, he said.

And who's hating the Christ here, she asked. Me? Them children?

The preacher hadn't noticed the children. Carter had followed Ellen when she left the yard, and the others, curious, had run after them both. Now the children stood at some distance from the well, watching.

Carter saw shadows emanate from the preacher, surround his grandmother. His own helplessness overwhelmed him. His fear stole his voice and froze his feet to the ground.

Reverend Paul Crane also felt helpless. His fear arose from his inability to control his own feelings; at that moment he loved Ellen Bridges fiercely. He loved her in the way a person can only love someone whose life he holds in his hands. His love for her filled him like lust. It echoed off the mountains and flowed in the river currents. His love that was lust and fear gurgled up from the well. He was overcome with Righteousness.

No, Ellen said, No.

She backed up against the well where the cold wet stone told her everything about the darkness behind her.

The preacher pushed Ellen Bridges into the well.

She made no sound as she fell.

The preacher turned toward the children.

Instantly and as one, they approached him. Edmond Calloway set baby Alva on the ground without taking his eyes from the preacher.

Reverend Crane loudly vowed to himself and to God he would stand his ground. He would never run from children, even if they were possessed by the Devil as these here were.

But together, the children were so strong.

Together they pushed the preacher up and over the wall of the well.

With his last breath, he cursed the children, the mountains, the month of April, and Babbling Springs, Tennessee.

Then he was gone.

The birds stopped singing.

The river rapids lay down flat as a pond.

The sky turned red.

The children stood silent. At first they didn't notice Davis MacAllister lying on the ground, blood running from his head. In their rush to send the preacher to his death, the children had smashed Davis against the stones of the well. When they saw him on the ground bleeding, all but his brother Charles and Carter scattered. Charles shook his brother until he awakened, then helped him home, where the boys told their mother Davis had fallen while jumping from rock to rock in the river. Within days, Davis suffered his first seizure.

When all the others had gone, Carter sat by the well until Nora McGill came for water and found him there with Reverend Crane's old mule. When Carter told her his gran was gone and the water in the well was spoiled, she took Carter and the mule home to the boarding house. Later, she spread word that Ellen Bridges had run off with the preacher. Carter didn't deny her story, and none of the children ever told what happened that day.

On the night of the murders of Ellen Bridges and Paul Crane, the spring that had fed the well retreated into the earth. Strange insects rose up from the depths of the well, hovered buzzing for a day, then disappeared.

For the first time, no spring ran through the town. It had been called Babbling Springs since White men first set foot in the valley. The mayor renamed the town Sinking Springs. The inhabitants had to go to the river for water, and no one lingered there to gossip, there being nothing to lean on, and the river feeling so wild compared to the well.

Nora McGill's father was near death; nevertheless, she let Carter stay. One day he begged to go see his grandmother's house, so Nora took him. As the two stood before the empty cottage, it collapsed. Dust spread across the ground, choking them. For the first time since his grandmother had disappeared into the well, Carter cried. He cried so hard he couldn't walk, and Nora had to carry him home; she put him to bed, where his tears soaked his pillow and his bed sheets too. That night a spring burst forth from the mountains north of town, not far from the Harpe place.

The town named the new spring Sudden Spring, and they built a well they called the New Well. The mayor considered changing the name of the town again, but his wife reminded him that the name Sinking Springs would keep the inhabitants of the town humble.

* * *

Ellen Bridges sincerely expected to see God after she died, but that wasn't her fate. The first thing she saw was the children throwing her murderer into the well on top of her. From that moment, she found herself watching them from her new place, which was neither on the earth nor in heaven. It took some time before she realized she could still sing. Her first songs were simple. She sang about having no bodily senses. About watching children. About loving them. These songs sounded almost like air. Ellen felt her new whispery melodies blessed the children who had avenged her death.

As time passed, she wanted to sing songs to guide the children, to help them make beautiful lives. She began with Carter, attempting to sing a song to ensure his success. But while the song was at first buoyant and optimistic, it soon turned frightening. In spite of her intentions, Ellen found herself singing about how her grandson learned to watch death so as to protect his own life. She tried to stop the song, but so long as Carter was in her sight or heart (She still called it that since love continued to live within her), the song about him continued.

She tried directing her attention to the Adair girls; being wealthy they seemed to have the best chance at beautiful lives. But the songs for Emily and Polly turned more fearful than those for Carter.

Ellen sang about one child after another, each time finding that instead of singing the future she wanted for them, she sang a future incomprehensible in its horror and sin. When she tried to stop singing, she found she could not. She was near despair, when she remembered how her first songs when she lived had caused harm, but by the end of her life she had learned to turn them to good. She believed she could do the same from beyond death, so every time a song turned evil, Ellen worked hard to turn it back to her intent.

If she could not, she began a new song.

Because she had lost her sense of time, Ellen didn't know how many years passed. A great war came like a vicious storm; some of the children died. When the war ended she still sang about those children who remained, but more to comfort them than to direct their lives.

Nearby, she sensed the preacher, ominous as the fog. On the day he died, when he uttered his curse, a shadow had risen out of him. And from amidst these mountains, it watched.

1866

Johnny Harpe

Hey Johnny Reb! Where's your arm?

Damned Federals think they're funny. Known some of these bastards since we was boys. They wasn't my friends then neither. But even though my horse Out of the Fog and Edmond Calloway was my only friends, these here weren't my enemies back then. But nowadays everyone knows who fought Federal and who fought Secesh, so if I want a drink I got to take the taunting that comes with it. I ain't in the mood. Seems to me it's about time these bastards quit reliving their Lincolnite glory days.

Got any real money, Johnny Reb? Maybe in your right hand?

That's Matthew Thompson. He's always been a son-of-a-bitch; since the war he don't never take the trouble to hide it. Soon's he speaks, my only fist takes on a life of its own. My knuckles slam into his ugly snout. Next I know we's out the door of The Hammer and The Axe and into the street. Rage rises in me, but it rises in him too. It always lives inside us both, just like everybody. All of us going through the world like it ain't hate drives us from place to place, hour to hour, day to day. If any man in this country does a good thing, it's to hide the hate inside hisself.

Thompson's blood sprays across my knuckles. Mine runs out my nose. Everyone around us yelling, not caring no more who's who or what we stood for once. They just want to see blood. We got to fight 'til one of us can't get up. For a change, this time it ain't me stays down. I kick Thompson one last time before I spit on the ground near his head. Then I turn away toward the path home. My shadow spreads out under the gaslights like a hideous one-armed ghoul.

* * *

It did look like I was going to leave that war intact. End of April '65 come the surrender and we was in Bentonville, North Carolina. A group of us gathered for the walk home, more than three hundred miles. Pa had turned gray and grizzled by then, not near the fierce man of four years before, though he was just as likely to lose his temper with me.

Early in the morning, the lot of us started to walking, staying as much as we could to the woods, which was nearly as destroyed as the towns. If we seen or heard any people, we laid low 'til they passed. I could hear others laying low as we passed them, too. No man could trust another no more.

One evening toward sundown when we ain't found nothing to eat all day nor the day before, we heard someone's coming, so we hid behind some rocks. What comes by but a horse, all on its own, a saddle still on its back. One of the men among us raises his rifle. I yell so as to scare the horse but I'm too late. The man fires and the horse drops. The men, Pa included, swarmed that horse before it breathed its last breath, cutting into it with knives, turning it into meat. They built a fire right next to where it fell and started to cooking. The smell of burning horseflesh choked my nostrils. I was shamed to fury when I found my mouth watering and my stomach rumbling. Still, I resisted eating it. I seen enough of horses getting killed in the war. So I walked off on my own. What happened next is just more proof that if God exists at all he don't give a good god damn about his creatures, animal nor man.

I heard more rustling and thunk it might be another horse. I weren't going to let another one get kilt so instead of hiding, I walked toward the noise. It weren't no horse I found, though. It was a crazed soldier. His ragged uniform told me he was on my same side, but I could also see he was in no condition to determine who I might be. He come at me with his saber swinging. Like a fool I hold out my hands and call for him to halt, I'm friend not foe. He slices into my right arm, then swings again. He keeps slicing at my hand, my arm. I tried to block my chest and belly but that just invited more cuts into my arm. I'm thinking I'm a dead man when a shot rings out and my attacker drops to the ground. I turn to see Pa standing there with his rifle raised, calling me a damn fool. Without even asking me am I all right, he went back to finish devouring the horse.

I stand there by the dead man. He looks just like all the dead men I seen the last four years. I kneel down and reach in his pocket. He ain't got no food or money. Just an old lighter. I put it in my pocket. It's become a keepsake of the worst thing ever happened to me, and I find myself lighting it and staring into the flame whenever I've got enough whiskey in me.

When I sat down among the men none looked at me. I wanted to wrap my arm and hand, but I had nothing 'cept the shirt on my back. It's still cold at night, so I let myself bleed. Later when we's on the march again, we found a stream. I washed my wounds and packed mud on 'em to stop the blood from flowing. We kept walking, me feeling weaker and dizzier every hour, seems like.

The next days I spent stumbling in maddening pain, trying to keep mud made from dirt and dew on my wounds; it seemed some nights and days passed before we stopped at a river. There I washed the dried mud off to see my skin purple-brown with black crust around the gashes in my arm and hand. All of it was slick with some kind of ooze. One of the men happened to look over at me trying to wash off the crust and ooze. He turns to Pa and tells him if I don't get some help, I'm going to die. Pa come over to look at my arm for the first time since he saw me get cut, then he cusses me under his breath.

Later that day we made our way out of the woods to a farm. The woman there told us she'd been butchering her own cattle, 'til the Yankees come to take 'em all. She said she can take off my arm, 'cause that's all can be done for me now. Pa cussed me again. Ignoring him, the woman fetched some corn whiskey, made me drink 'til I thought I'd vomit. After that the men held me down while she took a saw to my arm. Last thing I remember is the red blinding pain.

I woke up days later in a bed, tucked in with blankets, a pillow under my head. The woman comes to tell me the men, my pa included, went on, assuming I would die. She'd been nursing me and praying over me, she said. She told me to say a prayer of thanks, but then she wasted no time saying it for me. Her name was Rebecca, and she took care of me 'til I was up and walking. It was then we found I couldn't do no work around her place to repay her. Rebecca put me in a cart and drove me to the nearest town. In that town was where I first encountered the way people was going to treat me for the rest of my life, some who couldn't stop staring, others not able to look at me at all. It took me near an hour to summon the courage to inquire about the direction of Sinking Springs.

I walked for days, stopping at farms where people took pity on me, fed me, and let me sleep in their barns. I knew that if I had both my arms these same people would have shown me the barrels of their guns, so in that one way I was thankful. By the time I reached our farm I was dirty, feverish, and tired of seeing pity on the faces of all who looked on me. It cut me to the quick when Ma's heart near to broke on seeing me, my sister Lucy near fainted, and Pa looked away in disgust. Folks in town was worse, 'specially those who fought Union and come back whole.

* * *

After the fight with Thompson, I brush myself off and head on home. Before I go inside, I stop at the barn where I got my horse, Out of the Fog hid. Only my sister Lucy knows he's here. She was outside stargazing and dreaming of Willie Reed when she seen me take the horse into the barn.

You can't keep a big animal like that a secret, she said.

I told her I'd figure something out. Don't tell, I said, Give me sometime.

Pa'll find out. You'll see, Lucy said as she left me and the horse in the barn. Much as it angers me, she's right. If I keep him here, Pa'll find him sooner rather than later and hitch him to a plow, or worse, make make meat out of him.

Tonight when I go in the barn, still shaking with rage from fighting, Out of the Fog's there in the stall, calm, waiting on me. I wish he could tell me what he seen in the war. Or maybe I don't wish it. I wonder what a horse would remember of the terrors of battle. Bullets flying, other horses dropping to die in the mud, men running up over their bodies. Out of the Fog remembered how to get home, so I reckon all them other pictures of war are somewhere inside his mind, too. He nuzzles my face with his nose. I'd just as soon sleep out here with the horse than go inside. But that's a sure way to attract Pa's attention; by morning Out of the Fog would be in the field. I figure he done enough work in the war. Ain't his fault my brother Tommy took him to fight the wrong side. I let the horse nuzzle me one more time before I drag myself in to bed.

*   *   *

Morning comes too fast. I got to get out of bed, haul myself to the table for a breakfast I ain't got no hunger for. You'd think I'd appreciate it. Food cooked for me every morning by a mother who loves me.

At first it did comfort me: my mother's love, the smell and taste of home-cooked food. Then came the moment when my mother cut my meat for me, stupid Lucy gazing down at her plate so as not to stare at me, Pa leaving the table. This ritual has become every day.

Now a year out, to think of breakfast, or any family meal makes me twitch like when we soldiers was out in the field so covered with lice our very skin moved. I find myself wishing for those battlefields, when I was a whole man among the cannons, the bullets, the comrades dead and alive. When I was a hero to our Confederacy. I sure ain't no hero now, I think as I watch Ma cut up my sausage, a task I could likely manage myself, but she insists, like it's the one way she can show me she sees what I been through. Soon as Ma sits down she asks Lucy if she expects to go walking later with that Yankee scum Willie Reed.

Since the war Lucy has adopted a kitten purr that rankles my whole spirit. In her tiny singsong voice, she says she supposes so.

I don't often agree with Pa, but I do on this topic. When he tells her he don't like it, I tell her I don't like it neither. Ma takes it on herself to point out how moody poor sad Willie Reed been since he hobbled back from the war. I bite my tongue. I don't tell her to look to her own breakfast table if she wants to find someone's suffered from the war.

Right then, Pa points out one of Willie Reed's true qualities.

He don't work, Pa says.

I'm about to agree when I see Pa's eyes're on me, letting me know it ain't just Willie Reed he's talking about. I pretend I don't understand.

Lucy simpers, protecting Reed's imagined virtues. He helps his ma, she coos.

Helps her eat any food she got, I say.

Does that fact quiet our Lucy? No, it don't.

Seems to me he's special, she says.

A fire starts in me lit directly from her stupidity. I know Ma likes to keep at least a pretense of manners at her table, but I can't help it: I spit on the floor.

Not at my table, son, says Ma.

Pa glares, but I know he would of been the one to spit if I didn't do it first.

Lucy's undaunted, though. She goes on to finding something magical in Willie Reed. She starts to chirping 'bout he has a mystery to him. Pa puts her straight right quick.

There's no mystery to laziness, girl, he says.

That still don't stop our Lucy, who now makes up fairy tales about this Federal son-of-a-bitch. Telling how he lives in some enchanted world, how he just can't abide this one. That's all I can stand to hear and I tell Pa he shouldn't let her step out with Willie or he'll find himself saddled with both Reed and his tainted offspring.

Lucy's face turns red with being mad at all of us, but mostly me.

You know you got secrets I can tell brother, she says. You might be careful what you say about them I love.

I ain't got no secrets, I say.

No? She almost sings it.

Let me eat my food in peace, both of you, orders Pa.

Lucy glares at me.

I'm done, I say.

I get up and go straight out to the barn. I got to get Out of the Fog away from here before Lucy tells or Pa finds him.

⁕ ⁕ ⁕

Truth be told, I most always liked animals better than people. Birds and horses in particular. Though I ain't always treated birds right, a thing I ain't proud to say. But horses. I ain't never mistreated a horse. I never feared them, neither, not even when their chests was above my head. Pa had an old brown one to work the farm and no matter how many times I got told to stay clear, I'd run in the barn, straight to his stall. Pa wouldn't even give that horse a name 'cause he said it was just for work. But I had a name for him in my mind: Moonrunner. I named him that 'cause I was sure he saw the moon outside through the gaps in the boards on the barn at night, and dreamed of running in the moonlight 'til we couldn't find him nor make him work no more.

When I got big enough to reach Moonrunner's flanks my brother Tommy taught me how to brush him and feed him. This was the best part of my day. I was the youngest boy, so I had chores to do with the women and the men both. Sometimes little Lucy come along but she mostly got in the way more than she helped.

Once I got grown enough to go down to town every now and then, I found the world's filled with horses. My brother Tommy would hook Moonrunner to a cart, then my brothers and me would ride down to sell vegetables so as to bring back meat and other things like cloth and needles that Ma needed. Moonrunner would plod in front of that cart just like he pulled the plough in the field. In town I saw how different horses move in different ways. Most of 'em wasn't as big and slow as old Moonrunner. And they come in all manner of colors. On Main Street I saw horses the color of nuts in the forest, and horses the deep black color of the river at night. Every once and again I'd see a white horse looking like it's made of snow, with crazy blue-sky eyes or even sometimes pink eyes what made me think of the devil.

The black horses was my favorite. I got it in my mind that one day I'd have me a black horse. I asked for one on my birthday, but I got britches, a piece of chalk, a board, and a trip to school. At first I was excited 'cause it meant less chores, but I soon found school was much worse than the field or even Ma's kitchen. I went to school as seldom as possible. Since six-years-old I known the Lord's Prayer by heart and I understood the ways of animals. What did I need of school?

One morning when we was all on our way down to school—that was when we was all together and alive: Tommy, Frank, Ethie, Cora, me, and Lucy—we was nearly there, when seems all of us together felt drawn to walk right past the schoolhouse. For once, Lucy didn't pull at my hand. She seemed to know right where we was going. We walked through town, out of town, 'til we found ourselves in Ellen Bridges' front yard where was other children from town, too.

There in Miss Ellen's yard I met Edmond Calloway who would one day be my best friend, and his sister Alva, just a baby, who I would learn to love as she grew. From that day, we went to Miss Ellen's to play much as we could, only going to school enough to convince the schoolteacher we only missed school when there were chores to do. This was a happy time, 'til the day the preacher come.

He came on a normal day. Like always, we had followed Miss Ellen to the well 'cause none of us liked her out of our sight, we loved her that much.

Miss Ellen had just pulled the bucket of water up, when the preacher appeared from nowhere, riding a ancient mule. Him and the mule was both so shabby and spindly, none of us thought to fear him. But when he leapt off the old mule's back to grab Miss Ellen by the shoulders, we was all too scared to move.

Miss Ellen fought the preacher like the wildest wolf in the woods, biting and growling. But the preacher overpowered her. He pushed her hard against the well and she fell down into the darkness.

That was the moment Edmond first heard the voice of the all-knowing Universe. Send him down! Edmond shouted, and the all of us, we knew what to do. We swarmed the preacher, biting and growling just like Miss Ellen had. Even though Tommy and Frank was older, it was Edmond and me climbed up on the well. We pulled while the others pushed and we sent him down. He went down screaming, never hitting the bottom. Cold air come up from that well and set us all to shivering.

We was all shivering, catching our breath, when we noticed Davis MacAllister on the ground bleeding at his head. When his brother run over to him, it was like we all realized what we had just done. All but the MacAllister brothers and Carter Bridges scattered and ran, Edmond stopping just long enough to grab up baby Alva. We didn't look back, and none of us has spoke about it since. Davis was the only one got a permanent reminder of that day. He's had fits ever since, and they are a fearsome thing to witness: him shaking on the ground with the whites of his eyes showing, screaming like a dying rabbit. We made fun of him to hide how scared we was that we might catch his sickness.

For a while I dreamed about Miss Ellen, the preacher, and the well. But time passed and I started dreaming about horses again. One morning I woke with a strange feeling, like something was calling me outside. It was the first time anything had called to me since us children was drawn to Miss Ellen's house. I shook off my sleep and went out in the yard. It was so early the fog was still up, damp on my skin, making me wish I didn't leave my bed. I had just about given my feeling up for another dream when I heard air blowing through nostrils. I thought Moonrunner must of got out to finally take that nighttime run, but when I turned to look, the shadow in the fog weren't Moonrunner. The horse what stepped out of the fog was dark and strong, with muscles you could see even in early dawn starlight.

My black horse.

I put my hand on his neck. It was cool and wet. His hair was coarse, but it patted smooth and sleek. I kept my hand on his neck while he walked beside me right into the barn like as if we always been friends. I stayed there with him, the both of just standing there looking at each other's eyes 'til breakfast.

Thank you for the horse, I said to Pa when I went in.

He says, What horse?

Tommy went out to the barn and come back to tell Pa there's really a horse out there.

Take it to town, said Pa, See who lost it.

You might think I sorrowed, but I didn't. I knew they'd be back that night. I knew that was my horse. They did come back and I named him Out of the Fog, 'cause that's how he come to me.

First thing, Pa tried to put him to work, pulling the same plow Moonrunner been pulling. Out of the Fog wouldn't have none of it. He bucked 'til he pulled free.

That horse got to earn his keep or he goes says Pa.

So I taught Out of the Fog to pull the cart to town, and I showed Pa I was grown enough to do the trading. My horse wouldn't abide anyone in that cart but me. Usually though, out of respect for him, I didn't ride. I walked beside the cart and talked to him the whole way there. Sometimes when we finished in town we'd go out to the Calloway place. Mr. Calloway took a shine to Out of the Fog, always checking to make sure his shoes was fitted right. He even made him a bit and didn't charge. Mr. Calloway was a kind man who thought children should play. He always said we'd have plenty of time to work ourselves to death. He'd look after Out of the Fog while I run off with Edmond and Alva.

Little as she was, Alva was always with us. She weren't like my sister at all. Alva understood everything. My sister spent her time sewing and brushing her curly blonde hair. Alva's hair was straight, black and wild. The three of us, me, Alva, and Edmond, climbed to the bald of the south mountain, explored deep in caves, swam in the rapids of the river. We made our own world with its own rules. I didn't know it then, but it was bound to be the best part of my life.

* * *

In 1861 the first of the war come through. Them soldiers was supposed to be ours but they come from Virginia or some such place. They came in and took over Sinking Springs. They even come up to our farm, ordering us to hand over our food and our animals. Pa made a deal with them; they leave the chickens and the crops, and the Confederacy would have him, his sons, and his horses. It was so early in the war. We all thought it would be over in weeks. If they had come in later there wouldn't of been no deal they'd make, 'specially where it concerns food.

My brother Tommy, who I had looked up to more than anyone 'til that moment, betrayed us all that night, said he was fighting for the Union. A few hours later, he lit out and took my horse with him. I think that's the only time my pa and me ever had broken hearts at the same time.

There wasn't much time 'til I had to go, so I went to see Edmond, to ask if he'd come with me.

Friend, he said, You're about to fight for the wrong side.

Yankees going to come take our land, Edmond, I said, Yours and mine.

No they ain't, he said.

Slaves going to rise up and kill White men across the south, I told him, They're going to take everything.

They ain't, he said, Someone filled your head with lies.

You ain't joining the Lincolnites.

It's the right thing to do, Johnny.

Edmond, I stammered, Edmond. That means a day could come...A day could come when we might...

We might meet in battle, he finished my sentence.

What will you do?

I'll do what righteousness leads me to do, he said.

His words cut me to the quick.

You'd kill me dead Edmond? You going to kill me and bury me like a bird? Say one of your half-cocked prayers over me?

If it's the right thing to do, he said.

You call yourself my friend, I said.

I do, he answered.

You ain't no kind of friend, I said, Not to me. Not to Tennessee.

Not to our way of life.

I'm friend to all that and more.

Yet you would shoot me.

Yes.

For the second time in just days my heart broke. Before that I didn't even know a heart could break more than one time. I didn't have no more words for him, so I left him there.

Next thing I knew I was marching in the infantry with Pa, my brother Frank, and Moonrunner. I'd never left Sinking Springs before. I didn't even know there was places without mountains. Now I went everywhere, marched down steep roads and flat roads, wide roads and narrow ones. My bloody feet marched across fields and farms, through forests and towns. Everything was strange.

I learned that any broad, flat place, any meadow or field, meant men and horses would die. I grieved for Out of the Fog, hoped my own brother Tommy, not some strange Federal, was riding him. For me, horses had come to be the only creatures with dignity I saw. I'd ask officers could I take care of the horses, which caused many jokes about how you can take the boy off the farm but you can't take the farm from in the boy, and worse, too. The jokes made me mad, but made Pa madder. I tolerated it all so I could be with the horses. Every day the horses showed me how much better than men they was. Even when they was wounded. Even when they was sick. Even when they was dying.

When a horse got hit, when bullets sunk in their flesh, the sound of surprise and betrayal they made could rip a man's soul apart. If they could, they'd keep running, lifting their hooves like as if nothing happened. Then all at once they'd collapse to the ground. Their ribs rising and falling, their eyes fixed like they're already staring straight past this world. The only way you knew when a horse died was to see its ribs stop moving. Men, they scream the whole time. They bend their bodies so unnatural like. Men fight to keep their spirits inside their bodies. After a time I got so I could watch a man die. I could listen to him yell for his mother, so loud and full of yearning for home. It was the same whether he was killed from a bullet wound or was shitting himself to death, writhing with fever, or trembling with cold. I prayed I wouldn't get sick, and I didn't. That I wouldn't be shot. And I wasn't.

After Stones River, my brother Frank died of the shits. That was hard to look at. My own brother lying in filth, flies all 'round him. We dumped him in a shallow trench with all those died of bullets or disease after that battle. When everyone was asleep I went to where they had filled in the trench. I said what I could remember of Edmond's prayer for the dead:

> *Round and Round.*
> *Round and Round.*
> *Life begets Death.*
> *Death makes life anew.*

I kissed the dirt that covered my brother and the others. Whatever dirt touched my tongue, I swallowed.

After that, I took care of horses, marched, shot men. Truth be told, I shot some horses too, though I tried not to. When they fell, I feared birds might eat their bodies, so I shot as many birds as I could after every battle, even though I felt guilty I couldn't bury them. When I could, if I saw a shot horse still breathing, I'd creep up to slit its throat so it wouldn't have to lie there dying with men it never asked to fight beside. Nighttimes I'd pray that if Out of the Fog fell on a battlefield there'd be someone just like me to cut his throat.

* * *

Yesterday was the first time since I got home that I went down to the river where me and Edmond and Alva used to play. I went in the daytime and I stayed while the sun set, the moon rose, and the fog drifted across the surface of the river. I was occupied with the reflection of the moon on the water and thoughts of how I would manage my whole future with just one arm, when branches cracked behind me. For just a second I thought I had survived war and amputation only to be killed by a bear a mile from my own home. I drew my knife, thinking I could stab a bear in the throat or heart. I spun around, knife up. I held back from stabbing, though, and thank God I did.

Because standing right in front of me was not a bear, but my own horse, Out of the Fog, what I hadn't seen in five years. He stood there looking at me like why did I take so long to find him. I wrapped my arm around his neck. He nuzzled my shoulder where my right arm should be, forgave me for not coming home whole. He smelled like the forest and the setting sun. In the shock and happiness of seeing him, I realized my brother Tommy, who my family never talked about, must be dead.

A strange thing happened then. I wept. At long last, the searing pain of all the death rose up in me. It burned in my tears. In my mind I went back through the war, saw every field of bones and rot. Every crying woman we robbed and

41

raped. Every child we left starved. Every four-legged creature that died because we hated other men. While I wept I
knew my sorrow and anger would never leave me. I would
see the war's reflection everywhere. In the woods and the
river. In my horse. In everyone I loved. Finally I understood
how the war had ruined me.

Out of the Fog waited for me to get ahold of myself.
When I finally run out of tears, though not rage and sorrow,
I thought to take him home. Then I thought again. Pa's only
interest these days was to get the farm going again. Out of
the Fog didn't survive the war so he could be a workhorse
pulling a plow in a field like some old mule, or poor Moonrunner who got worked to death. Moonrunner had pulled a
plow on the farm, then he pulled artillery on the march,
until he couldn't pull nothing more. Finally our cook made
a stew out of him. I didn't eat that day or any day 'til we
went back to hard tack and the occasional wild turkey or
stolen pig.

I figured Out of the Fog lived in the woods this long, he
could keep on. I'd come down to see him, I told him, try to
bring him an apple or some treat whenever I come. He
seemed to understand and agree.

But as I headed for the tavern I heard his hooves hit the
path behind me. Seems Out of the Fog didn't agree with my
plan after all. So I took him home and hid him in the barn
before I went to town. Later when I went to check on him's
when Lucy found him out. I got to take him somewhere
he'll stay. Only place I can think of is the Calloways.

* * *

When I storm out of breakfast this morning, I go straight to
the barn to get Out of the Fog before Pa comes. Partway

down the path to town music floats up toward us. Out of the Fog goes skittish. He dances back and forth; if I didn't know what he'd been through, I'd think he liked the music. But I do know. I ain't much less skittish myself. So I stop to wait 'til he stills. Once he's used to the noise, we go on down. When we get to Main Street, we have to stop again. This time I put my hand on his neck to keep him calm. There's horses and wagons coming down the street, the wagons painted bright Colored, with pictures of animals on the sides. A circus parade, shining on the dirt road. The dogs that roam our town bark at the music and nip at the wheels. A man with a megaphone stands on the fanciest wagon, saying if we come to the circus we'll see lions and acrobats. I wonder where they plan to put their tent up. They're headed right now for the Colored village at the west end of town.

But then he says, Out east of the town where you think there's nothing but a dried up well and an empty piece of land. Come to this place, and you will see magic!

He means Miss Ellen's place. Part of me feels sick but I know I'll go. I got to see how it fared through the war. If it still feels like only bad things can happen there.

After the parade passes, I take Out of the Fog across the road and through the woods to the Calloway place. As I get close I think about how surprised Edmond would of been to see my horse come back to me. He'd have a philosophy about it for sure. I bet he'd bless Out of the Fog, and me too. Then the four of us, me, Out of the Fog, Edmond and Alva, we'd go down to the river. I get lost in the happiness of my daydream and forget I only got one arm now. I ain't seen Alva in near five years. And I killed her brother, my best friend.

* * *

At Chickamauga the thing happened that I had prayed would never happen. Edmond and me met on the same battlefield. I didn't see him at first. Because a Federal was coming at me. He ran so fast he got close enough I could see his diseased teeth. Even through the odors of gunfire and fear it seemed I could smell his putrid Yankee breath. I shot him dead before he reached me. When he fell, Edmond stood behind him. At first, we stared at each other wondering why we looked so familiar. Not even folks you love look the same in the midst of battle. When he raised his rifle he looked so sad, and I suppose I looked just as sad when I aimed my rifle at him.

Then Edmond did the wrong thing. He forgot he was a soldier. He let our friendship take ahold of him. He lowered his rifle.

Edmond Calloway, I said, You need to raise that rifle back up.

I know he heard me even with gunfire and cannons and men screaming all around us. But he just stood there. Seemed he almost had a smile on his face.

This ain't a place for childhood feelings, I said, Lift up your gun.

I hated him for standing there like that. He had no right to make this harder for me. Then he turned his back, and this was more than I could tolerate. He walked away like I was no one. Not worth talking to, not worth killing. So I shot him. In the back. Like a coward, I shot the man I loved most in the world in the back.

* * *

Alva don't know I killed Edmond. And I ain't telling her. I won't risk her hating me. Then where would I take my horse? It's best for her and for Out of the Fog if I don't tell her.

First thing I see when me and Out of the Fog come into the Calloway yard is the children, Alva and Edmond's brothers and sisters. I heard her pa's dead and her ma's near to it. Alva's taking care of the children now. They all come running up to see the horse. The bigger ones, the boys, Robbie and Nathan, they remember Out of the Fog from when they was small.

I thought he runned away, said Robbie. He reaches for the horse. I think Out of the Fog will rear up, but the boy has a way about him, a little of his elder brother. He touches the horse on the flank, then on his head, and the two's friends. I've brung my horse to the right place.

A little girl holding an even littler girl says, Where's your arm?

Lost it, I say.

You can't find it no more?

Not never, I say. She seems satisfied by that so turns her attention back to the horse.

Alva steps out of the cabin. She must be eighteen now. I walk toward her, see her eyes glowing like violets in half shadows and half bright sun. She got dark purple-black shadows under her eyes. She's beautiful. Long black hair like I remember. I stand there waiting on her voice. Behind me, I hear the children playing with the horse. I'm thinking about how I look. Skinny, one arm, hair in my face like a horse mane. I should of left the horse in the yard and gone back home.

Johnny Harpe, she finally says.

I feel I ain't never heard my name pronounced before.

You ain't set foot here since the war, she says.

I'm sorry, I say.

She looks beyond me to the yard. Is that Out of the Fog? He come back?

My pa would put him to work.

He ain't made for that, she says, But he can't stay here. I got nothing to feed him.

I'll take care of that, I say, Look. Robbie's taken to him.

Robbie's like Edmond with the animals she says.

Hearing her talk about Edmond and the animals makes me think back past the war. To the time him and me met. Not the first time, that was at the Bridges place. All us children did our best to stay away from each other after that. Later, when I was big enough to have a slingshot, I'd wander the woods, hearing my pa's voice in my head, telling me I'm good for nothing, yelling at Lucy for being underfoot. One day I was in the woods with my slingshot when I seen some vultures on a possum carcass. I hate vultures, their ugly wrinkled heads, the way they dance on things what's dead. I was thinking which one to shoot when a sound like a little hammer starts to banging above my head. I look up and damn if a bird isn't up there pecking a door into a tree. I forgot about the vultures, aimed my slingshot at the black bandit mask on the woodpecker's red pointy head. Next I know he's laying on the ground, his yellow eye staring up at the yellow sun.

Right then some twigs snapped. I readied myself to shoot some bigger game, but out of nowhere Edmond Calloway stood beside me, looking at the bird on the ground.

You can't eat that, he said.

We both gazed at the dead woodpecker.

After a time, Edmond said, I suppose we should give it a funeral.

He picked up the bird and carried it to where the ground turned soft near the river. We used sticks to dig a hole, then Edmond laid the bird in, covered it up, and spread some of the light-filled river rose blossoms on the grave.

Let us pray, he said.

He sounded just like a preacher, so I bowed my head.

Edmond said a prayer both me and Alva would come to learn by heart. The whole of it, what I couldn't remember later when I was grieving my brother, went:

Round into the ground.
Round up to the sky.
Round down to the river.
Round into the trees.
Rising in the sap.
Rising in the roots.
Burning in the fire.
Flying in the wind.
It lives. It dies. It rises.
God.

After that day me and Edmond joined up. I'd kill, he'd bury and bless. Mostly birds: vulture, crow, bobwhite. I killed a duck once, his green head so beautiful I scarcely wanted to bury him. One of us should of taken him home for food, but we couldn't decide which of us it belonged to. Edmond saw it first; I killed it. The only fair thing was to bury it like the other birds.

One day, not far from Miss Ellen's old property, we saw

a red-tailed hawk. It stared at us so hard, looking like it known us and had no liking for us.

Barely daring to say it, I asked Edmond, Is it the preacher come back?

When Edmond didn't answer, I raised my slingshot. He knocked it out of my hands.

Can't you hear that music, he said.

I listened. I heard only a rustle in the tops of the trees.

That bird is sacred, Edmond said, We got to go away from this land and stay away.

I still didn't hear nothing, and I still wanted to kill that bird, but I trusted Edmond, so I picked up my slingshot and we left.

When I was twelve, Edmond was thirteen, and Alva must have been seven or so, that's when we started to playing Down by the River. First we'd all three pull up thorn branches. We'd make a crown of them for Alva, and me and Edmond would take off our shirts so as to wrap thorns around our waists. Then we'd walk, one behind the other down to the river. Alva first, then me, then Edmond. When we reached the bank, Alva stepped into the water. Then the three of us sang a hymn. It was a prayer first when Edmond wrote the words, but then Alva made a melody for them:

Blood in your body. Blood is water.
Blood is God. Water is God.
Lay down in the water.
The flowers of God are planted in you.
The flowers of God will bloom from your body.

Then Alva would close her eyes and lie down in the river. Edmond and me would throw flowers on her. We'd listen to the currents, the faster water toward the middle of the river, the eddies in the shallows, the tiny waves sliding across Alva and across the shore before they backed up and headed for the deep. Finally Edmond crouched down to lift Alva from the water. We'd build a fire to sit by 'til Alva was dry enough to go home.

As we got older me and Edmond and Alva made rituals for almost everything we saw or did in the forest. For hunting animals, for the falling of leaves, for the ice over the river, for the buds in the spring. It seemed too soon the war come to take it all from us.

On the day I fought with Edmond about what sides we was taking, when I turned away from him, there stood Alva. Not a baby nor even a little girl no more. Her violet eyes and her black hair stopped me in my tracks. I hadn't even noticed her growing up.

He didn't mean it, she said.

He ain't really going to fight Union?

He is, she said, But he ain't gon' hurt you. Not never. You're our brother.

He can't be my brother and fight against me.

Then fight beside him.

I can't.

I'll make songs for you both, she said.

When I left the Calloways that day, the memory of Alva's hymns got mixed up with the music drifting so softly in the forest, the melody like a vapor closing in on me; my throat tightened around the song, suffocating me. I started to run like as if I could outrun the sound. But Alva's music was in me just like Miss Ellen's, spreading through my mind like the ripples of the river when a stone gets thrown in.

❖ ❖ ❖

Today I stand in front of Alva, knowing I didn't even pray for her brother after I killed him. Nevertheless, when she opens the door to her house I step in. Like most places nowadays her house don't fit my memory of it. The main room was always a shambles 'cause of all the children, but now it looks just dark and poor and run over. I can't tell whether it's shadows or dirt clings to everything in the room. It smells like mold, like sick, like shit, all smells I got to know good in the war.

At first I don't see her ma. Then yellow eyes shift around inside what seems a pile of rags on a chair. Look like some night bird come to take vengeance on me for what I done to Edmond. But then them yellow eyes slide past me, rest empty on some broken shadow in the corner.

Alva stands beside me. I know you was on opposite sides from Edmond, she says, But time's passed. You're welcome here.

I know I should thank her. Say something kind at least. What I do say's not just stupid, but heartless, too.

Heard your ma don't talk no more I say.

No, she don't, says Alva. She don't even know what happens around here. Then Alva rests her hand on my forearm just as though I had offered up comfort instead of stupidity.

I've missed you forever, she says.

I don't know how the next moment happens. I hear her voice and next I know we kiss. I can't remember when we turned away from her mother and toward each other. She pulls me into a room even shabbier and darker than the main one. Again, time disappears. We're on the ground on a pile of torn, stinking blankets. When she pulls at my shirt I realize I can't do this. I can't let her see the wreck that used to be my arm. What if I fall on her.

I'm sorry, I say. So sorry.

I try to pull away but she won't have it.

It's what's meant to be she says as she pushes me onto my back and climbs on top of me.

I want to ask her where she learned this. There was whores in the camps who knew these tricks to control a man. I wonder is it possible... The war did such corrupting things to so many people.

I been waiting so long for you, she says.

I forget my suspicions. I been waiting so long for her too.

My embarrassment returns when it's time to dress. Alva's back in her shift in seconds, while it takes me minutes to put on my britches. She watches me, which makes it worse, so I turn my back on her. I'm relieved I resisted removing my shirt.

When we come out the room, her ma's eyes still glow through the darkness. I know her stare's meaningless, but seems there's a knowing in them, what I did with her daughter, what I done to her son. All I want now is to get away from her and them accusing eyes, so I pull Alva outside.

On the sunlit porch, Alva's hand in mine, I can't believe I didn't know I wanted this. Now I'm here, it seems so clear. I think back to when we was children, how much I loved to be near her. But then Edmond intrudes into my mind; I send him back to the muddy, bloody ground I left him on.

Standing so close to Alva in the cold spring air, hearing the river rush around the rocks in the distance, I think maybe life can be like none of the past ever happened. Even my horse is calm like he ain't never left Sinking Springs, nor ever seen the ugliness of war.

Out of the Fog still takes up the children's attention. He surprises me with his tolerance of them.

You really gon' feed that horse, Alva asks.

Yes, I say.

All right then, she says.

I want a reason to stay by her, or a reason to come back, even before Out of the Fog needs to eat. I remember the circus.

There's a circus come to town, I say, Can you go? You and the children?

Tonight?

Can you leave your ma?

She won't even know we're gone.

All right then, I say.

I'm feeling some peace for the first time in a long time, when what do I see but good for nothing Willie Reed stepping into Alva's yard, carrying a pathetic pile of sticks. Bad enough this Yankee deserter trash caught my stupid sister's eye, now here he's out at Alva's place, proving he's a no account just sniffing 'round whatever woman might be young or ignorant enough to have him.

I try to jerk my hand free of Alva's 'cause my first instinct tells me kill him. But she hangs on. Likely it's for the best, 'cause if I killed him now I'd get hanged for it. It ain't easy to remember you can't kill the very same men you was ordered to slaughter just a year ago.

Alva says, He brings me kindling sometimes. It ain't nothing but a kindness.

Of a sudden I have to get away from her. As I pull away, I promise to come back to feed the horse.

And the circus, she asks.

I don't know, I say.

I'm looking at Reed, not her. As I pass him I feel that urge to murder come up strong inside me, but I keep going. I try to make my feet head home, but I find myself crouched in the bushes just beyond her yard, like some lowest form of spy. I remind myself it was me in Alva's bed, not him. Some darkness in me whispers I couldn't have been the first. I know I shouldn't listen. I know I should go on home, leave Reed to give her the wood. Trust her that told me I was what she always waited for. I don't even know if I can chop wood. I ain't never even tried. Fact is, I didn't bring nothing to her door but another thing for her to take care of. My insides boil when I think how Willie Reed considered what she might need while I was thinking about what I want. At this moment, I hate myself as much as I hate him.

Hiding in the bushes like a coward and a spy, I watch Alva take Willie Reed by the hand. Those same sweet hands what touched me just an hour ago. Already she's using those hands to touch another man. I can't discern what she's saying, but the evil inside me tells me I know damn well. My hate surges right into my gullet to where I've got to spit it out. That's a mistake. They hear me spit and look over toward the bushes where I'm hiding.

You need something kilt, Reed asks her.

No, she says, Animals don't never trouble us.

I need to get away 'cause I want to kill them both right now. I jump up silent as a man fleeing an enemy, and I run.

Back in the woods it's hard for me to even remember that just a few hours ago this path felt sacred to me. This day, most of it, felt like it had some magic to it. Before today I'd thunk myself beyond loving or being loved. For just that time with Alva I tricked myself it weren't so. My heart feels like a stone. Where it was hot with rage, then love, then rage again, now it's gone cold and dead. I start for the tavern but remember I ain't got no money, so I set out for home.

When I get there I see Pa, Lucy, and Ma, all out in the field, all earning my keep. No wonder Pa hates me. My throat dries up, craving whiskey. I'm already a burden and a shame, why not be a thief and a drunkard too? I know where Ma keeps her witch money. Pa told her she ain't to go out treating people with herbs and such to earn witch money, but she does it anyway. She can't say nothing about the money being gone without Pa discovering she's still doing god knows what for the women in town. I dig down inside a bag of beans and take all the coins without counting. None of my family notices me when I walk back down the path.

Inside the tavern I order a drink, swallow it, order another, then find the darkest most full of spider webs and dried vomit corner. Sitting on a rotting wood bench, I sip my whiskey, flick my lighter, start to feel better. When I close my eyes I feel Alva against me; inside my head I hear the song of her voice. I should go get her, I think. Use this money to take her and her brothers and sisters to the circus like I promised. Then my thoughts stray to Willie Reed with his crazy mind and his two strong arms. I swallow the rest of my whiskey, then I have another.

With my third drink my mind wanders to Miss Ellen's land. How will it feel with a circus on it? Them people putting on an entertainment at a place what's cursed? Ain't no one talks about that land. Folks pretend Ellen Bridges run off with the preacher, 'cause who's going to call little children murderers. When our army trained on Miss Ellen's land, we lost men at least once a week to some stupid accident. Can't say how many died just learning to fire their own rifle. I heard any army what camped there during the war lost their next battle and most of their men with it.

I'm seeing the bottom of my glass when Wade Butson sets another one in front of me. He fought for the South too, but the truth of it is that my own side taunts me near as much as the Yankees do. Everyone knows what happened to my arm. Wade was among those there when it happened.

You planning to have some fun on my account, I say as he sits down.

No, he says, With Yankee so-called peacekeepers and gloating Federals all around, it's time we honorable men stick together. We can't afford to disunite ourselves or take after one another.

He gestures at the untouched drink in front of me.

Go ahead, he says, You won't owe me nothing.

I'm reaching for the glass when a whole group comes in: Richard Caldwell, Jesse Sanders, Gantly Fletcher, Toby Handon. All of 'em was among those who left me behind when my arm got cut off. Caldwell's got money from work for the railroad so he buys a whole bottle of whiskey for the lot of us. As the bottle's passed around, they start telling stories about the war. I ain't right clear on how the very occurrences what was a horror during the war have come to be something to joke about when men get together afterwards. We find ourselves laughing at the way a new group of men come on the battlefield one time, froze solid, wouldn't shoot their guns. We had to run over their bodies when it was our turn to charge.

I'm surprised to find I enjoy this talk, that I like being drunk with other men, the same men I avoided when we was fighting together and even since we got back. I keep waiting for them to devil me about sticking with the horses in the war, but they never do. They don't say nothing about my arm, neither. The bottle keeps going around, and with every drink we become better friends.

When the day turns to evening Butson says we should all of us go to the circus. Alva's face flashes in my mind, but I've drunk enough whiskey I got no trouble forgetting her.

Handon slaps me on the back.

Let's go, Harpe, he says.

My legs wobble some when I stand. Caldwell props me up when I near lose my balance.

You got trouble holding your liquor, Harpe, he says.

I'm fine, I insist.

Let's go then, says Caldwell.

It feels natural to fall in with them, almost as if we're on the march.

Lucy Harpe

I walk with Willie Reed down by the river, like always. Seems lately he's more distracted than ever. I tell him about my day with Ma, how Johnny and Pa been fighting again, but he barely listens.

Shadows fall from the trees, crisscross the ground and the water, making it too cold for the light shawl and sunbonnet I'm wearing, so I say I want to go home. He don't say a word, but he turns back. We walk the path away from the river while the dingy shafts of sunlight fade to milky blue night.

I'm glad when we reach town. The newly repaired gaslights comfort me, give me a moment of light before we climb the steep dark path to my family farm. As we step onto Main Street, I hear grunts and shouts. Among the voices I recognize my brother Johnny's angry hoarse cussing. I look down toward the tavern. Sure enough, there in the street a jumble of men roll, thrash, and grunt, my brother Johnny among them.

We should go help him, I say.

Johnny's only got but one arm, but it don't keep him from fighting like he's still a whole man.

No sense in that, says Willie, It's just fist and skull. We step in, we make it worse.

He's right. I know Johnny. If I step in or especially if Willie does, it'd be like stabbing a hornet's nest with a broom handle. I say a prayer in my heart for my brother as Willie walks me on home. When we reach the yard, like always, he says he'll see me tomorrow.

Like I been saying for almost a year, I say, Goodnight, Willie.

He turns away. As I watch him disappear in the dark, a chill passes through my heart and I wish him back next to me.

It's dark, is all my pa has to say when I go in.

Did you see your brother, asks Ma.

I tell Pa I'm sorry I stayed out so late. I tell Ma I ain't seen Johnny. Truth just leads to trouble.

I don't know what time it is when I hear Johnny come in. He don't even try to keep quiet. It's a wonder Pa don't get up and send Johnny out to the barn to sleep, for acting like such an animal.

* * *

It's only breakfast but already Ma's worried about what I might do in the evening. She says it so sweet but I know she's trying to hint her disapproval. Her voice has that lilt to it.

You going out with Willie Reed this evening, she asks, soft as butter.

I suppose so, I answer, just as sweet.

Pa don't mince words. I don't like it, he says.

And Johnny's got to repeat after him, as if I care what my one-armed brother does and don't like. Now the whole family sets to describing the many flaws of Willie Reed 'til Ma sums it up for all of them: That boy been nothing but moody since he got back from the war, she pronounces, so soft it's almost affectionate.

I have to admit to myself moody don't even begin to describe the strangeness in Willie since he come back. I blame his misguided choice to join the wrong side in the war. I used to think I understood him. But now, however much I look in his eyes, I can't see his true feelings. I rely on things I've known since we used to hide behind the school-house, me patting his pretty brown hair, so different from my blonde. Johnny says we was at the well together too. But I only remember that day like a dream. Ma says the way Willie is now weren't no surprise. She says he was borned sad, and cursed too. He was bound to join the Federals, and bound to suffer the consequences. My ma knows the stories of all the families in Sinking Springs and she tells them to me sometimes when we're sewing of an evening. That's how she came to tell me the story of the Reed family.

❖ ❖ ❖

Ma says Willie's pa, George Reed, was a poor White cracker come from Carolina. He left his orphaned brothers and sisters behind to walk over the mountains looking for work in the Tennessee marble quarries. They say he walked all that way with onions in his pockets for food, and the smell never got off him. At first, he didn't understand Tennessee marble's limestone, what needs patience to be cut in blocks with a hammer and plug drill. Sometimes too, they use black powder to get the marble out from the side of the mountain, which makes the work dangerous. It don't pay much neither.

Still, Mr. Reed learned the work, eventually earning enough to get a little piece of land at the west edge of town just past the Negro village, where he built him a little house. He even had a garden with corn, and naturally, onions. Ma says just working at the quarry, coming home to eat, going back to work again, got lonely for Mr. Reed. Luckily, about that time a Mr. Long who worked in the quarry with Mr. Reed invited him to have supper with his family.

Now this Mr. Long had three children, and among them he had a daughter, Bertha. They say she was strange and quiet, but when Mr. Reed come to their house for supper, she acted sweet and attentive to him. She smiled at him, kept refilling his plate though her brothers glared at her. Mr. Reed felt obliged to eat 'til his belly got past full. He had never experienced so much friendliness or fullness, so when he returned to home, his little house felt a dark and empty place. The next time he went to work, Mr. Reed asked his friend if he might return to visit with his daughter.

Within a season, Bertha Long became Mrs. Reed. She moved into the little house at the west edge of town, where she set about sweeping and tidying. She added sweet potatoes to the onions and corn in the garden. On Saturdays Mr. Reed would hunt so as to provide game for the delicious stews and soups she cooked. They loved each other, so before long he got a child in her. Now this seems like it'd be a happy thing, but Mr. Reed had come out of a home with little money and many children. He had failed to consider his young wife might fill his home with hungry mouths to feed. Ma says he claimed when he thought of children he felt a scratching in his throat what could only be relieved with whiskey.

Mr. Reed tried to convince his wife to see the witch in the woods. He told her she was too young for children yet. He reminded her how happy they was alone together, how with the money he earned at the quarry, their small garden and his hunting, they were just comfortable. Mrs. Reed refused absolutely, a thing he should've known, as her nurturing nature had drawn him to her in the first place.

Ma says Mr. Reed got took with the notion his home in Tennessee would become like his home in Carolina, that he'd be nothing more than a poor cracker with a house full of starving brats. So one day he told Mrs. Reed he was going hunting, but instead he went to find the woods witch. After a whole lot of begging, giving her money, plus promising her fresh game every month for a year, he was able to convince the witch to cast a spell on his wife to prevent her from having babies. To help the spell along, he had to sneak a potion into Mrs. Reed's soup. He worried it might make her sick, but on tasting her soup hisself and feeling nothing, he thought it harmless. Mr. Reed knew his wife would be heartbroken at the loss of the child, but he told hisself he'd make sure to fill up her life with his love and devotion. He would keep her so happy she'd forget about children. When she lost the child, he comforted her. Not knowing her husband's part in her misery, Mrs. Reed accepted his comfort.

Two months later Mr. Reed was astounded when Mrs. Reed announced another baby coming. He stormed out to the witch, who assured him his wife wouldn't have no babies.

But she's pregnant, said Mr. Reed.

You din't ask for her to have no pregnancies, said the witch.

Mr. Reed was horrified. He stopped taking game out to the witch, hoping she'd cancel the spell if he didn't fulfill his promise. When Mrs. Reed lost a second baby, Mr. Reed vowed he'd never put a baby in her again. Mrs. Reed didn't understand why her husband turned cold to her. She sunk into silence, her heart aching every time she looked at him. He watched her skin grow more pale each day. One night he awoke to hear her sobbing in the dark. He took her in his arms and she became pregnant once more.

Not knowing her husband's part in her woes, Mrs. Reed went far out into the woods to look for the witch for to ask her help in keeping the baby in her womb. When after searching some hours she found a mound the size of a small woman, she knew the witch was dead. When she next went to town she discreetly asked the local gossip about the witch. That's how she found out my ma, who was young then, and Jewell Smith, a free Colored woman who lived in the Negro village, had learned together from the woods witch; in fact it was them had found her corpse and buried her. Mrs. Reed decided to come up to the farm to see Ma. My older brothers and sisters was borned then, but not me nor Johnny.

Ma says when she put her hand on Bertha Reed's belly she knew right then Bertha'd been cursed. Mrs. Reed wept and begged, but Ma told her she ain't never lifted no curses. She said she was midwife and healer only. Even if she should try, there was folks in town, and there still is, who might of named her for a witch if they heard anything of curses, even if it's just a lifting of them. Ma told Mrs. Reed she likes it right here on our farm. She didn't have no interest in moving out to the woods where folks think witches belong. But Mrs. Reed wouldn't stop carrying on. So finally Ma couldn't stand to see such deep sorrow no more. She thought how she'd feel if any of her own babes had been cursed inside her belly.

Before she'd mix the herbs for the spell, she warned Mrs. Reed a great sacrifice would be required. Mrs. Reed asked what it was she could sacrifice; she didn't have much aside from vegetables for soup and the clothes on her back. Ma explained the sacrifice weren't something a person chose; a person don't get to decide what they lose, nor when they lose it. Mrs. Reed said she'd sacrifice anything to save the life of her child.

So Ma mixed the herbs for the spell. She gave Mrs.

Reed one batch to drink in a tea. The other she wrapped in muslin and bid her hide it under her pillow, there to remain until the baby was born. Mrs. Reed did as Ma said. She drank the tea, she tucked the herbs under her pillow, and sure enough her belly grew.

Mr. Reed was relieved and nervous to see his wife happy in her pregnancy. He had stumbled across the wood witch's grave while hunting, so assumed death had broken all her spells. He decided to allow this baby to be born, then seek out someone to prevent any more. They could take care of one child if it would make Mrs. Reed happy.

When Mrs. Reed woke early one morning with the pains that told her it was time for the baby to come into the world, she bid her husband go for Ma. She told him to go to the quarry after, for she might labor all day. She didn't want to frighten him should she cry out. Mrs. Reed assured Mr. Reed that when he returned in the evening he'd have a fine son. Mr. Reed did as she bid him.

Ma went down to help bring the child into the world. Mrs. Reed did labor all day, and then into the night. Ma began to think that after all, this baby was still cursed, that it would be born dead. For her part, Mrs. Reed was so consumed with the work of childbirth, she didn't even think of her husband, or of how he would get his supper when he come home. Several times someone knocked at the door, but Ma shouted at whoever was outside they should come back later.

Just before the moon began to move toward morning, the baby was born, healthy and bawling. Mrs. Reed named him William George, after her father and her husband. Ma bathed him, then put him to Mrs. Reed's breast. That was when Mrs. Reed noticed the coming dawn and asked after her husband.

Remembering the knocks on the door, Ma opened it to see Sam Boyd sitting outside.

What's happened, Ma asked.

George Reed got hisself kilt in the quarry, answered Sam.

Ma told Sam to go on home. Then she went inside to tell Mrs. Reed she had made her sacrifice.

Ma says she's worried all these years that maybe she herself would have to make a sacrifice on account of removing the wood witch's curse. When she lost her children one at a time in the war, she thought she had paid. But now she says she's afraid there's more payment still ahead. She feels it in her bones; her greatest price's coming because of me and Willie Reed. She thinks he just suddenly showed up here to see me after the war due to a curse on her. She don't know how long I've loved him.

* * *

When Willie first come to school he didn't know how to spell his own name. Since I was good at spelling, soon's I learned my letters I showed him how to make his W big and his R too. When the other children teased him for being poor and shy, I sat with him, without neither of us saying a word. Most times it felt peaceful to me. Times, though, I'd get bored. Then if someone called me to play a game, I couldn't resist. I'd leave Willie's side; sometimes I'd even forget about him. I'd be playing tag or some other game, and of a sudden I'd feel a presence. When I turned around there'd be Willie, watching me. So I'd have to leave the game to go off with him. It weren't something I could help. We was woven together like the high voices and the low voices in the hymns at church.

What I liked best about him was that even though he was a boy, he didn't seem to mind at all that what I loved best besides playing games was wandering through the woods picking wild flowers. I don't know how flowers act in other places, but here in Sinking Springs they arrange their colors according to how close they are to people.

Nearest town, we have white flowers, and pale yellow, with light green leaves, not even green as my eyes. I think if their stems and leaves was just a little deeper of color, these town flowers would look just like me. Even with this little difference, though, I still think of myself as a town flower. I'm pale in my skin and hair, and I prefer people's company mostly, always have.

Times, though, back when my whole family was alive, sometimes my brothers would fight, and Pa would yell at all of us about what kind of work we should be up to, and Ma and my sisters took after me to learn some chore like sewing or cooking, those times I'd crave the quiet, cool of the woods, and the fairies whispering by the river.

I'd slip away from the farm, down through town, into the woods. Almost soon's I got under the trees, I'd see a change in the flowers. Their stems and leaves darkened, some of them deeper, brighter green even than my eyes. The blooms just inside the woods sprung up almost gold, like they had soaked up all the sun they could, holding on so as not to wilt in the chill of the shade. These sun-filled flowers mostly died off during the war, or maybe just got trampled. Of late I've seen some of 'em struggling up, more brown than gold, but looking determined to recover. Further in, dark purple and green flowers grew close to the ground amidst the deep brown-red bushes. These was always ready for the war, with colors that could hide blood, and sturdy stems, branches, and vines that could withstand marching feet just as well as they could wild boar or bears. I used to like to think the fairies lived under the purple petals. Willie picked me some purple flowers for a present once, and he couldn't understand why I wouldn't stop weeping. He kept telling me fairies ain't real, which made me cry all the harder.

Close to the water's where the strange red river roses grow. Sometimes I felt brave enough to go to the edge of the river at the yellow-pink time of day when the flowers glow like blood and fire, while the last of the sun's light bounces purple-blue off the ripples in the river. I ain't never touched them flowers, though. In my imagination they're hot as the sun. When I was about ten years old, I brung Willie down to see them. He wanted me to touch them, to prove they wasn't hot, but I wouldn't do it. So together we looked at the flowers, then we looked at the water, then we went back to town, back to our homes. I was punished when I came in. My sisters and brothers had looked for me all day; also I hadn't done any work in the house or on the farm. After that day, Ma kept me close. I had to walk to school with Cora or Ethie. I only got to play with Willie at school, if he came. I loved him. At night I'd dream we was running through the woods, giant glowing flowers and sparkling fairies all around us.

Nowadays the woods seem full of cold shadows. The river's different too, rushing away from town, whispering secrets only Willie can hear.

* * *

I never dreamed Willie would fight for the Northern invaders. That he'd come back from the war with his insides harder than hickory wood. I'm sure his true self must be in there somewhere. Why else would he keep coming to see me? It must be love driving him, whether he knows it or not. And I can't bear to hear anyone say cruel things about him. Not Pa, nor Ma, and especially not Johnny, who's got no business to talk bad about anyone. Johnny didn't even lose his arm in the war. He lost it by way of his own stupidity on the way home. Yet, here at breakfast, they're all determined Willie Reed should be our conversation. No consideration for my feelings.

He don't work, proclaims Pa.

He helps his mother, I point out.

Helps her eat all the food she got, says Johnny.

I know in a way they're right. Willie don't work. And though she's getting on in years, Mrs. Reed keeps growing that garden, shooting squirrel or possum, or whatever else might run up close enough to the house for her to kill it. Folks say she throws everything into a pot of water hanging over a fire and calls it soup. I believe though, that like me, Mrs. Reed knows there's something different in her son. A way of seeing the world we can't fathom. A need to find his way in his own time. I try to explain this to my family.

Seems to me he's special somehow, I say.

Johnny spits on the floor.

Damn right he's special, he says.

I don't like his tone. Like he always does lately, he sounds like he'd like to cut someone with his voice alone.

Not at my table son, says Ma.

It ain't real clear whether she means the cussing or the spitting. I think he scares her. She got to do everything for him, but he rails against everyone all the time. I also know his horse come back and he's keeping it a secret. Pa could use that horse to help with plowing and planting.

I hint to Johnny I might just tell about him hiding that horse.

At least Willie Reed ain't keeping any secrets, I say.

Johnny slams his chair back, wipes his hand on his britches just the way Ma hates, and stomps out of the house. We all, me, Ma, and Pa, go on with our breakfast like nothing happened.

* * *

Though Ma and Pa knew each other all their lives, they never expected to be married. Pa always knew he'd be a farmer even though it's hard to grow crops in these mountains. It's what his pa, and his grandpa before him done. Ma was the daughter of the quarry manager. She never meant to learn from the woods witch; that all came about cause she was wild and rebellious. Ma says everything about her parents' formal, spotless clean home crushed her spirit. Her parents forbade her to go into the woods, so she went there as often as she could get away with it. She'd take off her shoes, run deep into the woods 'til it was cool and dark. That's how she come to encounter the woods witch.

The witch lived in a home she had dug out of the side of the mountain. There she kept a fire burning outside her door. Over the fire hung a pot. Whatever boiled in it caused a strange, bitter steam to rise into the air. From where she hid, Ma could see where roots and herbs hung inside to dry. Ma was crouching there spying when she sensed someone else in the bushes. She looked around to see a Colored girl, just about her own age. That was Jewell Smith, who'd later be Jewell Boyd.

You ripped your dress, Jewell whispered to her.

And Ma, petted child that she was, told her, I got so

many dresses I could just throw this in the river and my ma wouldn't never notice.

Jewell shushed her, but it was too late; the witch had heard them. Ma says the witch near to swooped in on the girls, that Jewell and her didn't see her feet touch the ground. Ma says the witch's face looked like leather. She had just two or three teeth hanging down from gray gums. Her eyes was a mix of brown and blue like none Ma'd ever seen except in stones.

Who are ye, the woods witch asked.

Ma says both her and Jewell just stared at their feet, too scared to answer.

You got names, asked the woods witch.

Jewell told her name first.

Your Pa works in the quarry, said the witch.

Then Ma said her name.

Your Pa runs that quarry, said the witch, He'll be coming to a bad end. That man who works other men to death. Suffering breeds suffering, on down the generations. It all comes back.

Her words scared Ma and Jewell both. Ma says she wanted to run, but she held her ground, and so did Jewell. The witch admired their courage, so bid them come back, and she would teach them. So Ma and Jewell Smith learned from the woods witch, and that's why my Ma knows about medicines, charms, spells, and bringing babies into the world. I wish she'd teach me, but she says those ways is disappearing. We're better off with doctors; that way we don't have to worry about any magic coming back at us.

Later the woods witch's words about my grandfather did come true. He got caught stealing from the company, pretending there weren't no money to pay the workers, and putting their wages in his own pocket. A hunter found him strung up in a tree in the north mountain woods back past where our farm is. No one knows whether he done it himself or someone done it to him. My grandmother was so ashamed she jumped in the river and drowned. Ma's sister and brother had already married and moved away.

So Ma married her only suitor, Tom Harpe, who's my pa. The first baby born to them was my brother Tommy. From what Ma says, he outdid all the hopes a mother and father could have. Obedient, smart, quick, and strong. He didn't need school to learn letters or numbers. Soon's Ma taught him at home he could read and write, sign papers, and help with farm accounts. Even as a small child, he could mend a fence, drive a plow, and work all day, whether to plant or harvest. He always made sure Ma had water from the well to cook or clean, and he never forgot his prayers. Pa and four-year-old Tommy built our barn.

* * *

Johnny says it was Tommy took us out to Miss Ellen's place. That it was him and Edmond Calloway led the way to killing the preacher. That it was Tommy told us all never to speak of it again. I only remember Tommy as the bright shining light of my parents' lives. Then came the war, and seemed the light went out of the whole world.

I'd just turned sixteen when the war started. Old enough I wasn't thinking as much about fairies and flowers, so I took notice of what happened around me, which was mostly that folks acted angry and afraid all the time. Pa said the U.S. government was coming south to tell everyone how they got to live and to take away our right to vote. As I couldn't vote anyway, and neither could my sisters, we didn't really understand what all the fuss was about. Pa said too, that the U.S. government was going to take White folks' land and give it all to the Negroes. I wondered if our slave Malachi knew about this plan. He'd worked for us since before I was born, so if the Federals was going to give our farm to a slave, I supposed it would be him.

Malachi had a wife who lived in the free section of town. She did laundry to earn money to free him but seemed every time she got close to the amount, Pa would raise the price. Pa insisted he was the best owner around because he let Emeline, Malachi's wife, visit Malachi at his quarters, a cot in an unused stall in the barn. It did seem to me that Malachi had a nice life; we loved him and he had food every day and a place to sleep.

Then came the day he rode down to see his wife without Pa's permission. When Pa and his friends brought Malachi back that night, he was bloody and sad. He didn't get up from his cot for a week. Ma said he'd taken a chill and we all pretended to believe it. When Malachi walked off the farm after Mr. Lincoln's proclamation in January of 1863, I thought if the Yankees won he might be coming back with his wife and family to claim our land as rightfully his.

It came as a relief when Pa volunteered my brothers and hisself to the Confederacy. Where would we live if the Negroes had our land? The night Pa told my brothers they was going into the Confederate army, that was when Tommy shocked everyone by calling Pa ignorant. Then he announced he was fixing to fight for the Union.

In the following silence, Ma picked up her spoon and started to eat, so we all did the same, hoping the moment would pass and life would just go back to the way it had been. But Pa and Tommy didn't pick up their spoons.

Pa said, You ain't my son if you turn traitor to our way of life.

Tommy said he knew that's how it would be. He took up a saddlebag he'd already packed and walked out the door.

First Ma, then my sisters, then me, started to cry. I could see Johnny wanted to cry too, but he didn't. Him, my next oldest brother Frank, and Pa just finished their supper. The next morning we found Johnny's horse Out of the Fog had vanished. We knew it was Tommy stole it. By the next day Pa and the rest of my brothers were gone too.

Next after my brother Tommy was my sister Ethie, born only ten months after him. When the war started, she was fixing to marry the butcher's son, Philip Sparks. The two of them got along like bread and butter. Soon as Ethie finished her chores, she'd go outside to wait for Philip. She always seemed to stand up just before he appeared around the last curve of the path before our yard. He looked to my thirteen-year-old self like the tallest, strongest man in the world except for Tommy. I think that's how Ethie saw him too. Phillip planned to be a doctor. Pa ridiculed it for a soft profession, but Ma believed in the future of medicine, and she was proud her daughter would be married to a professional man.

It like to broke Ethie's heart when Philip too joined the Confederate army. He said there'd be need on the battlefield for anyone who knew anything of medicine. There wasn't nothing to be done about it. Anyway, he had to go. It was that, or be conscripted by one side or t'other. He would of been ashamed to buy a substitute.

The training ground set on Miss Ellen's land, which is cursed, so from that time and in the battles fought later, disasters happened there. Philip had only been gone a few days when Ethie received a letter saying he had taken it upon hisself to learn to shoot regardless of his position as a medical man. He had mishandled his rifle and accidentally killed hisself.

After Ethie opened the letter she stood in the yard reading it over and over, like the news might change if she read it enough times. She weren't crying, so until Cora went out to read it herself, none of us knew what had happened. Cora brought Ethie in, showed us the letter, then Ma put Ethie to bed like as if she was sick. Ethie wouldn't stay in bed, though. She wandered the house at night; she paced the yard in the day. She wouldn't eat nor drink. She kept talking about how Philip needed her. She said they was supposed to work side by side on the battlefield.

Twice Ethie roamed down to the training ground saying she was a nurse, arrived to help Doctor Philip Sparks. The first time Ethie went down there, an officer brung her back. The second time, a cavalryman had just shot hisself in the foot. Ethie patiently helped the doctor remove the bullet, then she cleaned and dressed the wound. She wrote us a letter all about it, and about her new occupation as a nurse for our Confederacy. She still believed she was helping Philip, but in spite of her delusion, the army found her useful. They took her with them when they left, and occasionally we'd receive letters after this battle or that.

One afternoon in 1863 we received a letter from a kind soldier who wrote to tell us how Ethie had followed imaginary Philip into the aftermath of the battle at Mill Springs. The soldier related how she moved from one corpse to another, speaking to Philip about how many there was to tend there. It happened that one of the soldiers lying on the battlefield wasn't dead. He took her for the angel of death, and so as to stop her from taking him to God he shot her in the heart. Ma knew it was bad news soon as the letter arrived; she was already crying when she opened it.

My brother Frank, a year younger than Ethie, only outlived her by a year. The dysentery what followed soldiers everywhere caught up to him. By now it was 1864, and the war that was supposed to be won in weeks had gone on for three years.

At home, for months the weather wouldn't never warm up. When it finally did, the rains came and came and came. We couldn't plant early because of the cold, and we couldn't plant late because it was too wet. We had some hay and corn, but even inside the barn they rotted in the damp. We had just a few chickens left, and one time a duck Cora caught right off the river with her bare hands. We were so proud of her. We saved the chickens for eggs and we ate the duck. It was so delicious that when the rain let up, Cora went down to the river to catch another.

She did catch a duck, but she also come back covered in insect bites of a kind we'd never seen the like of before. At first Ma didn't worry so much. She packed mud on the bites, broke the duck's neck, and give it to Cora and me to pluck. We set to our chore, but after a little while Cora didn't look right to me. Seemed she couldn't concentrate on her chore, and she wobbled like she was about to fall off her chair. Her face turned pale as death, like she seen a ghost. I screamed for Ma but before she could even get to her, Cora went limp as a dead rabbit. Ma laid a quilt on her, but Cora's sweat soaked right through. Then Cora started to bleed at her nose.

Go for the doctor, Ma said.

That's when I got scared. Cora must be in a terrible way if Ma couldn't do nothing for her. I ran down the path, into swarms of strange black insects. They buzzed something like mosquitoes, high pitched. There was thousands of them, sounding like the air itself was screaming. Somehow, they took no interest in me, so I kept on. When I got to town, I saw people slapping themselves, bleeding not just from their noses, but their mouths and ears too. I saw old Bart Landry quit moving like he'd froze in place, then fall over. Those bugs set to him, even landing on his open eyes. I thought sure I was witness to the endtimes, but still I hurried on. When I reached Doc Irwin's house, it was shuttered and locked. I banged on the door 'til Jenny Pearson, walking by slapping at her arms and bleeding from her mouth, said Doc ain't a going to help us. All the rich folks got their houses locked up tight.

I remembered then I ain't seen no insects 'til I got near town. There was none up at the farm, so I determined to go back home as quickly as possible. I was fixing to ask Jenny did she want to go with me home, but she had laid on the ground, her arms and legs so limp, looked like someone took out her bones. My sister Ethie would of helped her, but me, I ran. When I reached the cooler air of home, there weren't no more bugs, but my sister Cora was dead.

I told Ma what was happening in town. Naturally, she started weeping harder than she already was, all the while ranting 'bout curses. She stayed up all that night mixing herbs and I don't know what all else together in a pot. In the morning Ma bathed Cora with her concoction, then we spent the whole day digging a hole. We wrapped Cora in a sheet, rolled her into the hole, and covered her up. Then Ma and me went back in the house. We didn't eat no supper that night. We didn't have the stomach for it.

Within a day, birds came like a low black sky, hanging over town and forest alike. It took them only days to devour those insects. Some of the birds sickened and died, but most didn't. Once the insects were all gone, those birds that survived ate up what small crops people had managed to grow. The birds ate up all the seeds of all the flowers and they ate up all the nuts from trees. They ate most of the worms in the ground, and most of the fish in the river. They even dug wild roots out of the ground. Finally, there was nothing more for them to eat, so they began to die. For some time, birds would die in flight and fall from the sky.

Then came the packs of dogs, feasting on the dead birds. Wild animals followed right after. Sometimes a fox, a wild cat, or a bear would go right into town, kill a dog or snatch up the corpse of a bird in its mouth, then disappear up in the mountains. The wild animals were followed by vultures, strutting about but not dying. The crows wasn't dying neither. Both of them's still in Sinking Springs, mostly crows, now, and dogs, too, all of 'em bold in a way animals never was before the war.

Not that long after, Davis MacAllister and Polly Adair brought Polly's snakebit sister Emily to die in our house. Ma said 'cept Cora, she never saw poison go through a person that fast, there must be some greater evil at work. For once, I agreed with Ma. As soon as Emily breathed her last breath, Davis had one of his fits. Ma and me were beside ourselves with a dead girl on our table and a boy flailing on our floor. Once Davis woke up Ma sent me down to the store to fetch Davis's uncle Asa. After Asa picked up Emily, and the four of them left, Ma and I just went to bed. There was nothing to say. We had to sleep off that day so we could be ready for the next.

* * *

Pa come back from the war last April, thin and covered with sores. He wouldn't talk about where Johnny was. Finally some letters come from a woman who been tending him, but Pa wouldn't let Ma answer, nor would he go fetch Johnny.

Let him walk home like a man, he said, If he can walk home without losing any more limbs, maybe he'll be of some use to us.

Johnny did make it home without losing any more limbs, but he wasn't much use to us anyway. I asked Pa when Tommy might be home. He said Tommy was dead to us, alive or not. He said Tommy knew better than to show his face in Sinking Springs. He said I was never to say Tommy's name again.

I had been waiting secretly for Willie to come home. He didn't get here 'til near September. First time he come up to see me, Johnny stood in the yard glaring at him, ready to continue the war right here in our yard. That day Willie went right back home without saying nothing to me. Next day he come back. Johnny was in the barn so I went out and met Willie at the top of the path. We walked down to the river. I expected him to talk to me, to tell me about his adventures, but he didn't say nothing, just stared into the water.

Did you miss me, I asked.

He answered me he had thought about my hair and my hands. I took this to be a declaration of love.

❖ ❖ ❖

This morning, eight months later, now Johnny's out of the house, I tell my parents how I've been thinking, if I just knew what to do, I could comfort the mad out of Willie, and he'd be all right.

That boy ain't never gon' be all right, says Pa.

He's a grown man, Lucy, says Ma.

Pa says, If he can't take care of his own mad, there ain't no one gon' take care of it for him.

And with that final proclamation, Pa gets up from the table, brushing crumbs from his shirt onto the floor.

I got work to do, he says as he goes out.

When Ma stands up too, I understand both my parents have said all they're going to say about Willie Reed. Working's a sign that talking on a subject's done. Me and Ma go out to wash the dishes together. Neither of us say a word. We work together like we've learned to work over these years, both of us knowing what to do. But today, words bust out of me.

Ma, do you hate Willie so much, I ask.

I don't hate no one, she says.

More words come flying from my mouth: I think I might love him.

Ma scrubs a plate in silence.

Directly she says, What makes you think that?

Because, I stammer, Because no matter what I know in my head, how he's poor, how he's strange, how he's likely not even a good prospect for a husband. I can think all that and know it. But when I see him, it's like. Like there's something just pulling me toward him.

It's called pity, girl.

It can't be that simple.

It is that simple, says Ma, A woman sees some broken suffering creature, she can't help but pick it up and try to save its life.

But what if it can be saved, I ask.

How many of them broken sick birds and squirrels you children brung home do you see 'round here?

It ain't the same.

Ma says it with the conviction of a Bible verse: Creatures get damaged, they stay damaged.

Some heal, I say.

Ma stops working to look straight at me.

Lucy, honey, know this. There's always a sign of the damage. A missing limb, a limp, a scar. A mad or sad that don't heal no matter what.

Ma gathers the dishes. Work again.

What do I do, I ask her.

Seems she's just going to take the dishes into the house, but finally she does answer me.

You think careful girl, she says, I've told you the stories. You don't know what kind of trouble you might bring on us.

I can't tell her how me and Willie's already been bonded. And Johnny too, for that matter. I don't even know what she'd do if she found out about how we murdered that preacher. Anyway, seems to me I been thinking careful since the day Willie showed up, strange and distant, but looking for me. I know he'll be here tonight, too. I have to admit, though, walking with him by the river's been causing me more discomfort of late. Would I be able to say no to him? If I didn't want to go, could I tell him I want to do something else? I decide to test myself. I'll speak my mind, tell him I want to go to town, or any old place that ain't that river.

❋ ❋ ❋

In the early evening Willie comes into the yard; I walk out to meet him.

Lucy, he says.

Willie, I say, About the river.

There's a circus, he says.

A circus?

Pa comes outside to tell me I can't go walking out tonight.

Willie's taking me to the circus, Pa, I say.

With what money?

I got money, says Willie.

Please Pa?

Pa knows I ain't done one thing for fun in five years. He waivers.

Please, I say again.

You can even hear a glare in Pa's voice when he says, You bring her right back after.

I will, promises Willie.

Honestly, I can barely hold in my excitement as we head down the path.

As we near town Willie says, It's set up at Miss Ellen's.

I almost go right back home.

It's no good can come from that, I say.

We been through a war, Lucy, Willie says, Ain't nothing a circus can do to us, no matter the land it's on.

I want him to be right. It would be such a relief to have some fun.

Polly Adair

Polly Adair, shrieks my mother, How can you be with child?

I cannot help but sass her. Far as I know, there's only one way, I say.

She ignores my tone, too absorbed in how I'm blighting my family name, my upbringing, and the memory of my dear, innocent departed sister who would never have shamed herself by conceiving out of wedlock.

I raised you to be decent, Mother says.

I cannot help it, the truth flies from my mouth:

You barely raised me at all, I say, Florence raised me, right up to the minute the Federals forced her to be free. Since then, near as I can tell, I've been taking care of you.

I should never have let you go walking with that Yankee soldier, she says.

She's referring to Peter Allan, Union peacekeeper, father of my child. I pull my favorite silver flask from my décolletage and take a very unladylike drink. This is too much for Mother to bear. She snatches the flask from me.

There will be no drinking your father's liquor!

What father, I say, He's been gone long enough, I reckon I've inherited his liquor.

Be quiet girl, you talk like the devil's whore, she says.

This riles me. Because how did I become the devil's whore? And which devil might she be talking about, the gray devil or the blue? Those were the devils that used me as whore. I love the father of this child.

I will not say these things to my mother. Not because she was there when I was attacked, and she already knows; not even because I want to convince her Peter is different from those that, if I'm a whore, made me it. The reason I won't remind her is because she has sent the whole war from her memory. I look into her eyes, which are somehow enraged and vacant at once.

I say, Now the devil's whore is fixing to have the devil's baby.

My mother pretends not to hear me. She turns once again to the subject of my phantom father, asking me in her best shaming tone, what he will have to say about all this when he returns.

Father's dead, I answer.

It may sound cruel, but this is a truth I want her to know. Because of her dislike of truth she only has a sliver of a chance to hear it when uttered in the boldest of language. And as usual, my truth telling has no influence. Mother keeps on with her fantasy, insisting Father is just missing. Just slow getting home.

We have not seen nor heard from him for five years, I say.

Still she doesn't hear me. Still she continues to rant, laying my sullied reputation before my father's stern, if absent, judgment, finishing with a grand flourish of her dust rag, which I can see was once one of my dresses.

* * *

I don't know if I'll ever forgive my father for leaving us alone here. He could have bought a substitute, but his Confederate pride outweighed his common sense. Because we're in the center of town, and because we were once wealthy, soldiers always made our home among the first of their stops, whether they were passing through or embedding themselves. Early in the war, the first Confederates to arrive at our door claimed to know my father. They asked politely to be fed. We invited them to sit down to the dinner table with us. We packed them provisions when they left. Our Confederate money was still good in the store, so we were able to buy more food. Those early visitors seemed like guests; they respected Mother and Emily and me, even if a few of the younger ones flirted with my sister and me, and a few of the older ones leered. No one tried to touch us.

When the Federals came through it all changed. I opened the door to them, but they behaved as if we had forced them to kick it down. They swarmed the foyer, spreading through the house like an invasion of ants. They pointed their bayonets at us. They ordered Florence, our slave, to be free, and she ran out. I don't know what became of her.

The Union soldiers broke our furniture, taking away pieces to use as firewood. Then they picked me up and carried me forcibly to my room, where they hurt me in my own bed. One after the other. I didn't even know a woman could be hurt that way. All the while I could hear Mother screaming in the kitchen. I could not imagine that men would do the same thing to her as to me. I have never asked her. I saw a soldier grab Emily. Though I try my best never to think about it, I can easily imagine what he did to her. After that visit, my sister never spoke again.

Throughout the war the Union and the Confederacy took turns capturing Sinking Springs. Whichever army held the town would surge into the house. When they found nothing to steal, they'd take their anger out on Mother, Emily, and me. Sometimes they'd try to turn our house into a hospital, but the other side would always come in, take their wounded out and lay them in the street. Which to be honest, I was grateful for. Those men never stopped moaning, bleeding, and calling for their mothers, and their wounds emitted the most foul odor.

None of them, Confederate or Union, knew about the barrels of whiskey my father kept in a secret cellar out back. He had covered the cellar door with dirt before he left. After the second wave of men left, I went into Father's office to find his flasks, hidden behind books just like I remembered from when Mother forbade him to drink in the house. I went outside, dug up the cellar and went down, filled every flask, put them back in Father's hiding places, then went back out to rebury the cellar doors. I go back out only when I need all the flasks refilled, and only at night.

Eventually, we knew how to prepare for any soldiers, North or South, who came through. When we heard them coming, we pushed Emily up into the attic, I promptly got drunk, and Mother retreated into her state where nothing that is happening is actually happening. In a way, I envied her ability to disappear without aid of spirits. As time went on, it took her longer and longer to come out of it, and I fear it may be her primary condition of late.

I don't remember clearly when everything but the whiskey was gone. We went to the store one day to find our money was no good. Some kindhearted folks would leave us bread or beans or some apples by the back door. We never sought to find out who, as we wanted to avoid the humiliation of thanking them.

Everything was even worse for a few days when strange buzzing insects swarmed the town. We had to shutter the whole house, and no one brought us food. I determined to survive on whiskey, until the situation forced Mother to reveal the candies she had hidden beneath the floorboards.

It's the filth of soldiers brought insects here, insisted my mother, Their filthy bodies, their filthy crimes, the filthy dead.

This was a rare moment of clarity for her. I wished she'd have more of them.

After the insects, came the birds and the dogs. They have never left. Evil is nothing if not tenacious.

One afternoon, I took Emily with me up into the woods to gather chestnuts. She still didn't speak, but the sunshine seemed to lift her spirits. She even smiled. Then Davis MacAllister stepped out from behind a tree, and everything changed in an instant. He told us the devil brought him to the forest, and though I said I didn't believe him, some premonition told me that perhaps I should. That premonition was realized when he pulled out a knife, telling us he was going to cut locks of our hair. We turned and ran.

Emily had sprinted ahead of me, when suddenly, she stopped. She slowly turned back toward me, the terror on her face sending me into a panic. She took a step toward me, but couldn't take another before she fell to the ground. When I ran to kneel beside her, she pointed at her ankles. I don't even know how many little snake bites were there. And only evil Davis MacAllister to help us.

He took his time walking over to us, and he took his time carrying Emily to the nearest house, which was the Harpe farm. I thought surely Mrs. Harpe with all her witch knowledge could save Emily, but nothing she tried made any difference. I was holding my sister's hand when she took her last breath.

Then Davis had a fit, which served him right. My memory of everything after that is foggy. Lucy went to get Davis's uncle Asa. The four of us went down to my house, Asa carrying Emily. I thought my mother would blame me, but her grief was bigger than blame. Someone built Emily a casket. The day Mother and I stood in the graveyard watching them pile dirt on top of our beloved Emily felt like a terrible, horrible dream, worse than any violence that had happened. And around us, wartime life went on.

Then peace came, and with it, the peacekeepers.

By that time, our anonymous helpers must have been hard pressed to feed themselves, as they only left us a few bruised apples, along with small chunks of stale bread; sometimes some dandelions, which we did not know what to do with. I tasted the flower once and it was bitter. Mother used them to brighten up our wreck of a house. Inspired by the weeds, she decided it was time to clean up the house in preparation for my father's return. She told me not to worry about money. Father would be home any time. All would be well.

Luckily, only one of us was that deep in a fantasy world. I began to consider work. Because I can read and write, it occurred to me I could be a teacher, although I haven't much patience with children, or anyone, really. The schools had not yet reopened, though. I thought perhaps our minister would know where I might find some work, so I set out for the Presbyterian church to ask him.

As I neared the town center, I hesitated. The peace-keepers still occupied the Fort—what we came to call the courthouse since the Confederate and Yankee invaders had begun to take it over in succession—our own town business came to be conducted in the Methodist church, or the home of the new mayor, who by some miracle or treachery, managed to retain most of his belongings.

I took a breath, crossing in front of the Fort. Just as I feared, a soldier said good morning to me.

His name was Peter Allan, and he was the tallest, prettiest Yankee I ever saw. His eyes were like the summer sky, his hair as brilliant as the sun. The very sight of him made maudlin, sentimental ideas flood my mind, which until that moment had been plagued with the dark terrible memories of these recent years. To my embarrassment, my stomach rumbled.

Have you eaten, he asked, his voice smooth as fresh milk.

I insisted I had.

He pulled a pear from his jacket, saying it was a shame I wasn't hungry, as he was uncertain what he would do with this very ripe pear. He himself had eaten, but some kind soul had given the pear to him.

I know my eyes on that fruit must have been like a fox on a rabbit in the dead of winter. Peter Allan lifted my hand by the wrist, turned it over, and placed the pear in my palm.

Then he asked my name.

When I told him, his expression darkened. Polly Adair, he said, I've heard fellows talk about you.

I know my complexion reddened at that moment. It doesn't matter if a girl did a thing by choice; it only matters she did it. I couldn't look at him.

He did a strange thing, then. He touched my burning cheek.

I'm sorry for what happened to you, he said.

I need to be on my way, I responded.

Where might you be going?

As it seemed he already knew the most shameful part of my history, I told him I was looking for work.

You're too good for that, he said. He said he received more rations than he could use. That he had credit at the general store, too. He asked for the honor of helping my mother and me, just until my father should return home, or I should marry.

God help me, I accepted his offer. I accepted his offer, even with a voice in the back of my mind asking me why a complete stranger would offer such a thing. I did not even ask him who it was told him about my mother and my absent father. I did not ask him what he wanted in return. He was so pretty, his voice so sweet, and I had a fresh pear in my hand. I did not continue on to talk to the minister; I went back home.

That evening the basket that appeared on our back porch contained substantially more supplies than usual— even a little soap— which I admit did make me wonder if it was a comment on my hygiene. Mother responded to our new supplies by stating the grocer had finally filled our order correctly.

After three days of groceries, Peter Allan himself appeared at my door soon before sunset. When I did not invite him in, he astutely realized it might distress my mother and myself to have a soldier in the house. He politely offered to take me out. Coming up behind me, Mother saw the uniform and assumed the war had resumed.

For God's sake, she said, Let him in before he tears down the door.

I did as she asked.

Mister, shouted my mother as he stepped in, Your kind already took it all and my daughter's virtue, too. Why can't you just leave us alone?

Oh madam, he said, You misunderstand. I don't want to take anything. I would like to walk out with your beautiful daughter if you can spare her.

Spare her, asked Mother, What does she do around here?

Peter Allan settled his blue eyes upon me, making me forget my mother was even there.

Let's go see the sunset, he said.

I've seen it, I answered.

Have you seen it today, he asked.

He looped his arm through mine and escorted me out of the house. We wandered, seemingly without destination.

The war treated you badly, he said.

That would be a fair statement, I responded.

I suppose you have a bad opinion of soldiers.

That would also be a fair statement.

Maybe I could change that.

I don't know how you could.

When did you last laugh, he asked me.

Strange. I hadn't thought about laughter in so long. I used to laugh with my sister. We laughed at our parents, at the boys who courted us. Somehow laughter had slipped not just away from my life, but from the town, from Tennessee; I would wager it had slipped away from most of the country.

Do you think you can make me laugh, I asked him.

Not today, he answered, Not yet.

Then you expect to see me again, I said.

I do, he answered.

After that evening, both the food and Peter Allan continued to arrive at the house. Each time we went out walking, we went a little further from home. To the west toward the Colored part of town, to the north toward the Harpe farm where my sister Emily died, to the south toward the river; but never toward the center of town and the Fort.

In all these walks, I saw no sign of his intention to make me laugh. Peter Allan was never amusing. In fact, he rarely spoke. Mostly we walked quietly, occasionally commenting on a flower or the weather.

We cringed at the flocks of birds crowding the sky. We

dodged the mangy dogs that ran free seemingly everywhere, some alone and some in packs, all terrifying.

One evening a rabid dog blocked our path. Peter shot it, then to my surprise, he wept. I stood impassive. The death of a dog doesn't make me sad. That poor beast was foaming at the mouth, its teeth bared, its legs stiff; but its eyes were terrified. It was a relief when it yelped and fell quiet, when its wild eyes closed peacefully.

Peter went to the nearest house to borrow a shovel. He dug a hole, and when I looked into it, I suddenly thought of all the soldiers attacking each other like rabid dogs, eyes filled with fear, obeying a disease with no understanding of what was happening to them. For most of the men I had known in this town, my father among them, a hole like this was likely the best fate they had. I told Peter I would see myself home; I could no longer watch. He didn't respond; he was laying the dead dog's body in the grave.

The next day Peter and I went to the river. When we reached the shore, he kissed me. Just that, that time. It was just a kiss, and when it was over, his hands still rested on my shoulders and my skirts remained all in order. In my astonishment, I laughed.

Miss Polly, he said, I meant to make you laugh one day, but I didn't think I'd accomplish it with a kiss.

I apologized. I didn't know how to explain to him how his simple kiss freed me. The delight in realizing there was no violence to follow. I'm not sure what I stammered out, but it wasn't that. Whatever I said must have been amusing, because he laughed too. Then we held hands while we walked and walked, while we listened to the river, the breeze in the trees. While I listened to the music in the sky that I knew he couldn't hear.

In time the day came when I did for pleasure what had

only ever been a violation. I can only use the word astounded. How could this be the same act? Did the same heart beat in my breast? Beat just as hard, but with desire instead of terror? The shock of it overwhelmed my emotions; I found myself in love. With love came hope. And levity. And compassion. My ridiculous mother seemed charming to me. I pitied the horrible dogs and birds that overran the town. I lived for the time I would spend with Peter Allan.

Because he lived at the Fort with other men, and Mother never met a closed door that wasn't begging to be opened, we were driven to express our love in all manner of wild places: We lay on large, flat, moss-covered rocks at the edge of the river; we hid behind the dying trunk of a fallen tree in the woods. When winter came we found a cave that blocked the wind and protected us from the snow. Peter bought a blanket, which we kept there, neither his nor mine, but ours.

We met at the cave whenever we could, sometimes more than once a day, so it's a miracle it wasn't until spring that I missed my monthly troubles and began to lose my breakfast every morning. At first I was dismayed, but then it dawned on me that I was going to have a baby, become a family with the man I loved most in the world. I could barely contain my excitement. Soon after my discovery, I suggested to Peter we stroll along the river rather than go straight to our cave. He acceded. As we walked along, noting how the waters had risen now the snow had melted on the mountains, I took the opportunity afforded by the talk of spring and renewal to tell my beloved about my condition. Imagine my amazement when he backed away from me.

Oh, Polly, he said.

To my ears, he was speaking a foreign language.

We were just passing the time, he said, We warmed up the cold winter.

Passed the time until what, I wanted to know, and soon wished I had never asked. We were passing the time until his wife and son could join him in Sinking Springs. Until he had saved enough of his pay to repair for them one of the homes abandoned during the war. And when would the wife and son arrive? Tonight. Peter swore he was just about to tell me. He had no idea of my condition. I wanted to hit him, but I could barely breathe. I had to get home. He didn't even try to stop me as I ran away from him.

The next day Peter came to my house, and at first I thought he had had second thoughts; he had come to realize how much he loves me. For a moment, I foolishly entertained the idea that he might leave his wife. But when I came outside to speak with him, he encouraged me to drink Pennyroyal tea. He said he'd buy it, that the loss of the baby would look just like natural monthly sickness. I told him I would consider his suggestion. He said to come see him if I needed money for herbs.

I could never have predicted the way his visit changed my attitude about the thing growing inside me. Suddenly I saw it as an invader in my body and in my life, nothing more than a reminder of what a foolish child I am. I know I could get what I needed from Mrs. Harpe; all women in town know this by the time they are fourteen or fifteen. I also know making medicine from Juniper berries can be dangerous, and that the result doesn't look at all natural. I've seen women after Mrs. Harpe visits them. One woman I know, using the medicine because her baby was the result of a visit from a Yankee brigade, died from taking too much in spite of Mrs. Harpe's warnings. She was determined to be sure it worked. I didn't live through this war just to die trying to kill a baby. Maybe I do want it, I thought. Why couldn't I be a mother? I could do no worse than my own mother. I could love it, and it would love me back. I decided to tell my mother, and here we stand.

* * *

Mother puffs herself up to her proudest height, the top of her head reaching nearly to the height of my nose.

We will not bring a bastard into this family, she declares, By the time your father returns, you had better have a husband. A good one with a good name.

This is comical. Good name or not, every one of the few men left in town has some kind of limp or a vacant stare, or an arm chopped off like what happened to Johnny Harpe. Or else they are peacekeepers like Peter, and I've seen how that turns out.

I don't need a husband. I can easily say I married secretly and my husband died in the war, I tell her.

What do you know about raising children, asks my mother.

As much as you, I answer.

But then my doubts return. I think I had better ask Peter for money so I can buy the medicine. While I'm thinking on him and money, it occurs to me: He owes me much much more than that small amount. He owes me for his cruelty and my shame. Most of all, he owes me to keep silent whenever I might chance to see his wife.

I go to the Fort to find him standing outside, looking important.

Lieutenant, I say, May I speak with you?

I ignore the ugly, secretive laughter of the nearby peacekeepers. I wonder what precisely they know, and how his wife will remain ignorant with all these nasty, blustering men around.

I need to talk to you, I insist.

I'm posted atop, he says.

We climb to the roof, him helping me up the ladder. When we reach the top, he speaks over my head, as if I'm distracting him from something at the peak of the mountain.

I can have the money to you by tomorrow, he says.

I miss the former gentleness in his voice so much.

I'm keeping this child, I say.

I cannot describe the pleasure I feel at his shocked and fearful expression. During his stunned silence, I take in the view.

Out over the trees I can just make out the river. The mountains loom all around, holding us like an enormous cradle. It seems something's happening at Ellen Bridges's old place. I wonder who would want to go there. That property is cursed.

You can't mean that, Polly, he says.

But I can.

You know you'll ruin both our lives.

Yours more than mine.

I don't think so, Polly. No one will ever marry you. You know people would blame you for destroying my family.

What matters, I say, is that your family will be destroyed.

Please don't do this, he begs.

As much as I'd like to prolong this moment, I need to get to the point.

I want money, I say.

I told you I'd give you the money.

Not just that money. I want enough for Mother and me until the time I do get married.

I don't know that I could manage that. My wife—

You can figure it out, Peter, I say, After all, it's much easier for me to do nothing, let nature take its course, let my belly grow, than to go through the trouble and pain of making it go away.

All right, he says. His once sparkling blue eyes turn gray as the clouds before a storm. His mouth sets in a straight hard line as if he had never smiled and never could. I find this so satisfying.

Starting right now, I say.

I don't have much.

It's more than I have.

He reaches into his pocket, pulls out some coins.

Thank you. You can put the money in the baskets of food you'll continue to send, I tell him.

If I'm giving you food—

We need both.

And you'll get rid of it?

I will, I say.

Our business concluded, Peter quickly climbs down the ladder, leaving me to make my own way down, my skirts catching in my boots. I tell myself, from this moment, Peter Allan is a ghost. I decide to go to Slacom's store to cheer myself up with a hair ribbon.

When I come in, I see it's Davis behind the counter. At least it isn't his terrifying uncle, Asa Slacom. Back when we had money, there were times if I came into the store to find Asa there, sneering at customers as he waited on them, I would walk right back out, never mind how much we might need whatever I was there to purchase. During the war, everyone stayed inside when Asa and his Home Guard were out and about. I'm pretty sure he didn't favor either side, because people with both Federal and Confederate Allegiances disappeared, as did Negroes and some women, mostly poor ones that no one noticed or cared when they vanished.

Davis tending the store comes with its own fears and bad memories, though. I'm always afraid he might have one of the fits that have plagued him since he bumped his head on the well. I only ever saw him have one once, but it was under the worst circumstances: the day my sister died. Even though he had just been playing a childish prank, nevertheless I blame him some for Emily's death. We never would have run into that field if he hadn't chased us.

I try to remember that day as seldom as possible, though I sometimes dream of Emily covered with snakes. Once I dreamed of her skeleton, snakes slithering in and out of her empty eye sockets, weaving through her ribs. I woke sobbing so hard mother plied me with nearly half a flask of whiskey despite her dislike of spirits.

Can I help you, Davis says as I enter the store.

I gather myself, approach him, my best artificial smile adorning my face.

Hello, he says, How are you?

Fine, I say.

What can I do for you, he asks.

I do not like his voice at all. The only word I can think of to describe it is furtive. There's always a feeling around him as though he's hiding something.

I'd like a hair ribbon, I say.

Would you, he asks, What might you need a hair ribbon for?

For my hair, I answer.

He smiles at me as if he knows something about me.

Of a particular color, he asks.

Blue, I say.

Like your sister's eyes, he says.

I shouldn't be surprised he would say something so cruel, but I can be cruel, too.

Maybe something in a deep brown, like your brother Charles's eyes, I say.

I need a drink. I consider pulling the flask from my bosom and drinking right here in front of him. Just to change the mean expression on his face.

He sets a roll of blue satin ribbon on the counter.

Will this do, he asks.

Yes, I say.

What length, he asks.

Long enough to go around my head, I say.

He stretches a length of ribbon across the counter.

Will this suit you, he asks.

Yes, I say.

He pulls a little penknife from his pocket, the same knife he threatened Emily and I with. I'm determined not to react.

Don't y'all have scissors, I ask.

I prefer my knife, he says, See, it's sharp enough to cut this wood.

He holds up a little wooden figure.

Do you recognize her, he asks.

I peer close as I can without taking any steps toward him. The figure does look familiar.

No, I say.

It's Miss Ellen, he says.

I feel a little dizzy.

I don't think its right to carve her likeness, I say.

He tells me he's carved the likeness of all of us.

I have to go, I say.

He slices the ribbon, holds it out to me.

I try to take it from where I stand.

Perhaps I should tie it on you, just to be sure, he says.

No, I say, No thank you. How much?

A penny.

He's smiling at me with his enormous white teeth. He prides himself on them, I've heard. Doesn't even drink tea or coffee. I know this is much less than the price.

Davis, I can pay.

We're old friends. And if you want something extravagant, you should have it.

I think he winks at me, like somehow a lascivious gesture will make me attracted to him.

I don't consider a hair ribbon extravagant, I say.

Well. Given the times, he says.

One of those damn crows has hidden itself in the rafters. It squawks as though in agreement with Davis.

I toss a penny on the counter, reach for the ribbon. He seems reluctant to give it up, so I tug. Finally he lets it loose. There's a greasy fingerprint where he held the end. I need a drink. I need this day to end. When I open the door to the street, the store fills with calliope music. Davis comes around the counter to join me at the door. He breathes through his mouth and I can smell his breath. It smells like judgment, secrets, and peppermint.

A wagon passes down the road. Painted on its red-orange side is a strange animal. An elephant, I think. But I always thought elephants were massive, with big ears. This painting looks like a hairless dog with a snake on its face.

A circus, I say.

Davis snorts. A wasteful entertainment, he says.

I tell him I saw it setting up at Miss Ellen's place from

the roof of the Fort. I immediately regret my words when he stares hard at me.

How did you come to be up there, he asks.

I like the view, I reply, The soldiers sometimes let me go up.

He keeps staring at me. There's something different about you, he says.

I pretend I don't hear him.

I haven't been there since, I say, To Miss Ellen's, I mean. A group of shabby horses trots by. I must admit they have a nice way of prancing that almost makes you forget their condition. They remind me of myself.

Finally, the last of the parade passes by, a group of ridiculous old men in baggy clothes and greasy white faces with hideous painted red smiles.

I must be going, I say after the last ugly man has passed.

Are you going, he asks.

I just said I'm leaving now.

I mean going to the circus, he says, I don't intend to.

I wonder if he knows he's rubbing his head while he says it. I suppose you wouldn't want to go there, I say, After what that accident did to you.

No, he says.

I need to get home, I say.

He doesn't answer, just goes back in the store.

I return home to find my mother on hands and knees, scrubbing the floors. When I question her, she tells me we cannot have a welcome home ball for my father with these filthy floors.

The filth won't rub off, she says, What will Mr. Adair say?

I never did understand why Mother calls Father Mr. Adair when she's speaking to her children. When Emily and I were babies, we called him Mr. Adair until Florence explained to us we were supposed to call him Father.

Is that my white party dress, I ask.

No call for you to wear white anymore, she answers.

I decide not to argue with her today, though I'm angry she seems to have taken all of today's water for her illusory chore. I had hoped for more than just washing my face with the water in the pitcher in my room. I have to admit I have never reconciled myself to seeing her do slave work, or to doing it myself for that matter. I'd rather let the dust pile up.

I find a flask, plop myself in one our once-fancy chairs with its stuffing ripped out by soldiers in search of the gold they believed my father must surely have hidden. Of course, my father didn't hide any gold. Or if he did, he hid it even better than the whiskey. As I drink and watch my mother clean, I begin planning how and when I will go see Mrs. Harpe for the medicine. This leads me to think about Peter Allan, which in turn brings his wife to mind. What does she look like, I wonder. What is it about her that he prefers to me? He could easily have abandoned her after being away so long in the war, just like my father abandoned us.

It occurs to me Peter will likely take his family to the circus. If I go, It would be a simple and discreet way to see her for myself. The more I drink, the better I like the idea. I determine that I will go. I could even take my mother so as to be inconspicuous.

There's a circus in town, I say to her, We should go, see some entertainment.

My mother looks up from where she scrubs an imaginary stain off the floor.

Why on earth would I do that, Polly? Do you not see how much work I have to do? I would assume you would want to stay home and think about how to solve your current dilemma.

I've thought about it, I say, And I think you have worked enough for today.

How would you know how much work is enough, she says, I haven't seen you do a lick of work in your life.

I'm going by myself, then, I say.

Go ahead, she replies, Put the last nail in the coffin of your reputation.

If you say so, Mother, I say as I go up the stairs.

What to wear is my next concern. We hid away a few dresses, but lately Mother claimed them as the only dust rags worthy of our regal and broken furniture.

I have one of Emily's dresses hidden. I rolled it up and stuffed it in our attic, first to hide it from soldiers, then to keep it hidden from my mother. I have to climb onto a chair to push the attic door open. I feel around, and at first I can't find it. My heart floods with sadness. It's all I have left of my sister. Then my hand touches cloth. I pull the dress down and replace the door.

I shake the dust out of the dress. It smells a little moldy, but if the animals smell as bad in the circus as they did in the parade, I don't think anyone will notice. Carefully, in case the fabric has become fragile, I try it on. It used to be small on me, but five years of near starvation does much for a lady's figure, even a lady with child. The mahogany color of the dress contrasted Emily's blue eyes and blonde hair; it's a match for my brown eyes and auburn hair. When I put the dress on, I imagine I'm both of us, a combination of my body and experience, and the delicate, laughing, kind woman she might have grown to become. I tie on the blue ribbon. Emily would have been so pleased to see me wearing such a pretty decoration. I allow myself to miss my sister for a few breaths.

When I come downstairs my mother looks at me and bursts into tears. This is the very first time I've seen her cry throughout all our troubles. It frightens me. She has much to sorrow over. What if she should never stop weeping?

I miss Emily, too, I say.

Mother dabs at her eyes with the same rag she used for dusting.

We'll see her someday again in heaven, she says.

I have never been able to conceive of what heaven might be; nevertheless, I agree with her. I want her comforted as quickly as possible so I can leave. She sniffs one last sniff before returning to her housework. I slip out the door.

Delia Boyd

My poor, gone baby brother. Born at the start of the war, Mama named him Promise, 'cause the world was gon' be different for him. She's gone now, and Papa too. We was just the two of us, me and Promise, and he was my responsibility. I wasn't 'sposed to let him get sick. I feel like I might sit in this spot 'til I'm gone too.

Carter Bridges must of knocked but I didn't never hear it. Of a sudden he's in the room. I ain't seen him since he practiced his picture making on me, Mama, Papa, and Elijah. I heard Carter went off to make pictures of the war. And I also heard he came back. When he first returned I thought he might of seen Elijah and want to let me know, or at least come out here just to see me, but he never did. I assumed he just forgot about me. Now there he stands, Carter Bridges. In my home, bringing memory after memory all the way back to the day at the well, which ain't nothing but a bad dream to me now, wrapped up in so many other bad dreams, with this one now the worst.

Carter looks at me so tenderly I think maybe he's an apparition. But he comes over, stands next to the bed where Promise lays so still.

How long he been sick, he asks.

Just three days.

Fever?

Burned so hot I couldn't hardly touch him.

Carter puts his hand to Promise's forehead, like he might find him fire-poker hot instead of stone-cold dead.

You call the doctor?

What doctor, I say, The White doctor? You think he comes out here? Since my Mama been gone Colored folks on our own, scrabbling together what we can remember from her and from folks' old grans. We get what medicine we can from the forest, hoping no White man gon' come through telling us we're stealing nature.

I hear my voice rise with anger, though I know he ain't responsible for none of this. He don't know what none of us been through here. He was at the war and he lives in the town. Near as I know, he only stays around White folks. I don't know what brung him out here tonight, though he always did have a knowing. I wonder did he have a vision of what happened here the way he used to see the future when we was children. I don't ask, though. I don't want to know what he knows.

He says he'll help me bury my brother. He asks should he build him a box.

What for, I say, Promise, he never did hold still. He wouldn't want to stay in a box. Best we wrap him in his blanket. Best we just bury him.

The idea of my little baby brother under the ground starts me weeping again. Seems every hurtful thing's rising up from where I hid it inside me, coming spilling out my eyes like a river.

Carter wraps Promise in the blanket and picks him up. Sorrow itself sings in the air.

I must of helped bury my brother. Next thing I know I'm kneeling by a mound of dirt under a tree. Carter's packing moss on top, then stones. When he's done it looks nice, like part of the forest. Then he kneels down beside me. I don't want him here no more. And though it seems ungrateful, I ask him to let me alone.

You all right out here, he asks, like as if I ain't been out here all my life.

I listen: animals, wind, leaves, water, music. Everything in its place.

Yes, I say.

I'll look in on you tomorrow he says before he goes off into the woods.

I don't care whether he comes back or not. I lay both hands on the stones atop my brother's grave.

I'm sorry, I say to him, I didn't know anything else I could do.

I kiss one of the stones before I take myself inside.

• • •

This morning, I swear its Promise wakes me, just like he done for the past four years. But my eyes open on a cold empty room. I think to fix breakfast but cooking for just me's too sad. I go out to stand over my baby brother. My mama would of known how to heal him. I wish she'd taught me those potions she learned from the woods witch. She cared more I learned reading, writing, and numbers. She felt strongly I should be a teacher in the new world after the war. She didn't live to see nothing I'd become.

• • •

During the war the Home Guard'd come out here sometimes. They'd circle our house, shouting ugly words what made me feel dirty and ashamed. I didn't understand why Davis MacAllister would be part of this. Me and Elijah played with Davis and his brother Charles out at Miss Ellen's place. Davis played as much a part of pushing the preacher into the well as any of us, 'til he hit his head.

Maybe when he was laying on the ground the preacher's evil come up out of the well and got inside of him.

Mama and Papa knew no one was ever really safe. Was a time they would hide some of them who run from Kentucky or west Tennessee where the plantations are at. We never talked about who these people were, but I knew they was like my papa. Slaves who got free and run. I was curious about them. Once I asked a man 'bout the scars on his back. He seemed inclined to tell me his story, but Mama stopped him. She scolded me for not minding my own business, then for asking a person to relive their hurt. People got to put off all their chains to keep going in life, she told me. Ain't fair to make them tell their memories. I didn't understand her then, but I do now, now I got my own memories to weigh me down.

Somehow my family always managed to hide those we sheltered. My mama had a knowing—not visions like Carter —more a sense of things. Maybe it come natural to her, maybe she got it from studying with the woods witch, but she could always feel it when the pattyrollers was coming. There was an old hollowed out log behind our place, and we'd send our guests out there 'til the danger passed. Usually after a day or two, our guests would move on. Maybe they'd hide a bit among the free people in the village, but usually they'd go north to where the Yankees could help them.

One time it was a woman traveling alone stayed with us. She was quiet and nervous, jumped at every noise. Her second night we woke in the middle of the night to find her with a sack, stuffing whatever of our food she could fit into it. Papa told her she was welcome to the food. If she'd asked, he would of given it to her. She didn't believe him, I reckon, cause she dashed out the house.

In the morning when Papa and me went out to fish, we found her hanging from a tree. When I saw her I screamed and screamed and screamed. Papa didn't hush me. He let me scream 'til I was screamed out. He told me don't forget, you know evil when you see it. I remembered how I helped to kill that evil preacher, and I felt so proud, I almost told him about it, but I remember Mama told me never to speak of it. I was otherwise honest with my papa, but he was a man who believed in God and the bible. I think I do have some of Mama's magic in me. 'Cause I can still hear Ellen Bridges in the wind and the water sometimes, and I feel the preacher in every sin I commit and every sin I see. I smelled the preacher's foul breath in the air while I stood screaming under that hanged woman. I didn't feel him nowhere around my dead brother. I must of done right by Promise.

I know it was the Home Guard took my parents, right from our home, while I was in town visiting with Elijah. I know that somewhere up that mountain across the river, they was hung from trees until they rotted and dropped. I don't know why they took my parents away instead of hanging them outside my house. Maybe that was one kindness Davis did for me, talked his brother and the rest into taking them where I didn't have to see the horror of it.

Some folks tracked the bodies of their kin got taken by the Home Guard, and what they found was fearsome and terrible. I know it was cowardly of me, but I didn't try to find my parents. I preferred to imagine the angels come down and lifted them straight to heaven, bodies and all. Maybe even plucked them right out of them evil men's hands.

My parents weren't the only ones taken that day. Or the days before or after. People who'd just gone out to fish or was on their way to work would never be seen again.

Everyone knew what happened. That's when we under-stood how dangerous the Home Guard was to all of us. Folks knew if they rose up against them, their family and friends would be threatened or killed. We could only hope if we waited to the end of the war, everything would change. God was with the Yankees and he'd punish the likes of Asa Slacom, and all that rode with him.

Elijah didn't believe in waiting. He believed we'd have to fight every step of the way, starting with fighting like White men fought: armed. He said after the war, we'd have to keep on fighting. He told me to never be ignorant about the intentions of White people. He said for me to hold onto my land come hell or high water. That I'd maybe be lonely sometimes. That something could happen to my parents, to him, but to keep holding this land because me owning it free and clear's something rare and valuable.

I lose my sense of time standing over my brother while the sun rises high in the sky. Though I don't feel like I got any appetite, my stomach growls. I decide it will calm my spirit, and later my belly, if I catch some fish. As I'm gath-ering my pole and bucket, Carter Bridges appears again. I find I'm glad to see him. Today I notice he's become a grown man, with a kind face and a kind manner. He's brung me some cornmeal, eggs, sugar. He says he's sorry for everything.

I'm not sure what he even means. It's words people say when they don't know how to help you. Now with my grief for Promise so strong and all my griefs flooding in to join it, I feel the grief of Elijah, too. Another body I ain't seen dead.

I speak before I think: You seen Elijah in your travels?

No, he says.

This makes me sad. Not for me who was already grieving, but for Elijah. I hoped he had maybe seen a familiar face sometime in his time at war.

I must look like I expect Carter to say more; he tells me he heard Elijah died in a fierce battle.

A picture forms in my mind of my beautiful Elijah amidst smoke and death. The bloody scene fills me near to bursting with the pain of it. I know Carter thinks he done me a favor telling me this. I gather my voice together and tell him what he likely wants to hear: I suppose I'm glad Elijah died brave.

* * *

I known Elijah all my life, because his papa's both the preacher and the teacher in the village. My papa made us go every Sunday to the house that was already school during the week. So Elijah and me was together six days a week mostly. We was near the same age, so we'd sit together whispering, inviting smacks with the ruler on weekdays, and stern glances from my mama or his on Sundays.

His mama let him come out to our place to play sometimes, so that's how the two of us ended up in Miss Ellen's yard with all them White children. Elijah would of said the three of us. He was born a twin, with a brother. His mama told him they was born holding on to each other. His brother's name was Elkanah. They was early and tiny, but his mama said they still nearly tore her apart, and for days after they was born no one knew who would die first, the babies or the mother. But all three lived.

A year later both babies took sick. My mama went over there and did all she could. She said those babies clung to each other just like on the day they was born, and so it came that Elkanah died in Elijah's arms, same way he'd been born. Elijah claimed his brother never left him. That Elkanah grew when Elijah did, and always stayed by him. I thought he was playing make believe 'til Carter saw Elkanah in Miss Ellen's yard.

Elijah's the only one of us told a grown person 'bout what happened to Miss Ellen and the White preacher, and that's how my mama come to be the only grown person to know. She had gone out into the woods that day to call us for dinner. When she couldn't find us, fear took hold on her, and her fear was so strong it led her right to where we was at. Miss Ellen and the preacher was already gone down the well, and most of the children had already run off. Mama snatched me and Elijah by our collars and dragged us out of the yard. I felt sorry to leave Carter alone, but Miss Nora took him in later, so it turned out all right.

The White preacher pushed Miss Ellen in the well, Elijah said to my mama.

Don't lie, Elijah, I said.

I knew that kind of story's one that could get us punished. And I didn't want a whooping, even if it was for my own good.

But Elijah couldn't be stopped.

We pushed him in after, he said, He kilt Miss Ellen, so we kilt him.

Elijah's telling stories, I said, That preacher come with a handful of flowers and Miss Ellen, she fell in love with him and they both run off. They didn't even take his old mule, and they left Carter behind, too.

Elijah kicked up a fuss, said I was the liar, that we kilt that preacher, all us children.

Mama stopped, let go our collars. She crouched down to look Elijah in the eyes.

You ain't gon' tell that story no more, Elijah Ware, not to no one. Then she turned to me.

And you ain't gon' speak of it neither, Delia Boyd.

She didn't have to tell me. I wouldn't of, never. Something in her eyes must of scared Elijah good, 'cause he never told that story again. We didn't talk about it to each other, nor to Carter neither. After a time, seemed like it never happened. We didn't hardly see none of those White children no more 'cept Carter, who'd escape his chores at Miss Norah's boarding house to come out and play in the woods with us. The three of us—four if you count Elkanah—did everything together for a time. Soon's we was done with chores or school, we'd run out in the woods. We'd play acorn battle, or hide 'n seek. Sometimes we swam in the river or fished. It was a happy time. For me and Elijah it got even happier when we fell in love.

Then we didn't feel so much like playing with Carter no more. We'd walk and talk for hours. Me, I wanted to be a teacher, just like my parents wanted for me. Elijah's parents wanted him to go to a college up north to become a preacher or a doctor. That ain't what he wanted though. He wanted to be a lawyer, then to be in the United States government, so he could be one of those making the laws. He had a powerful imagination, it seemed to me then, but who knows what he would of done had he lived through the war.

Elijah had wanted to go to the war in 1862 when he first heard they was taking Colored men. He did go, but when he got to the place they was gathering he realized right quick that Black men was doing nothing but slave work. They wasn't allowed to have guns, nor to see battle. They was just cooking and cleaning up after ill-mannered White men. Doing the dirtiest of work: lugging slops, gathering the dead to throw in trenches. So Elijah took the treacherous road back home, traveling at night so as to hide from pattyrollers and the like what would capture a Black man to sell into slavery even if he's born free and got the papers to prove his freedom.

January 1864 Elijah heard they was arming Black troops in Chattanooga, so he left again. In a letter from Dalton, Georgia he told me he was expecting to march toward Nashville, where I suppose he died because there was a big battle there, and no one never heard from him again.

❖ ❖ ❖

Today I tell Carter I wish Elijah had lived to do the things he planned to do. Carter's unnatural quiet; could be it hurts him near as much as me to think about Elijah.

Maybe we should talk about something else, I say.

Carter jumps on changing the subject so fast I don't think I hear him right.

There's a circus, he says.

A what?

A circus, on my grandmother's land.

Why would we go there, Carter, I say.

My hands tingle, remember the rough cloth of the preacher's clothes—sometimes I tell myself I meant to pull him back—but I know the truth of what I did. I helped push him in. But that man even smelled evil, like old mule and wet ashes. He had to die for killing Miss Ellen. All of a sudden a terrible thought invades my mind: what if helping to kill the preacher gave me a secret taste for killing, what if something got inside me, waited for an excuse... What if I could of saved my brother? What if that White doctor would of come out if I asked. Was Promise really that sick?

Maybe I didn't have to. Now my tingling hands remember a different rough fabric, my own pillow...

Carter's still talking.

A circus might change the way the land feels, he says, Put our fears to rest.

It ain't fear, I say, It's a dark memory.

Maybe it's just land, he says, Might could be it got all its darkness because we stayed away, let our memories take over.

I suppose, I say, Could be doing everything in a new way is how to go now.

I think so, he says.

You brung me all this food. Could you come to supper first? Before we go to the circus?

He says he will.

Then he stares at me like as if he sees the second coming in my face, and I know he's having one of his visions. I ask him what he sees.

Nothing.

I know he's lying. If the vision's bad enough he won't tell me. And in that case, today I don't want to know it. I don't need fear piled on top of sorrow.

I got to go see Willie, he says.

We say goodbye and see you later. When he leaves, I go down to the river. The rest of the day I fish, I clean, I cook. Before I know it, we're sitting across my table and Carter ain't eating.

I'd a thought you'd come to supper hungry, I remark.

He don't answer, but he eats. I admit I do like having a familiar face across the table from me. We finish all there is, but it ain't time to go yet. Our silence grows into discomfort. Then I remember I still got them pictures he made of my family, so I go get them from where they sat all this time under my bed in the wood box my pa made, along with a cloth doll my ma made for me, and the first flower Elijah gave me, that I had let dry so I could keep it always.

First we examine the picture of Mama. Her name, Jewell, suited her. She was rare and precious. She stood tall like a queen; even doing housework, she was graceful as a bird. My mama knew everything of herbs and potions to heal a body and a soul. She learned it from the woods witch, who had once lived even further into the forest than us. Strangely, her learning companion was Matilda Miller, a White girl who'd grow up to be mother of the Harpe children I played with in Carter's yard. Most of them Harpe children died in the war one way or another. Mama said when she met her in the woods, Matilda was rich, though she ran barefoot like a beggar.

* * *

Mama had crouched behind a tree, secretly watching the witch, when she spotted two dirty, bug-bitten white feet on the ground next to her. When Mama asked who's there, up jumped Matilda Miller, tearing her fancy dress. When Mama pointed out the rip, Matilda bragged she had a thousand dresses. Mama said Matilda and her whole family was haughty like that. That's why the Miller family fell into disgrace and Matilda had to marry a man who farmed hard, rocky, mountain land. So as to learn humility.

That day Mama and Matilda met, the woods witch heard them talking. Instead of casting a curse on them, she taught them both all she could before she died. Eventually, Mama and Matilda both got married and went their own ways.

My mama met my papa when he was hiding in the

woods. He'd been living there and he'd watch her when she come to gather plants like ginseng, snakeroot, and the blossoms of witch-hobble bushes. One day he was trying to snatch a fish from the river when she came walking along the bank. Mama told me she knew him for her husband the first time she saw him. As soon as she appeared, a fish swam right into his hand. Mama helped Papa build a fire, and he shared the fish with her. By the time they finished eating, they was in love. He followed her home where she lived with her papa, my grandfather, who died when I was small. Her mother had died of the smallpox when Mama was six years old. Her papa raised her mostly hisself, with some help from women in the village while he was at work. He worked in the quarry, and he told my papa that down there they didn't ask no questions about where a man come from, so long as he can work. So Papa went to work in the quarry, and when he had saved enough money, he bought this little piece of land in the woods where he built our cabin with his own two hands. Mama was glad enough to live in the woods where it was easy to find all she needed to meet the growing demands for her root magic.

❋ ❋ ❋

Here in Carter's picture, Papa looks serious and stern, but he was the kindest man I ever come across. He was the only man I knew who was born into slavery, but he wouldn't talk about it. Said it was a thing I shouldn't have no way to picture. He wanted to start getting that memory out of his kin's blood, so by the time my children had children, there'd be none who had any sense of how it feels to be property. For myself, I thought he should be proud of getting away, of building his own home and his own family, but Mama and

Papa both warned me against pride, pointing out any time somebody fell because of it, like the Millers. I know my parents was proud of me, though. When I was inside Mama's belly, she had a dream I was a girl, that my name was Delia, and I was sister to the sun. When Papa took me fishing before dawn, when the sun come up over the trees, he'd say, Look Delia, there goes your sister; she lights the day like you light my life. I miss him so much.

The next picture's Elijah. Seems we can't get away from him today. Likely since me and Carter's together, whatever spirit's left of Elijah got to be here too. Carter looks at the picture but he don't say nothing. He reaches for the water, but I get hold of the pitcher first. I lift it too fast, spilling water on the table. And there goes Carter into one of his trances. This time I make him tell me what he sees.

Fish, he says.

I want to laugh, tell him far as I know fish ain't deadly.

We just ate fish, I point out, Maybe they took your imagination.

He says these're live fish.

I look at the table. It's just water there, Carter, I say.

But I know he's seen fish, so I ask if he thinks these fish might have some bad meaning.

I don't know, he says. He says the fish scare him, even though they're all pretty colors.

Your visions ain't always bad, I say. Remember that time you visioned me in a pink dress?

That was a good vision, he says.

And it came true. It did.

He don't say nothing more, so I say we should go on to the circus.

He agrees. I leave the pictures and our dinner things, spilled water and all, on the table. I can clean up later.

Willie Reed

The cave was mostly filled with my aloneness. The nothing, the dark, the ripple of the underground river. That freezing water what dug through moss, dirt, rock what cut the mountain 'til it made a cave where it could flow easy, far from people, way down in the ground, cold and quiet as I want to be. I know the answer, now. Water has its own ways. Then, now, forever. Water got its own ways. Ways what's different from men.

Sometimes other men did come into that cave. I could hear their arrogant voices, smell their cowardly sweat. I hid inside the blackness then. Sometimes they'd find what food I had, eat it all. Still. Even with the hunger the damp the others, I didn't want to leave. I dreaded that long walk home away from the comfort the quiet the stone walls, the hidden river what quenched my thirst, what told me secrets.

Then one day I heard men outside the cave.

War's over, they said.

I knew my mother'd be looking for me, looking for a hero to come home, take care of her. That I'd have to go home, even though she weren't expecting a living ghost stammering 'bout prison, its stench of men and death, all things rotten and rotting. She weren't waiting to hear how her own son lay in his own filth with other men, how he got took by the Secesh soon's he saw battle. How he got throwed in behind them tall wood fences where men, pigs, disease all lay festering together.

Would I tell my mother how I didn't figure my own way out but depended on other men stronger to take me from there? How I cowered in a stand of pines while guards put bullets through them that rescued me? That rather than go back to the war to avenge them what saved my life, I ran 'til I got in the mountains then kept running? I had seen the battlefield. Maybe it did look like vengeance and redemption to some, but I don't know how. It weren't no sight of pride, nor honor nor saving of a union nor saving of any man from bondage. It weren't nothing but mud made of blood and dirt. Nothing but men butchering men and land 'til the world choked on the smell of destruction. The smoke of suffering rises up from a battlefield like a poison fog.

Then they say war's over and just like that a man got to walk home toward his mother, every path a graveyard, every bird crying a funeral song, every animal a witness to the evil of man, the lowliest of creatures who brung hell to earth. Every tree and rock shamed me on that walk home down the mountain through the woods.

While I walked the bitterness built in me what was borned on the battlefield, in the prison, in the cave. I carried my anger like tinder 'til I walked myself into a fiery rage fueled with memories of blood and smoke. Finally I stood on the banks of the river in my own town. I heard the river whispering I might quench the fire inside me in its cool rushing waters. But I couldn't believe it; I didn't know how. The river has patience, though.

❖ ❖ ❖

Tonight I walk by the river with Lucy. I know I don't deserve her, never did, but all our lives she stayed by me much as she could. Always shined her light on me even though we share a sin from childhood.

Even though she carries that same secret as me she never was tainted. Lucy believed in fairies once. She said they was like lights in the forest, but I knew the light she saw come from her own self. She still shines it. I believe if I stay beside her, her light will shine into me and save me from all I was born into, all I've become. Though I come into the world the very day my pa died, his spirit didn't stay on earth to guide me. Worse, when he went, he took part of my ma. I ain't never known nothing whole but sorrow in my life. But Lucy. She makes me feel like I got a whole heart and a whole soul. I bring her to the river knowing she can't feel its mystery just like I can't see fairies. She comes along because it gives me peace to be here. She loves me.

Tonight we walk, same as always, but it ain't the same too; I feel her restless. The river, always the same always different, carrying life and death, but Lucy. She's 'sposed to be all light but her light's all asunder this evening. It glitters but it don't shine. She's cold, she says. I look at her, her long blonde curls her bonnet her shawl. All meant for sunlight but sun's mostly gone. Moon's already up, waxing to full, its reflection a white stain in the black blue purple river. Lucy says it again, she's cold.

I could warm her if I had the courage. I could take her delicate lily white hand in my hand what's big and clumsy, but warm. I can't though. I'm scared to touch her. I ain't never told Lucy none of what I seen or done in the war. Even my hands hold secrets. If she was my wife I could tell her. She would hear me then, she'd stroke my hair like when we was children, she'd love the fury out of me if she was my wife.

I'm cold take me home, she says.

We walk away from the river. It will wait for our return.

In town's a fight. Her brother, one-armed, hateful. Lucy cares about him. I tell her she got to leave him to fight, leave him to travel his own road even if it's hate filled. We walk on, I take her on home. I want to touch her on the darkness of the path, and in the moonlit yard. I can't even raise my hand up, though. I say goodnight and leave her outside her house.

April's a time for ghosts, so I go back down to the river to build a fire to keep 'em off me, at least tonight. My mind does quiet by the fire, 'til Carter Bridges come up on me searching for the boys we once was. We talk about the weather and fire. I talk about the war and the cold without saying nothing true about neither of 'em. When the fire goes out I stand up. I got to go home to my mother, I say. I leave Carter Bridges standing there with the river and the ashes.

Out late Ma says when I come in, Out late and covered with dew. I'll fix you some soup.

I tell her I don't need soup.

She fills the bowl. This is the way of us now.

When I don't eat she lights a candle.

I'll light your way to bed, son, she says.

I see all her sadness the way she waits for me to be what I ain't, the way she waits for me to do something, the way she moves a little slower every day. She lights my way to bed where she finally leaves me alone in the dark and the quiet. Still, sleep don't come.

When I get up in the morning there's the same soup, my ma in the chair like she ain't moved all night. Might could be she didn't.

Fire's out, she says.

I'll chop us some wood, I say.

Eat some warm soup first, she says, Fire just now went out.

I'll chop us some wood, I say.

I go on outside, breathe the air what comes with spring, with getting away from people, even my own mother.

When first I take up the axe my arm's heavy, I pull the

axe through the air slow, drop the blade, wrench it out, lift it again. This I do, lick after lick, 'til finally the rhythm of axe on wood the axe the wood work together the way I pull the weight of the axe up let it down free, it hits the wood, cracks it. This tree was already dead; I never take those that's living. Dead dried out things split easy. I raise and lower the axe, the wood cracks, splits. My breath works the right rhythm with it but here comes Carter again. Now he's come around me twice. I ain't invited him once. We was friends but then we wasn't and that was a long time ago. What we got in common I don't want to think about.

Carter wants to know did my ma ask for kindling.

Fire's out, I say, My ma ain't said nothing 'bout kindling nor any other kind of wood, she needs to keep soup warm, she needs wood.

Carter says I'm chopping too hard. He says these sticks'll start a fire but they won't keep one burning.

When he says it I think of sticks on water. I tell him how a stick can float down to town, past town. A stick can float straight out of Tennessee. I try to tell him the beauty: a thing starts out a tree, a growing living thing. Might be lightning strikes it dead or a man cracks it down with an axe, still, it can float. On a river it can travel anywhere, even to the sea. Maybe to something never ending. Carter asks am I all right.

I say it back to him, I say Are you all right.

He tells me yes. But it's a lie. I see the difference between his eyes and his words.

There's a circus, he says then, There's a circus set up out to my grandmother's place.

That well and its memories still sit on that land. My fingers grip the axe handle, I listen to the music of the axe and the air. Carter says he might go to the circus. Go out there to the circus and the well, he feels drawn to go, will I go too. I ain't got money I say. In my mind I see tents and animals over the ground where once us children was happy, before curses and death and war.

Let me give you some money, Carter says.

I swing my axe so close to him. I don't mean to, it's my shame my want of his money.

Bring Lucy he says. He's taking Delia Boyd he says, we should all be there make that ground something new not any way related to death.

Lucy's long blonde curls, her lily white hands. In my mind I see her smile whenever I come tell her circus when she expects the river like always.

I take the money, pocket it with my shame, go back to chopping. Of a sudden, Carter's telling me I got bloody hands.

Everyone got bloody hands now, I say.

Just as sudden, he calms. A vision, he says, They ain't been so easy for me to understand just lately.

Ain't nothing easy to understand no more, I say.

Carter says he'll see me later see me at the circus.

I touch the money in my pocket, think about Lucy's smile, her light.

When the wood's piled up I see the truth of what Carter said. It's more kindling than we can use even to start fires for neverending soup. I remember Alva Calloway's out there in the woods, everyone gone, she's taking care of little 'uns all on her own. Her brother fought Union like me but never come back, her pa dead of the Typhus, her ma a ghost haunting the cabin. And here me a coward I got my life, my ma, there's no balance to things that I can find. I gather the wood together.

When I come into the clearing, there on Alva's porch,

there's Johnny Harpe. There in her yard with his horse what his brother stole at the start of the war. That brother another man who fought the right side but didn't come back. The horse though, it come back so there's some good things you can't expect. Between the man and the horse, likely it was the horse deserved to live anyway. It's strange to me that horse come back to Johnny Harpe, he got so much hate in him, hate for me, other hate ain't had nowhere to go since the war likely because he left his arm there. People can see he ain't whole. Other's of us, you can't tell; folks can't see a man's ruined from the inside out. I see love on Alva. Strange it's on Johnny Harpe too. But instead of keeping his love on her he turns his hate on me. When it's time for me to fill Lucy with my love, for us to love each other, my rage will go out like water smothers fire.

Johnny Harpe steps past me, I take the wood to the porch. Alva touches my hand, her hand warm, small, soft, filled with love she holds for Johnny, him walking away. She's grateful for the kindling she says. She asks me do I want a drink of water.

I don't need it, I say.

The woods hiss.

You got varmints, I ask.

She says she ain't seen any. It's all right, she says, Thank you again for the wood.

I tell her it ain't nothing.

On the way out I keep my eyes open for varmints, but I don't see none.

When I get home I got time before Lucy, so I let my ma give me soup.

We sit quiet together, we eat. I'm grateful for her. I know she got no reason to be grateful for me. I know how much she wanted me, what she lost to bring me into this world. Maybe once I was the boy she wanted but I didn't grow to be the man she'd hoped to raise. Not yet. But now I got hope. When I'm married, Ma can finally be proud.

Finally it's time for Lucy, the walk takes me seems near as long as it took to walk from the cave to home. She's gon' expect me to ask her to the river but now I got money in my pocket, I'm about to say words she don't expect. When I reach her home, she come out right away.

There's a circus, I say.

Her pa come out, says no, says where's my money.

I show him Carter's money, but not my shame at where I got it.

Lucy's pa sees the money, Bring her right back after, he says.

I will, I say.

Lucy and me walk side by side. Her long blonde curls her lily white hands my shame-burnt soul. The crickets ain't singing the right song, the breeze blows wrong. We're on our way to the land we ain't never talked about. We don't talk about it still.

Carter Bridges

The crowds swarm the battlefield, turn out the pockets of the dead, steal their mementos and boots. Hogs devour the soldiers' entrails; vultures tear out their eyes. A picture I made but never showed. This is the picture that wakes me of late. The profaned corpses, enraged by violation and lack of recognition, have acquired voices that inhabit my dreams. They insist I wake, so I do.

Instead of lighting the lamp, I dress in the dark, go out into the night. It must be late, the tavern looms silent at the end of Main Street. The nearly full moon hangs high above the fog. I walk toward the river, listening for my grandmother's voice singing through the trees.

I'm not surprised to find Willie Reed on the riverbank, sitting alone by a fire. He don't acknowledge me, so I wait. I know he feels me there. Directly, he looks up.

Carter, he says. He could be saying any word for all the meaning in his flat, tired voice. His posture's tired too. His eyes have hung onto that fear I saw so often when I followed soldiers into battle.

I sit down next to him. We sit there quiet, listen to my grandmother's songs in the air. I don't ask him if he hears her. I assume by his stillness, he does. The fire dims. I pick up a stick, throw it in. It crackles as it burns.

Willie jumps. Cut that out, he says.

Cut what out?

That cracking like gunfire.

Fire was low.

Then leave it low.

Like as if it's taunting us, the fire rises into the sky, an orange glow spreading 'til it outshines the moon. Willie's calm, so I know it ain't real. A vision. I watch and wait. Soon enough the dark sky reappears, then the moon and stars, shining faintly through the fog. I don't tell Willie what I see, especially because I can't discern the meaning of it.

We watch the dwindling fire, watch the smoke and fog mix, fade into the night.

April's a cold month, Willie says, The preacher cursed the month of April. War started in April. April's always gon' be cold as death.

I'm worried about his mind. It ain't come back to him the way it should of.

Neither curses nor war make the weather, I tell him.

My head aches, he says.

You're thinking too much, I say, You keep it up, you might do something.

I might at that, he says, his eyes on the dying fire.

I ask him how he came to be out here, building a fire in the middle of night.

Searching the river, he answers.

Find anything?

No.

The water whispers to the night and fog. My grandmother sings a lullaby somewhere among the trees. The fire dims to embers. We can sense the deepest, blackest part of the river, out there in the middle, though we can't see it through the drifting mist.

We should both get home, I say.

Willie don't answer, but together we rise and move, me toward the boarding house where I live in the center of town, him toward the west edge of town, just beyond the Colored village, where he lives with his mother.

I've nearly reached home when I know sleep don't yet wait for me in my bed. I turn back toward the woods, but this time toward Delia Boyd. Something about the night, the vision of the fire, the insistent singing of my grandmother in the breeze, tells me it's time to look in on her. I ain't too worried; but I know enough to trust if I feel driven toward a place or person, I should go. I should of visited her long ago, but my guilt stopped me. Elijah's face slips into my memory. I don't let it stop me from keeping on toward the place where Delia and her little brother Promise live in the cabin her father built in the woods.

Though I see the flicker of a candle within, when I knock at the door Delia don't answer. The night rises up around me: owls, the rustle of leaves, the rushing of water around rocks. Directly I hear a muffled voice from inside the cabin. At first I think it's Delia singing, but then I notice her staggering, ragged voice. Slowly I push open the door 'til I can see shadows quiver in the spluttering light of the single candle that sets on a small table by a cot where Delia weeps over her brother.

She cradles him, strokes his head, his face. One of his skinny baby arms hangs off the side of the cot. I've seen arms hang this way enough in the war to know the boy's dead.

Delia, I say.

She don't look up. I edge toward her slowly, like as if she was a horse that might go skittish if I approach too fast. She keeps on petting Promise, her tears running off her face to drop on his narrow chest. I come closer, stand beside the cot. I say her name again even though I know she won't answer. I don't understand why I didn't see this in a vision. I could of been prepared. This don't look nothing like a rising, spreading fire, though likely to her it feels like one.

I kneel to take up the child's wrist, hold it hoping I might feel the slightest flutter of life. His little hand's already cool. No point in calling the doctor. I sit with the two of them while she cries softly; the boy's body grows colder. We'll need to do something.

You want I should make him a box, I say.

She shakes her head.

Want to take him to your friends in town?

Again, no.

I could bring someone to you.

No.

The wind and the river stop their whispering; the soft, comforting music of my grandmother's voice floats around us.

You hear that, I say.

She don't answer.

After awhile I say, You want we should put him straight in the ground?

Her sobs wrench from her guts so hard, seems they should shatter the moon.

After we bury Promise, she asks me to leave. There's nothing but to respect her wishes, so I go on toward home, hoping for some sleep with no dreams. When I get home I stash the war photographs away so they can't trouble me no more tonight.

They don't, but I wake in the morning thinking of Delia, worrying did she sleep last night. Thinking I should of stayed with her even though she told me to leave. I think maybe I should go see her. Comfort her until some time passes, then I'll unburden my conscience about Elijah. I'm dressing to go when I hear Nora McGill's voice outside my door.

• • •

Nora has been good to me since my grandmother died. She knew me when I was a baby, when my parents were still alive, so she knew about my visions. After she took me in, when her father got sick, she came to rely on me to help her know what might happen from one day to the next. Otherwise we lived normally. I helped her with the boarders; when I finished my chores she'd let me run off with Elijah and Delia. I had mostly harmless visions about Nora's father: him falling out of bed, spilling water on himself, knocking his food on the floor.

One morning, though, when I woke I felt the need to go straight to his room. By the time I got there he was floating out of himself. It was a sight to behold. A sight I'd get used to in the war, but this was the first time I'd seen it. Neither my grandmother nor that evil preacher had come floating up out of the well. I couldn't help it; I screamed.

Nora came running in, demanding I tell her what I saw, so I told her.

She told me to go get the doctor. By that time, though, her pa had floated up to the ceiling. No doctor could of got old man McGill off that ceiling. Sure enough, within minutes he was dead. I could tell Nora wanted to blame me, but she knew I don't make things happen, I just see them. If there's time I can warn folks. But there ain't always time, and they don't always listen.

❦ ❦ ❦

Nora calls to me again, breaking my reverie. Some folks have arrived to get their portrait made. I had forgot all about it. When the mother of this family wrote to make the appointment, she said her son sent them a picture I made of him out at the battlefields. Now she wants a picture of what's left of her family, made by the same photographer, to be a companion to the one he sent them. I dress before I quickly remake my room into a portrait studio by shoving clothes under the bed and setting up my camera. I finish just in time for Nora to usher them in.

Here they stand now, mother, father, a son who either did not fight, or who fought and lived while his brother fought and died. I shake the hands of the father and the son, nod to the mother. She's looking around my room.

She says, A little dusty for a photographic studio, isn't it?

I'm glad Nora's already left, or she'd rush my paying customers right back out the door; she takes pride in how clean she keeps the rooms, even mine.

I believe the landlady dusted this morning, I say.

The mother's gaze falls on my bed.

Oh, she gasps, as though she's witnessed something obscene.

The father says it doesn't show much respect for a lady, that I should be ashamed to have a man's bed in plain sight.

Under his breath, the son says, Jackass.

I don't know if he's talking about me or his father.

I do apologize, I say, hoping I sound polite, not contemptuous, Just now I can only afford one rent, so I got to work where I live.

The mother expels her breath like she's been holding it against some fetid stench. I can feel her thinking how her presence here's a sacrifice to her dead hero son.

Should we begin, I ask.

All three stare at me.

Let's get this over with, says the father.

Does he love this living son? Is he doing this to please his wife? These questions I can't ask my customers.

So I ask, Have you thought about background?

Something pretty, the mother says.

I search through the rolled canvases I keep in the corner, find one of flowers painted by a woman who specializes in such things.

I hang it on the wall.

Ridiculous, says the father.

I'm not standing in front of flowered wallpaper for eternity, says the son.

The mother prevails, however. This portrait is for my parlor, she says.

I open the curtains to let the sun stream in.

The mother covers her eyes.

Must it be so bright in here, she says.

I need light to make the pictures, I say.

I try my best to sound conciliatory. Finishing quickly is as much my wish as theirs. I want to go see about Delia.

If you'll find the pose you want, I say.

The three of them jostle each other until they stand side by side like a row of soldiers.

That won't do, I tell them. Try standing closer together, like a family.

They move closer to one another.

Good, I say, Now hold very still.

The mother scratches her eye.

Ma'am, I really do need y'all to hold perfectly still.

She drops her hand. The father straightens his collar. The son coughs.

I have some stands that might help you, I tell them.

I pull the posing stands from the corner of my room and set them up.

The mother reacts as if I've proposed chaining her.

I'm not standing in one of those, she says.

I can give you a chair, ma'am.

A chair will be fine, she sighs.

I set the men in the posing stands, the mother in a chair. At last, they're still.

When I focus the camera, the son shimmers for a moment, and I'm afraid I might see blood or some other mirage or premonition, but I only need to blink to make it stop. Then tears appear to glisten on the mother's cheek, but to my relief, they too disappear. Since I started taking pictures, my visions sometimes come through the camera. So many times I've looked through this lens, seen tears, measles, fever sweat or a bullet hole. Every time, tragedy followed.

Hold your breaths, I say.

All three inhale. I take the picture. They release their breaths.

The father says, Can we leave now, I have business to attend to.

I want to send them away, but I tell them we should do one more, just to be safe. I resume my place behind the camera.

Hold your breath, I say.

They do, and we're done.

As I leave the boarding house, I'm surprised to see a circus parade passing westward down the street, toward the Colored village. Curious, I think, maybe it's a Negro circus. But then a White man with a megaphone announces the circus will be to the east, in the vacant lot outside town. That's my grandmother's property. I make myself very quiet, wait for a vision or to hear her singing. Nothing comes. All that fills my mind is the memory of Delia crying over her brother's grave. I need to go to her.

On my way I stop in Slacom's store to buy some cornmeal, beans, and sugar. In the woods, I find eggs laid by some hens who got loose during the war. When I arrive at Delia's, the door to her cabin is open, and I can see her fixing up a pole for fishing. She sees me, but she don't invite me in right away, so I stand there like a fool, holding the basket out to her.

She stares at it for a while like she don't understand what it is. Then she shakes herself to her senses, says, What you got here?

Some corn meal. Sugar. Beans. Three eggs.

Where'd you get eggs?

Some hens gone wild.

Usually the varmints get them eggs before anybody can find 'em, she says as she takes the basket from me.

Are you all right, I ask.

No. But wasn't all right before, neither.

I'm sorry, I say.

We two stand there, at a loss for what to say next. When she finally speaks, she asks the question I had dreaded: Did you never see Elijah?

I tell her a lie.

No, I say. But I heard tell of him. I heard he died in a fierce battle.

This seems to satisfy her. She says she's glad he died brave, it was what he would of wanted to do, second to coming home to her a hero who freed people all across the south. Then she suggests I come back later to eat this food with her. It seems she might want to resume our friendship. I hope so.

At that moment I remember the circus. There's a circus, I say. It's setting up at my grandmother's old land. We could eat together, then go on out there to see it.

Immediately I feel ashamed. Her brother just died, and

I invite her to a stupid entertainment on another scene of death.

You sure you want to go there, she asks, You know there been bad luck on that land all through the war.

Same as everywhere, I say.

Suddenly, in her hair I see blue, green, and purple fish, swimming. I'm too fascinated to be afraid.

Carter, you're staring.

I'm sorry.

You see something?

No, I say, lying to her for the second time today. I need to get to Willie's, I tell her. I'll come back. We'll eat, then go to the circus.

All right, she says.

I bid her goodbye. I don't really have a plan with Willie, but while I'm at resuming friendships, maybe I should take up that one, too. He seemed lonely at the fire last night. He likely could use a friend, and maybe I could too.

When I arrive at Willie's, he's outside chopping wood. He chops slowly, barely glances at me when I come into his yard and sit down on a stump. When the wood gets down to the size of logs for burning, I expect him to acknowledge me, but he keeps chopping. He chops like he's keeping time with a tune inside his head, or maybe his heartbeat. He keeps on until he's got nothing but sticks. Then he splits the sticks.

Your ma want that much kindling, I ask.

No, he says.

Then you're chopping too hard. That'll start a fire, it won't keep it going.

Willie's next words don't make no sense to me. He tells me how the sticks will float. He tells me we can go, like floating wood, on out of Tennessee.

Then what, I ask.

He goes back to the wood. His hands on the axe drip blood.

What you done, I yell.

So many things, he says, Which one you asking about?

There's nothing on his hands. A vision. I don't know should I tell him. I decide I will. I saw you with bloody hands, I say.

He looks at his hands.

No, murder ain't something I done of late, he says.

He keeps on looking at his hands, like he might see blood on them after all.

You feeling all right, I ask.

Question is, are you feeling all right, he says, I ain't the one seeing bloody hands on him ain't doing nothing but chopping wood for his ma.

You're right, I say. I don't want to upset him any further, so I change the subject. You know there's a circus? Out at my grandmother's land.

He goes back to chopping wood.

I'm taking Delia Boyd out there. Maybe you could take Lucy Harpe.

He says he don't have money for that, so I offer it to him. At first he refuses, but I tell him it can just be a loan, he can get it back to me someday. I tell him I want to make new meaning of that place; it would be good to have as many of us there as possible.

He don't say anything about that, but he accepts, and goes back to chopping. Splinters fly all over the yard.

Maybe your ma will make you some soup, I say by way of trying to distract him.

We got nothing but soup, all the time. Ain't you got a fancy portrait to make?

Already done, I say.

He goes on chopping.

I'll see you at the circus, I say, and I leave him still splintering wood.

All that afternoon I help Nora with the boarding house. It feels like hours and days until I can go back out to Delia's to have supper. Before I know it, though I'm sitting at her table, watching her instead of eating. I can't help but to look for a sign of the grief she must be feeling. She don't show it though.

I thought you was hungry, she says.

I pick up my spoon and take a bite. She waits while I chew.

It's good, I say after I finally swallow.

She nods and we both set to eating.

When our plates are clean, it's not yet time to leave for the circus. I want to make some friendly conversation, but I don't know what to say to her. She takes pity on my awkwardness, tells me she still has the pictures of her family I made before the war. She don't mention I made them after her and Elijah stopped being my friends.

* * *

Awhile after I moved into the boarding house, Nora made me go to school, where other children avoided me on account of my family history. I was bad blood. After school, instead of going straight home, I'd wander in the woods, listening for my grandmother's songs. I didn't usually see visions among the trees, so my wanderings brought me some peace. One day I came across Elijah and Delia playing at battle with some branches. I was so glad to see them, as I was lonely. I asked if I could play.

My mama knows something bad happened out at your gran's place, said Delia, She told me stay away from you.

If he stays, though, we can play hide 'n seek, Elijah said. Out here in the woods ain't no one gon' know who we play with.

From that day I had friends again. The three of us would meet in the forest to play. Actually, there was four of us, though we didn't acknowledge it. Elijah had a brother, Elkanah, who had died. He was a twin, so though dead, he grew as Elijah did. I spotted Elkanah for the first time in my grandmother's yard. At first I thought he was flesh, so I spoke to him. When he didn't answer, I said to Elijah, You're brother don't talk.

I talk for him, Elijah said.

I looked over at Elkanah.

I think he got his own opinions, I said.

No he don't, said Elijah.

For a long time, seemed that was true. Though Elkanah always stayed near us, he never said anything; neither Delia nor Elijah mentioned him, so I never did again neither.

By the time we passed fourteen years old, Delia and Elijah was in love. I could feel that me, and Elkanah too, though tolerated, weren't really welcome. One day when we played a game of hide 'n seek, I came around a corner to see Delia and Elijah kissing. I looked around for Elkanah, but he was nowhere to be seen. I realized the four of us had outgrown our childhood friendship, so I left. I never came back 'til years later when I was practicing picture making on everyone I had ever known who might allow it.

The day I left Delia and Elijah behind was the day I first found Willie Reed down by the river. He was sitting by himself and at first seemed disinclined to play. When I took off my clothes and jumped into the water, I think that's the first time I ever saw Willie smile. He never did smile or laugh like the other children out at my gran's, even those few times he played a game with us. By the time we went to school, he was a figure of fun on account of his poverty and strange ways; if he come to school at all, he clung to Lucy Harpe much as he could.

That day I jumped into the river, Willie joined me swimming. After that, we'd swim most warm days. When the weather turned cold, we'd tramp through the woods pretending to hunt ghosts. I think both of us actually did see ghosts, but each was ashamed to tell the other.

When a portrait maker came to stay at the boarding house, everything changed. I was fascinated by everything about making pictures, from the camera, to the slides, to the chemicals. I forgot all about Willie as I became apprentice to the portrait maker.

Once I got my own camera, I didn't want to stay in a studio. I wanted to make pictures of how people lived, so I went around making portraits of anyone who'd let me. It turned out to be good practice for photographing the war. I already knew how to carry my equipment around. I only needed to set up a mobile darkroom. Nora had always given me a little money each week, which I had saved. So I was able to buy the tools of the trade, as well as a broken down wagon, and a pretty good mule. The portrait maker gave me extra supplies in payment for the good work I'd done as his apprentice.

* * *

Now as Delia stands up to search for those old pictures, I point out how I was just starting out back then.

You was already good at it. Anyone could tell it was a calling, she says.

She sits down with the pile of pictures, shuffles through them.

We all look so natural, she says.

She lays the pictures on the table one by one.

There's Papa, she says, Mama. Me.

I look at the picture of her for a while. Her smile. Even a little blurry, I can see a light of joy in her eyes.

Elijah had just asked me to marry him, she says, I wish I had a picture of Promise, too, she adds as she lays the picture of herself on the table.

I could of made one before we buried him, but I don't tell her that. She might be sad we didn't, or she might think me cruel, and send me away. At a loss for words again, I take up my cup of water and swallow all of it. She tries to pour me some more from the pitcher, but the water spills on the table. Immediately the puddle begins to shimmer; first blue, then purple, then green infuses the water. The colors take shape until fish flop on the table. I jump to my feet, so Delia does too.

What do you see, she asks.

Fish.

We just ate fish.

No. Live ones. Like trout, but all different colors.

It's only water there, Carter.

As if her words are magic, it is.

What do fish mean, she asks.

I don't know, I say.

You seem afraid of them.

I am. But they're beautiful, too.

She smiles. Remember how you once saw me in a pink dress? I teased you cause I had no such thing. But when I got home, my mama had that pink dress waiting for me. Someone who couldn't afford her medicines gave it to her as payment.

I do remember that, I say, That was one of the last days you, me, and Elijah—

We should go to the circus, she says, Forget the past and the visions.

We should, I say.

Alva Calloway

This cabin's so dark. I hardly got tallow enough to light this one corner, so I got to sit right here by Ma. She stays in her chair, stares at nothing. She smells like she's dying a little every day. I can hardly hear her breath unless I put my ear right up to her mouth.

The little 'uns's scared of the dark, so that's one blessing. They huddle together on the one straw mattress soon's shadows creep across these broken floorboards. There was more beds once but bugs and mice and who knows what all else been nibbling on everything in this house. Sometimes we get spider bit when we sleep.

I should sew up this pile of rags so I can try to put 'em on the children yet another day. I'm half inclined to let 'em run naked and wild. Why not? Ain't no hope for 'em anyway. I heard tell of another girl, not much older 'n me, in my selfsame circumstances; she took her baby brother and sister to the well, threw 'em in, then jumped in after 'em. They say the sin in her murderous body poisoned the well and all the water, and the whole town died. We lost a well to sin too. I was just a baby, but my brother Edmond told me about it and about how I was there. He had me to memorize all the names of everyone there that day. He made me to know we was all connected. To remember there's folks not kin what belong to me. He told me too, it was Miss Ellen gave me my music what sings in my head all the time.

After Edmond went off to the war to die, I'd close my eyes and sing the names to myself whenever bad things happened: Carter Bridges, Tommy Harpe, Frank Harpe, Ethie Harpe, Cora Harpe, Johnny Harpe, Lucy Harpe, Willie Reed, Delia Boyd, Elijah Ware, Polly Adair, Emily

Adair, Charles MacAllister, Davis MacAllister, Edmond Calloway, Alva Calloway.

When Asa Slacom and his Home Guard come out here to train a gun on Pa to make him shoe their horses for free, I'd sing the names. I'd sing 'em too when soldiers come into the house to make Ma cook them food we needed for ourselves and the little 'uns what just seemed to come every year on account of Ma liked to rock little babies. When the soldiers come for me, I found I wasn't hurt nor scared if I just closed my eyes and said the names. After I saw Davis MacAllister riding with his uncle, I stopped singing his name, and his dead brother's too. Edmond wouldn't've approved, but he ain't here to say nothing about it. He had me to believe there was some magic in them names, but hell has come for every one of us one way or t'other, ever since that day at the well.

Sinking Springs got a new well now, and if you go for water, there's always a body to tell a story how the world's disappearing a little at a time. One day it's a girl killing her own kin, another day animals devour every last person in a town, another day the weight of blood in the dirt of a old battlefield makes the ground to collapse in on itself, swallowing every person and every animal with it. There's a will for destruction in everything.

One day it will be my turn. I know I shouldn't think it. God gave me life, preserved it when so many others died, even my beautiful Edmond, even my father. I don't know what we been spared for, me and Ma and the little 'uns. Cause we're the meek? Edmond would of known the answer. It sure don't look like we're set to inherit even a piece of the earth, though.

My ma there, staring at nothing, never closing her eyes. She's lower than meek, I think. What's God's plan for that?

Each day I manage to get some pokeweed broth in her belly. In the mornings I listen to see if her heart's still beating. Every now and again I set little Rose on her lap, hope maybe she'll remember there's things she loves what stayed in this world. Ma just looks over Rose's head 'til the little 'un gets scared and fusses. The baby's crying don't move Ma neither.

I'm tired. I know idle hands is the devil's workshop, but mine don't care to do nothing no more. What for? Maybe I'll just sit here by Ma 'til we both turn to dust. Pretend the hungry cries of the children're the calling of birds in the forest. I know I can't though. I know I got to lay down at night with my brothers and sisters and hope to sleep my way into some strength for tomorrow.

When the sun comes up, it's all the same. My brothers and sisters begging for more food, me trying to get Ma to eat any at all. Robbie's almost old enough to work. I suppose if I sent him down to the quarry they might take him. But I hate to do it. What if something happened to him? Men all the time die in that place. I recollect how it was with me and Edmond at his age, how carefree we still was. We ain't out of everything yet, so I keep Robbie home. It's what Pa would of done.

Looking around this place, my spirit sinks. Every day it seems I clean while the cabin turns more broken and dirty around me. I do my best to patch up the chinks in the wall, but I ain't good at it, and soon's rain or snow come, the wood grows more rotten, or another hole opens up in the roof.

* * *

I'm about to take a broom to the spider webs what get spun anew every night when I hear more than the usual noise from the yard. When I go out on the porch, I can't believe my eyes. The children're gathered around a horse. Big and black, it can only be Johnny Harpe's Out of the Fog. But that's impossible. That horse took off north with Johnny's brother Tommy at the start of the war five years ago.

Before I fully comprehend the horse standing in my yard, I see Johnny there with him. My heart near to stops beating. Johnny's hair still falls down his face so you can barely tell he's got two eyes. He's lean as when he was a boy, but he's wiry now. His body looks almost angry in all its angles. Then there's his sleeve pinned up. I knew he lost his arm, but I had failed to imagine it. I focus on his face when I speak his name, which feels as tender in my mouth as when we was children. When he comes toward me I don't know what to do or say. I chastise him when really I want to fall on my knees in front of him to weep together over Edmond, my pa, the whole world what got lost on account of that war.

You ain't come round since you been back, I say.

He says he's sorry. He says it with such a weight to it I got to wonder what crimes he might be carrying on his heart.

I tell him I don't hold it against him he fought opposite Edmond. I mean it, too. One of Edmond's most important prayers was the one about forgiveness:

Feel: the dirt beneath your feet.
Hear: Water, wind, bird.
Smell: grass, flower, rain.
Touch your heart. Feel it pulse.
Feel time move. The world is here.
All is forgiven.

I can't ask Johnny what crimes he did. I can't weep, and I can't continue to chastise him, so I turn my attention to the horse, musing out loud how it come to return. Johnny says it just appeared, same's before. That his Pa'd try to put it to work like before, too. I understand then he's come out to leave that horse with me.

I go ahead and speak plain: He can't stay here. I got nothing to feed him.

My little sister Sara says the horse can have her food.

He eats more in a morning than you do in a month, I tell her.

I can see Robbie's already in love with that horse. He reminds me so much of Edmond with the animals. His reverence for creatures comes natural. Edmond even apologized to the horses before shoeing 'em. It seems the animals always understood and forgave him.

I'll come every day to feed him says Johnny.

I feel selfish thinking it, but I wonder if maybe in coming every day, Johnny might see our condition, maybe feed these children while he's about feeding the horse. For their part, they're jumping around begging and pleading to keep the horse. I tell 'em all right, so long as Johnny feeds it.

Then I ask Johnny in. Though I'm ashamed of the brokenness of our home, I want him to see it. We need help. I can see his discomfort soon's he steps in. He tries not to look at our poverty, same as I try not to look at his empty sleeve.

He tries to talk about Ma, but there's nothing to say in that regard, so I put my hand on his one arm. Words spill from my mouth of their own accord: My terror and sorrow when Edmond never came back. How Ma and I stood helpless, while Pa withered and died before our eyes. How Ma stopped taking care of the little 'uns. How lonesome I been, how I missed him especially.

He kisses me.

Before I know it we're naked on the ratty blankets in the next room. I've loved him for so long it all feels natural. I forget his missing arm, my near-dead ma in the next room, even my brothers and sisters outside. The moment's like a song I've always known; it fills me and gives me everything. When we finally lay there breathless staring in each other's eyes, the world feels so far away. But it ain't. Soon enough I notice the musty mold smell of the old blankets we lie on and the voices of the children make their way through the cracks in the wall.

We get up and dress. Though I don't feel shy, he seems to. I realize it's because he has to check for the pins in his sleeve, has to dress with one hand. I'm ready to help him if he needs me, but likely he won't tell me if he does. I imagine if I'm to be his wife I'll be the one pins his shirt, does the things he can't do. I'd worry about him not being able to support us, but his pa has that farm, hardscrabble as it is, and now since the war, Johnny's the only son, so the farm' 'gon go to him. Once the farm recovers from the war he can hire someone to help out. I wonder would we go to live with him and his family right away when we got married. This place won't last much longer. I know I shouldn't put all my eggs in one basket, but I know he loves me. I can still feel his love like a vapor rising from his skin.

We go outside, stand together watching the children play with the horse. He promises me again he'll feed it. Then he tells me there's a circus in town. That it's gon' be over where Miss Ellen used to live. He asks me do the little 'uns and me want to go. He says he's got some army pay left over he put away he could use to take us.

Seems to me that money could be better used, but I ain't never seen a circus. And I'm curious about Miss Ellen's land; will I remember anything when my feet touch that ground? As for the children, it'll be the first treat they ever had. I tell him we'd be glad to go with him.

He says he'll come back for us after supper. I wonder what do they have for supper at the Harpe's. We'll be having some broth, some chestnuts, maybe dandelion roots. I tell Johnny we'll be ready when he comes for us. I tell him I hope we don't need shoes. He says a circus is in a tent, they won't be looking at what's on our feet. He says he'll come for us just before sunset.

Right then Willie Reed comes into the yard to bring me some firewood. He's near as poor as me, but he's handy with an axe. He come out one time thinking Pa or Edmond must be out here smithing and he might could be an apprentice or even get a job. When he saw we ain't got no menfolk, he started bringing me firewood. I really should ask him to teach Robbie and Nathan to use an axe, and a rifle too. If they could hunt and chop wood, it might hold us over 'til me and Johnny get married.

Next to me, Johnny goes tense. I remember Willie fought Union. Maybe it's harder for Johnny to forgive and forget on account of his arm. He tries to pull his hand out of mine, but I hang on. In case he might be jealous, I explain how Willie come to bring me wood, expecting Johnny'll understand, but it seems he don't.

I can't be here, he says, I'll be back to feed the horse.

I remind him about the circus. The children hear and jump around, yelling in their excitement. The horse startles, so Robbie calms his own self down, so as to calm the horse.

Let Willie Reed take you, says Johnny as he walks away.

After Johnny's gone, Willie says, I can't take you.

I know that, I say.

Yonder past the yard the bushes rustle and Willie asks do I need anything kilt. I know what's there. Why would Johnny storm off just to hide so plainly? Maybe he'll come out when Willie leaves. Make it up to me, explain how he's just jealous. Then we'll all go to the circus.

But the bushes rustle again and I know he's gone.

After Willie leaves, I do what I can to fix us some food. We let the horse wander the yard. He seems content to stay with us. The little 'uns can't stop talking about the circus. I hold them off 'til near sunset, just in case Johnny comes to his senses and turns up to fetch us. He don't though. I feel a fool for all the hopes I had just hours ago. Still, I ain't done hoping. He'll have to come back to feed Out of the Fog. Then I'll be able to talk to him. We'll make it right.

The children'll be heartbroke if they can't go to the circus, so I got to figure a way to take 'em. My ma has a little money I been saving for the day we have a true emergency. Now I think instead of using it for something terrible, I'll use it to bring us some joy, just once. I explain to her why I'm taking the money, tell her we'll be back later. If she can understand me, I know she approves. She didn't bring us into the world only to suffer.

I gather my brothers and sisters. As we walk toward Miss Ellen's, toward our first circus, I think about Johnny Harpe and recite the forgiveness prayer over and over.

Davis MacAllister

On the day my brother died, the two of us went down to the river, where I dared him to a contest. We would put stones in our pockets to see which of us could walk across the bottom to reach the other side. Charles was always keen for a contest, so we filled our pockets and started out. The river ran cold, in spite of the summer heat. As I waded in, each part of me shrank from where the water touched me: ankles, knees, thighs, hips, belly, chest. When it reached my throat I said I wanted to quit, that I might have a fit. But Charles, three inches taller than me, called me a coward and a freak. This I could not abide. I walked on into the cold water, which soon crept up to my eyes. I shut them against the chill as the river closed over my head.

Near shore, small, sharp rocks dug into my feet, but the further I walked toward the center, the softer the bottom became. Soon I felt mud too thin, too slimy, slipping between my toes. I opened my eyes to a world awash with gold and brown and deep, shivering shadows. I couldn't see my brother. The water pressed against my chest. I spit out air, heard the underwater gurgle of my own voice. My throat constricted, trying to keep water from rushing in. I realized, coward or not, I couldn't make it across.

I pushed at the water with my hands but barely rose; my toes drifted through the silt, raising clouds that forced my eyes shut. I prepared to die. Then a voice said to me, Rise up. Rise up, for ye have been baptized. Rise up.

Try as I might, I could not heed the voice. My breath pushed hard against my chest. I was near to opening my mouth to suck in water when I saw my brother through the amber of the river. He did not seem to suffer the same terror or struggles as me. He was moving slowly, calmly, through the water. I extended my arm, found I could touch him. I closed my hand around his billowing shirt and pulled.

He turned toward me, eyes wide. A few bubbles escaped his nostrils. I put both my hands on his shoulders. He grabbed at them, tried to pry my fingers away. I held him tighter. I needed air. He was just tall enough that by straightening my arms I could lift my head above the surface. I gasped for breath, my eyes squinting in the sun, now too bright after adjusting to the murk. Beneath me, my brother jerked from side to side, tried to rise, to throw me off. I told myself as soon I took in enough air, I would let Charles go. I filled my lungs with air once, twice. The third time I inhaled I held it in, let go of my brother's shoulders.

As the weight of the stones pulled me under, my brother drifted away. At first I didn't understand what happened. But then I did. I thrashed beneath the water, trying to return to the surface. Once again the air inside my lungs pressed against my chest. It was then I remembered the stones. I turned my pockets inside out, let them float toward the bottom. As soon as I felt myself lighter I kicked until finally I burst through the surface into sunlight and the relief of breath. Gasping, I made my way out of the water to sit on the shore.

I won, I thought to myself.

Gazing across the river, I had the uncanny notion I had lived this very moment before. A shadow swept toward me, hardly bending on the ripples disturbing the river's surface. It was so familiar. In a rush of shadow and water, I understood who it was and that he had been with me all along. Finally, I could hear his voice. I knew then: I was chosen. I had always sensed the Preacher as a thing of the air. Now I understood: he lived inside me. I trembled with the joy of my specialness.

Then the familiar nothingness sent me nowhere. I woke on the bank with the sun low in the sky. As I sat watching the night crawl into the trees and into the red reflection of the sun on the river, the picture of my brother floating away arose in my mind. I stood up, called his name. A waking owl answered; the river lapped the shore so quiet and rhythmic it almost sent me back into a trance. I shook myself free and went home, where I told my mother my brother had hidden from me, that I had been unable to find him. I asked her had he come home. She stared hard at me, but she had no choice but to believe me; my brother often played pranks on all of us.

The next day a fisherman found my brother, pale and bloated, hung up on a branch below the waterfall west of town. The man who found him knew our family, so carried him home, where my mother insisted on washing him and tucking him into the bed next to mine in our shared bedroom. He smelled like the river mixed with soap. Slowly though, arose another smell, sweet and acrid. It traveled across our room in waves, now here, now gone. Lying there awake I absorbed it through my nose, my mouth, my pores. Every now and then I got up to touch him, his skin cold and smooth as a stone from the bottom of the river. I considered placing sticks in his hair, stones in his eyes, the kinds of tricks he played on me whenever I had a spell. But there was no sport in it if he wouldn't wake up furious.

My mother made no pretense about how she felt. She paced in and out of our room, ten, twenty times a day, all the while lamenting that the wrong son had died. When his body grew rigid, my mother decided she wanted a daguerreotype made of him. By that time, my brother smelled more acrid than sweet. At night his odor permeated the air, slippery and rotten.

The smell of sin, the Preacher told me. Then he bid me wash the body.

In order to avoid my mother's hysterics or the back of my father's hand, I rose in the middle of the night to accomplish this chore. I took a bucket to the new well for water. When I wiped my brother's face, the skin was too soft. I stopped.

The Preacher insisted I needed to continue, my brother needed to be washed by an anointed one.

I dragged the rag across his chest. The skin came up, a mess of stickiness in the dark. The smell intensified. I remained standing there, almost as still as my dead brother until the Preacher told me I had done enough and bid me go to bed. My mother found my brother's condition when she came in to say good morning to his corpse. She wasted no time calling my father in, so I did not avoid either the hysterics or the beating.

The Preacher told me not to trouble myself about failing at my task; the maggots would eat my brother's sins.

Undaunted, my mother continued to beg my father for a portrait of her favorite son. Finally, he beat her, then called his friends together to build a coffin. My mother clambered from the floor to send for the tailor. Within twenty-four hours, my putrid brother, dressed in a suit he would have hated when alive, was loaded into a box and carried from our room. Immediately my father dismantled his bed and fed it to the fire. The smell of death was the last of my brother to leave the room.

Life in our home changed after Charles was buried. My father retreated to the store, claiming it as the only place truly his. Around then he changed the name of the store from Slacom's to MacAllister's. My mother's brothers objected, but my father used his shotgun to bring them to understand the store belonged to him and would pass on to me. My uncles snickered at that.

That boy will never control as much as a bowlegged cow, said my uncle Asa, The way he stares at nothing, half the time he don't even know where he's at.

I know he said this because I overheard. Embarrassed and enraged, I untied all three of my uncle's horses and slapped their asses. Then I ran back home to throw myself on my bed. Even though it shamed me, I couldn't stop myself from sobbing into my quilts. My mother came to the door to watch me, but she never crossed into the room; directly she returned to the sofa in the parlor where she mostly sat since my brother's funeral.

Whenever my sobbing had subsided into an occasional gasp, the Preacher told me to be at peace. Vengeance would be mine.

Every one of my enemies was bringing demolition upon themselves.I decided that the best way to be sure I witnessed their destruction was to become a preacher myself. My family had never gone to church, and them being preoccupied, they never noticed my absence on Sunday mornings. I decided to attend the Methodist Episcopalian church because I heard they would send a man who aspired to pastoring to college in the city. I thought Nashville or Atlanta; both would bring me stature no one could demean. I convinced myself that as soon as they found a Preacher lived within me, they'd want to elevate me as quickly as possible. I didn't worry about my spells; I knew church folks would understand them as the holy state they are.

In all of this I was mistaken. The church sought to

control my every thought and movement. When I told him I wanted to speak at the pulpit, the minister chuckled. He had the nerve to pat me on the head, like a dog. He told me maybe someday, if I was a good boy. His words infuriated me so much, I determined he would know my wrath, and the wrath of the Preacher as well. That night I snuck up to the church and set it alight. I hid behind a stone in the graveyard to watch it burn. When the minister told his suspicions of me to the sheriff, the sheriff scoffed at him.

You know that boy ain't all there, he said, I'd be surprised did that boy know how to light him a match.

I wanted to be angry, but the Preacher told me no. He told me there are times when I need to hide behind the lies people tell about me. He told me to learn discernment.

Soon after my release from the Methodists, I came home one day to encounter a man leaving my mother's bedroom. Until that moment, I had loved my mother more than my father, regardless of her feelings for me. When I saw the man, I convinced myself I had had a trance; I never know when I do, after all, and though I had never hallucinated so vividly, it didn't mean I never would. To be sure of the truth, I began to lurk around the house, hiding behind furniture, slipping around corners, peering through windows.

During this employment I saw not only that same man, but others as well, and all of them gave her money. After they left, she would sit in the parlor, drawing pictures of dresses on scraps of paper. That's what she was doing the day I subtly confronted her.

Is Daddy going to buy you something new, I asked.

No, she said, not looking up, I'm just daydreaming.

It's a shame you don't have money of your own, I said.

My tone of voice must have given my knowledge away,

because she looked up. Our eyes met. I refused to look away, no matter how hard she glared at me with those black, bottomless eyes of hers, eyes exactly mine, so I have been told.

Yes, it is, she answered, before turning her attention back to her drawings.

She's got no remorse, the Preacher said.

I looked closely at her. Though she behaved as if I was no longer in the room, I noticed her hands, almost imperceptibly shaking.

That's just her fear of being caught, said the Preacher, Tell your father.

My father had a temper famous in Sinking Springs and beyond. My uncles, my mother's brothers, were also known for being easily provoked to violence. All of them were likely to accuse me of telling tales. I had to be careful. I needed proof. I had to be patient. I learned that the men came at particular times when my father was unlikely to return and my mother thought I was playing away from home.

I watched and waited until a day my father told me to help him in the store. He had a large order of cloth coming in and needed me to tend to the customers while he sorted, priced, and shelved it. When he was through, and we were alone, the time was approaching when the men visited my mother.

Sir, I said.

He didn't answer, as was usual.

Sir, I have something important to tell you.

He took up his feather duster, walked toward the shelves.

It's about Ma, I said.

Now I had his attention. He turned around.

There's been men in the house, I said.

I wanted to hold his eyes, blue as ice, hard as granite, but I couldn't. I said the rest to my shoes.

The men come about this time, I said, They give her money.

He didn't even blink. Go on now, Davis he said, Pick out some sweets as payment for helping me.

His voice didn't have so much as a quiver. I picked out some penny candy and left.

For days my father acted normally. Baffled, I continued to spy on my mother. On a day when I was watching through her window, trying to figure out why people would want to contort themselves in a way that would cause them to howl in pain and make ugly faces, the bedroom door flew open. There stood my father with a shotgun. He fired once, then twice. He was a good shot. Both my mother and the man were dead.

No one gave my mother a funeral. Nor did they bury her in one of the church graveyards. When I asked my father what became of her body, he walked away. Watching him, I was overcome with an excitation. Fire blossomed in my brain, the heat of it filled my head, crackled down my spine, tingled into my feet, where it burned itself off. I could see its remnants pass as waves out of the room. When nothing of it remained, I knew where to find my mother. I should have known all along. I knew only one place to dispose of a sinful body. I made my way to the well on Miss Ellen's land, where the Preacher had martyred himself to free us from Miss Ellen's witchcraft.

Standing by the well, I sensed its depth, the dark distance of the far, far bottom. I closed my eyes to see in my mind the bones of Miss Ellen and the Preacher, the rotting flesh of my mother. I leaned into the well, breathed the air.

No smell like that of my brother's putrefying body, only fetid water and moldy stone. No sound but a faint buzzing.

I listened inside myself, curious about how the Preacher felt to be so close to his own bones. His reverence on encountering the place of his crucifixion was so potent, it filled my very veins, once again sanctifying me through him. I don't know how long I stood there in a dreamy state, basking in the near bottomless black of the well. As my eyes focused back onto the world, the Preacher reassured me:

She's where she belongs, he said, Go now.

So I did.

Nearing town I was met with shouts and jeers. At first I thought it was directed at me. Then I realized the crowd's back was to me. I pushed myself between two men to see my mother's brothers Asa, Francis, and Lyman in the middle of the road. They had a man on the ground; they kicked and punched at him over and over while the man made feeble attempts to escape. Asa lifted a fist coated in blood. I tried to get closer but a woman held me back, placing her hands over my eyes.

You've no need to see this Davis MacAllister, she said.

Without my sight, the sounds of the scene grew in volume; beneath the shouting of the crowd came the grunting of the attackers and the panting of their victim, the soft thud of fist into flesh and bone, the shuffle of a boot as it swung across the ground to land almost silently in the ribs. I couldn't bear it; I covered my ears with my hands, sending myself into a vacuum of endless night and muted sound.

Then the Preacher said, Look.

I wrenched the woman's hands from my eyes, violently enough she gave me a slap on the back of the head.

Suit yourself, she said.

I will, I responded.

I looked. The man on the ground was my father. I stepped closer as Lyman swung his leg back, then landed a hard kick into my father's skull. Lyman's boot sunk in so deep he had to struggle to pull it out. My father, half his face collapsed, rolled onto his side to spit blood.

My left arm jerked. I swallowed, then swallowed again and again, gulping as if drinking pails of water. The jeers of the crowd faded away, replaced by a banjo tune. I knew the song, but I couldn't place it. I forced myself to take steps toward my father; Uncle Asa's face leered in front of me, then bright lights flashed before my eyes.

I woke up to the sheriff carrying me into my house. He lay me down on the sofa. They're gon' bury him, the sheriff said to my uncles.

I thought he meant me, so I forced myself to sit up. I'm alive, I told them. I meant to scream it, but my voice scratched its way out small, feeble.

You saved us hanging him for the murder of his wife, the sheriff said to my uncles.

That's how I learned my father was dead.

Days later, my uncle Asa went to the courthouse where he verified I was the heir to the store that had once been his sister's, his father having found all three of his boys too no-account and ill-tempered to run a business. I was also heir to the house. Given my age and my sickness, Asa had no trouble convincing the people down at the courthouse that he and his brothers should watch over me until I came of age to take on those responsibilities myself. I didn't need the Preacher or anyone to tell me they never meant for me to come of age. I thought of running away, but where would I go? Seemed to me, my fate was sealed.

My uncles wasted no time taking over the store, changing

the name back to Slacom's before they even opened for the first day. They moved into the house, took the bedrooms and gave me a pallet to sleep on in the hallway. They ordered our slave Amelda around as if she belonged to them and not me. They forced me to go to school; I hadn't been since Charles died. Not having to return to school had been one of the best things to come out of Charles's death. I had grown tired of the way the other children avoided me because their parents told them they could catch the sickness from me.

The first day I was supposed to return to school, I pretended to forget, and stayed on my pallet. Francis and Lyman found me, tied me up, and threw me over the back of a horse. They brought me nearly to school, where they dumped me on the ground. Where of course, the Harpe boys found me. They stood around me laughing until Edmond Calloway came up. He instructed Johnny Harpe to help him untie me, and he gave me his coat. I never did miss school again; but every day I remembered the humiliation of Edmond Calloway's pity and I never stopped hating him for it.

I also hated the run-down school, with its chinks in the wall, holes in the ceiling, one stove in the far corner barely raising the temperature in winter. Supposedly, the parents supported it, but most could not, or would not, give much. My uncle Asa was among the would nots. At least the new schoolteacher was a man. His name was Sydney Abbot. He had graduated Vanderbilt University in Nashville, and he wasted no time telling us he intended to refine our ruffian ways.

Mr. Abbot wore the same clothes every day, rain or shine, winter or summer: black trousers, boiled white shirt, black overcoat. I never could determine whether he had several sets of identical clothes, or had his landlady wash the same ones every day after school.

The Preacher was quick to note Mr. Abbot's speech, how he lacked ignorant country grammar. Prodded by the Preacher, as I walked to and from school, I would repeat things I heard Mr. Abbot say: I am well; I have never; All of you.

But it was his books that truly impressed me. In particular, I could not get enough of the *Iliad* and the *Odyssey*. I could lose myself for hours reading and re-reading battle scenes in the *Iliad*. Odysseus showed me perseverance and triumph. On the virtue of these books the Preacher and I disagreed. He preferred I spend all my reading time with my bible; he deemed all other books a sin and a lie. When I approached Mr. Abbot on the subject, he laughed; he told me the bible, like the *Iliad* and the *Odyssey*, had originally been written in Greek, and all such stories held value to the development of a man. The Preacher made me to know that it wasn't the language a thing was written in, it was who wrote it, and only the bible was written by God. So I read the bible. Not like I had in church, but like a book. I was pleased to find it just as full of violence and adventure as the *Iliad* and *Odyssey*.

My uncles mocked me of course, called me Saint Davis, pretended to bow before me. So I took to reading by the river.

That didn't last long, though. As soon as he determined where I was and what I was doing, Asa sent Lyman to drag me home.

Anything I did other than stock shelves at the store or chop wood for our fireplaces, my brothers made a rule against it, then beat me for breaking it. Sometimes the beatings sent me into a spell or fit, so I had the added anxiety of waking and trying to figure out what happened.

Lyman and Francis were less intelligent than Asa and made up for it by being twice as mean. When they came home drunk from The Hammer and the Axe, they tormented me not for the sake of discipline, but for fun. While I slept, they would sneak into the hall and tie me up with rope. Whenever they saw me in town, they tripped me as I passed. I suspect they also persecuted me during my spells, as I often returned to the world covered in small bruises, as though I had been pinched. I am certain they released spiders on me once. I never saw them, but I awoke covered in small, painful, red bumps. No matter what they did, I knew I was the secret victor; with every humiliation, the Preacher's voice grew stronger inside of me. Eventually, I would know what to do.

One morning I woke covered in molasses and feathers. When I emerged from the hallway, Lyman and Frances called to Asa and told him I had done it to myself.

I meant merely to contradict them, to defend myself, but a violent rage took hold of me. With all the strength I could muster, I dove toward Lyman and Francis; they only had to move aside for me to fall to the floor, feathers flying. The molasses made me stick to the floor, further enraging me. I clambered to my feet, lurched toward the dining room, where I managed to lift and smash a chair before Asa got hold of me. He cursed me as I struggled, causing feathers to stick to him as well. Francis and Lyman were howling, they thought the scene so funny.

Through his laughter, Lyman choked out, Boy, you roll yourself in molasses, visit the henhouse, then try to break up the furniture?

What's the matter with you boy, said Francis, Not

enough you're an idiot, you got to show yourself for a freak, too?

You did it, you did it! I shouted and sobbed until Francis slapped my face.

I am sure Asa knew they were lying, but he beat me anyway.

When he finally finished, and the cane he beat me with was sticky with molasses and blood, I ran from the house. Ignoring the stares of people I passed, I ran to the river, dove in, and swam. The river murmured to me; the Preacher comforted me. I came out of the water clean and new, knowing just how I would take my revenge, gain the house, and the store with it.

Asa kept arsenic in the store, as some of the townspeople had trouble with rats. White and powdery, arsenic can easily be mistaken for sugar or flour. First, I had to figure out how to get the arsenic, as Asa watched my every move. I waited long enough that all but I had forgotten the incident with the molasses and feathers before I went to the store to tell Asa I'd seen a rat walk boldly into the sitting room at home. Having a particular loathing for rats, he scooped out a bag of arsenic and gave it to me, telling me to line all the baseboards of the house.

I went home and did as I was told. Then I waited for Amelda to leave the kitchen to fetch water. While she was away, I poured arsenic, first into the flour, then into the sugar for good measure. When Amelda returned, I told her my uncles expected fresh bread that evening. She shook her head, commenting it was a good thing she had yeast on hand. I wished I had thought to poison the yeast as well.

That night at dinner Amelda served up the fresh bread. So as not to seem suspicious, I took a bite before saying I didn't feel well and excusing myself. By midnight all three of them were vomiting and running to the privy with the shits. Amelda ran for the doctor, who said they likely ate something bad. As he left, he suggested they continue to vomit until they purged themselves of whatever had sickened them. I vomited also, and had a seizure. When I woke from it, I felt light as air. My uncles lay on the floor. Beside herself by this time, Amelda ran for Jewel Boyd, who examined my uncles and me.

Jewell told Amelda that Lyman and Francis were dead, and Asa and me were still alive. She told Amelda to run because the blame would surely be placed on her.

Asa was alive. As he staggered out to get the doctor, still vomiting, I retreated to my room, which I had reclaimed as soon as my two uncles stopped breathing. When I heard the doctor come into the house, I stuck my fingers down my throat until green bile came up. It tasted so bitter and vile, it was easy to continue to gag until the doctor peered around my door.

It'll wear off soon, son, he said, Just be glad you didn't join the angels with your uncles.

As Jewel had feared, when he found Amelda missing, Asa assumed she poisoned us. As soon as he felt strong enough, he put the word out that she was a murderer. The people of our town were only too willing to believe an uppity slave had turned on her masters. Asa also accused her of stealing our valuables when she fled, which was not in any way the truth. A mob advanced on the Colored village, but found no sign of Amelda. Incensed, they burned houses to satisfy their thirst for blame and violence.

Asa buried Lyman and Francis in the graveyard at the Methodist church. Reverend Southerland delivered a sermon more about the threat of the people on the west side of town than about my uncles. For good measure he invoked some fire and brimstone on the heathens practicing black magic in the woods. On this, I agreed. If there had never been magic in Sinking Springs, I never would have hit my head on the well, I wouldn't have epilepsy. My whole life would have been different.

The Preacher assured me though, that all is as it is meant to be. That there is a plan for me. I just needed to learn patience.

With the last shovels of dirt piled on my uncles' graves, the old church biddies, happy I had come back to the fold, attempted to escort me to the apple stack cake they had put together for the occasion. I couldn't remember the last time I had even seen a cake, Asa being so stingy with money. I followed them willingly.

Asa had other plans for me though, long-term plans. I had no sooner taken a bite of cake than he took me by the arm and dragged me straight to the store without stopping at home to change out of our Sunday best. From that day, I worked in the store, usually from before sunrise until after sunset, seven days a week. I only had time to converse with Mr. Abbot if he came into the store when Asa wasn't there. I only had time to read if I had a fit, a big one, real or feigned; then Asa or the doctor would send me to bed, at least for a little while.

My real seizures usually started with just going to the dreamy place; sometimes that's as far as it went, and I'd find myself staring at nothing, with my uncle slapping me or yelling into my ear. Other times, I'd dream myself into seeing my mother and father, alive and happy in a way I never saw them in life; these times they'd call my name. When I tried to answer, everything disappeared. I'd wake up on the ground, and for minutes at a time I could hear people, even see them, but I couldn't move or talk. That's when Asa would call in a couple of the layabouts who lounged in front of the store to carry me home, where I would spend the rest of the day reading and communing with the Preacher. I knew the consequences of course: No work, no supper. The Preacher assured me of the holiness of fasting. You may feel weak, he said, but your spirit grows strong.

❋ ❋ ❋

When news of the war swept through Sinking Springs, I looked forward to a chance to show my commitment to the Confederacy and escape Asa at the same time. I knew he would pay for a substitute for himself. All bullies are cowards.

When I told Asa I was signing up, he laughed. Ignoring him, I walked out to Miss Ellen's land where men were signing up and training.

Since my visit to my mother's resting place in the well with Miss Ellen and the Preacher, I had made many pilgrimages out there at night while Asa slept, and I felt safe and comfortable on that land. I had never had a seizure there. Sometimes I sat by the well counting Asa's sins against me. Sometimes I listened to the Preacher reassure me I wasn't responsible for his death. The other children had murdered him. I would not even have been close to the well if the older boys hadn't swept the young ones along. Sometimes, the bones, the moon, 'tend the night would inspire me. I'd walk the property delivering fierce sermons about how those now brought low would later rule the world.

At first it seemed there would be no problem signing up for the Confederate army. I didn't see anyone who knew me well. And looking at me, no one could tell there was a sickness in me. I had grown tall, nearly as tall as Asa, and strong from working and lifting eleven hours a day. I had given my name to the captain and was moving on when Frank Harpe crept up behind me.

You taking him, Captain, Frank asked.

We need all good men, said the captain.

He ain't no good man, Frank laughed. And his brother Johnny laughed with him.

He done some crime, asked the captain.

He's filled with the devil, said old man Fuston, who had just been turned down for being old and decrepit.

That sent the Harpe boys into near hysterics.

If the devil falls on the ground pissing his pants, cackled Johnny.

I turned around just as Johnny threw himself to the ground. He shook his body in terrible spasms, jerked his arms and legs, rolled his eyes up in his head. Then he made a sound, a deep moan, like a calving cow.

All the men doubled over with the hilarity of it, but I could hardly hear them. I couldn't take my eyes off Harpe jerking around on the ground. I only knew my seizures from the inside. It occurred to me now that many people here, all the people in my life in fact, had seen me like that. In my mind, I begged the Preacher to tell me that wasn't how I looked.

Your trances are holy, he said.

Do I look like that? The question repeated over and over inside me. My vision blurred. I had time to think, Oh, no, this doesn't happen here, before the nothingness took. The men's voices receded further and further away until they seemed to come from the sky or underground.

My next sensible moment, I sat by the river, the rising

sun casting early morning pink across the surface. That meant I had lost an afternoon and a night. Never before had I walked someplace during a spell. A new chapter of my life had opened. I knew this.

Day by day, though, my life seemed very much the same, working with Asa, carrying, loading, shelving. When troops began coming through Sinking Springs, I was sure our store would go the way of most homes and businesses, but Asa had the gift of persuasion. Lincolnites thought he was a Lincolnite, Confederates thought he was Confederate. Both funded him for a Home Guard. Asa gathered other men who had paid for substitutes, and they would ride out, sometimes along the river in the woods, sometimes up one mountain or another. Sometimes they'd ride to the west side, just to remind the Colored people they weren't as free as they thought. From the doorway of the store, filled with envy, I'd watch them leave.

Eventually I noticed Asa hardly ever tormented me anymore. His orders sounded like any boss would give a worker. Because I was calmer, though I had a few tics, some time passed in which I had no fits, and very few trances. Bolstered by this feeling of being a normal man, I asked Asa if I could join the Home Guard. I thought he would mock me, but he seemed pleased.

You might could be a man yet, he said.

The next day when the Home Guard gathered, Asa brought an extra horse. When he called to me to join them even though I had never learned to ride, I thought that Asa had invited me only to entertain him and his friends.

To my astonishment, the invitation was genuine. Asa patiently taught me how to get on the horse and how to ride. Before long, I could gallop down the street with the rest of the Home Guard. The horses' hooves would kick up clouds of dust, causing anyone outside to duck into some shelter right quick. I had never before felt like I was part of something so powerful.

Fewer customers patronized the store during the war, the town being mostly women and children, with supplies hard to come by. So we had plenty of time to ride. Any men not elderly and sick, any strangers, and any man skulking through the woods, we sought out. We didn't worry about which army they were hiding from; we just took them to whoever currently held Sinking Springs. When we ran short of deserters, we turned our attention to the wretches responsible for the war to begin with. By 1864 no Negro dared to walk the streets after sunset. We took those who lived in the woods up the mountain and treated them to a bonfire.

The day we found the witch Jewel Boyd and her husband in the village, Asa suggested we go over to the cabin to destroy Jewell's potions and other instruments of spellmaking, but the Preacher bid me stop him. The Preacher said Delia Boyd and I are connected, like it or not. He said this wasn't Delia's time. So I told Asa there's no reason to go there. Without the witch there can't be witchcraft. Asa's friends, being lazy at heart, were glad to put less effort into our caper.

During these excursions, I never once suffered a seizure. Then in April of 1864 came the insect plague. One morning Asa and I went outside to find both of our horses dead, covered with insects that looked somewhat like mosquitos but larger, with black heads and dark green bodies. As we stood gaping, Otis Stike, who rode with us in the Home Guard, came running toward us, his mouth open in a silent scream. By the time he tripped over our horses, blood flowed from his nose and ears. As he fell, all the insects rose up like a black and green cloud before settling back down on Otis and the horses.

Asa stood there frozen. Of all the things he'd seen and done, these insects were what finally horrified him.

We need to get inside, Asa, I said, slapping at the bug that had just landed on my arm. Its bite couldn't rightly be called a sting. It was more like a blacksmith had clenched my arm between hot tongs.

Asa, I shouted over the swelling buzz.

Insects crawled up and down Asa's legs. I took his arm and pulled him into the house. As I slammed the door there came a piercing pain in my head to match that of my arm.

When I woke, I found myself lying by the door right where I had fallen. Blood splattered the floor, and at first I was terrified that what happened to the horses and Otis was happening to me.

I checked my eyes and ears: no blood. I felt around my head until I found a small cut, still sticky with my blood; I must have hit the doorjamb as I fell. I stood up, felt around the rest of my body. Aside from the welt on my arm where the insect bit me, and the cut on my head, I seemed fine. I went in search of Asa.

I found him in his bed, pants off, frantically scratching at his legs. The bites had opened up, oozing pus and blood. When Asa looked over to where I stood in the doorway, I was relieved to see tears flowing from his eyes instead of blood. His fingers scratched and scratched, further opening the sores. It seemed sure he would scratch himself to death. I went and got some rope. Asa was weak, so it was easy to tie his hands to the bedposts. Once secured, he thrashed and yelled. I left the room.

By the time the repulsive birds arrived to eat the insects, Asa had stopped yelling. When I went into the room, he was so still, I thought he had died. As I approached him, he opened his eyes and moaned through chapped lips. I untied him and brought him a glass of water. He gulped it down, asked for more. I brought him another glass, which he drank just as quickly. Then we examined his legs. They were covered with eruptions, some of them crusted over, and some still leaking puss and blood.

You are a hard man to kill, I said.

Get the doctor, he croaked.

Doctor's still not coming out, I said, According to the few people I've talked to who dared come out, the doctor's among those who believe the birds will turn murderous from eating the insects. But packs of dogs are coming in from I don't know where. Could be they're here to eat the birds that have started to drop out of the sky.

I don't believe you, said Asa.

I pointed at his legs. Did you ever think a thing like this could happen, I asked.

For answer, Asa tried to move his legs, winced with the pain.

You know it's sin brought this on us, I said.

Don't talk to me about sin, he snapped.

This town's riddled with it, I said, With murder and blasphemy. The people of Sinking Springs have souls as blistered as your legs. That's why so many of them are gone now, between the war, the Home Guard, and the insects. God chose not to take you. *Again*. I'd call it grace considering how you used to torment me.

Asa glared at me with a hatred I hadn't seen in him since before Lyman and Francis died.

You must have known it would come back to you, I said.

He swung his legs off the bed and tried to lurch toward me. He took only two steps before he crumpled to the floor.

You'll need help now, I said, You should be grateful I'm here.

Asa spit at me.

I had to stop myself from smiling. Looks like your only nurse is the one you tortured and beat, I said as I helped him up.

You were a brat kid. Didn't I give you a job? Didn't I let you ride with us? Risk you going into one of your fits to let you try to live someways normal?

I helped him back into the bed.

I need more water, he said.

He looked so defeated, I almost felt sorry for him.

Nevermind, Uncle, I said, The insects can give me a nasty sting, the birds can taunt me and fly at my head, the dogs can growl. None of them can kill me.

Then get some goddamn water, growled Asa.

The Preacher had always told me my time of power would come. Now here it was, and I could be merciful.

I went out with a pail to the new well. The birds hovered in the air and the dogs stalked me on the ground. In spite of my immunity to them, I still hated them. They couldn't harm me, but they followed me; the dogs trotted a few feet behind me; the birds fluttered from tree to tree. I feared if I had a seizure I would lose the Preacher's protection and the animals would devour me. The Preacher had reassured me many times, but I don't know what happens to him when I'm unconscious.

Asa was never able to walk normally again. Never again would he have a painless day. We'd work in the store, Asa sitting on a stool to take the customers' money in the mornings while I took care of any orders that made it to us through the armies, stocked the shelves, did all the physical work. In the afternoons Asa went home to do paperwork and nap while I tended the store. We hired a White woman who'd lost husband and sons to the war to do our housework and prepare our meals. She took very little pay from us; she considered serving two surviving men payment enough.

During the long, boring hours when the store was closed due to insects and birds, I learned to whittle; it kept my hands and mind busy. Before the Preacher convinced me I could go outside, I used the legs of our chairs; they were made of hard chestnut, so I gained control of my knife by sharpening each to a point. We had five chairs, so I removed the legs of three of them. When I had finished, I had twelve small spears. I polished them until they shone, then when I was able to open the store, I sold them as a way for women to protect themselves from dogs. They sold more quickly than I hoped; occasionally I see a dog lying in the road, one of my spears in its side.

Although it's likely I could have made and sold more spears, it was neither interesting nor challenging to continue to make them. As soon as it was safe to go out, I took to wandering in the woods up the mountain behind my house, picking up fallen pine branches that had fallen. I tried to whittle animals, failed at one after another: owl, raccoon, boar, bear. Eventually, I made a fish that almost looked like a fish; my near success gave me encouragement to continue. So I went back up into the forest to gather more wood.

As I finished collecting the branches best for whittling, I heard laughter. I peered through the trees, and there in a shaft of sunlight were Emily and Polly Adair, gathering chestnuts. I had rarely seen these two since the murder of the Preacher. Their father hired tutors so they could learn at home, rather than mix with any town or country people. The family always sent a slave to the store before the war.

I'm not sure how they survived since, but their mother must have mostly kept them inside; they had both eluded the insect plague.

The last time I had seen them was after my brother died. I had encountered the two girls striding down the street, dressed for church. Polly would have passed by, but Emily had stopped to scrutinize me.

Mother says the devil made you kill your brother. She said if we ever saw you, to run away as fast as we can, Emily shrieked.

Then the two of them ran away laughing.

Watching them dance about in the forest like two dryads, I knew I let myself give in to their charm. They were beautiful, one blonde, one dark, both with pale, pale white skin glowing in the sunlight.

Sinners both, said the Preacher, They have no fear of God or mortality.

After all this time, here was my chance to punish them for their insolence. I put down my bundle of sticks. Slowly, I moved from tree to tree until I was almost upon them. As soon as they became quiet, absorbed in searching for chestnuts, I stepped from behind a tree into their shaft of sunlight.

Polly stood up first.

Davis MacAllister, she said.

She tried to sound brave, to make the sound of my name into an insult, but her voice trembled, so slightly, a person not sensitive to it might not have noticed.

Emily stood up, but hid behind her sister. She wasn't as willing to show off alone with me in the forest.

What are you doing here, asked Polly.

I live here, I said.

No you do not.

I do, I said, The devil called me out here to make a bargain.

The girls held their ground.

No he didn't, said Polly.

He did, I said, pulling my penknife from my pocket. He told me to bring him two locks of hair, one dark, one fair. As soon as I bring him his gift, I can have anything I wish for.

I stepped toward them, brandishing my knife.

They turned and fled.

I followed them at a distance, just to keep them running. This is how I came to witness Emily Adair stepping into a bed of baby rattlesnakes. I stopped to watch her try to run to her sister, spreading the poison through her body. She fell just as she reached Polly.

I pocketed my knife, ambled over to them.

My sister's snakebit, cried Polly.

They were at my mercy.

I bent down and lifted Emily from the ground. She was so light. I could feel her already dying.

The Harpe farm is just over there, said Polly. Mrs. Harpe knows root medicine. She'll know what to do.

I carried Emily Adair, filled with poison, wilting in my arms, her weakened breath brushing across my cheek. It smelled like lilacs and honey.

The Harpe woman and her skinny daughter Lucy let us into the house, pointing me to a table, where I laid Emily down. When Mrs. Harpe lifted the girl's skirt, there was one beautiful pale foot and ankle—but the other—as the skirts were lifted we could see the black streaks of poison running under her skin from her feet, upward to where we couldn't see. But all of us knew that by now the poison coursed through her entire body. As if to prove it, she convulsed. I was fascinated. Her eyes rolled back, her body shook and writhed, her arms stiffened at her side. It wasn't like Johnny Harpe's imitation of me. Her movements were much more contained. There was a slowness about her, rather than the hysteria he had implied. The air around her felt holy.

Then the Harpe woman called for her madstone. All was frantic. Lucy rushing about, Polly crying over her dying sister.

Suddenly, Emily calmed. She seemed to stare at me, so I smiled down on her. She smiled back, wan and ghostly, so beautiful, already on her way to heaven. Then I remembered she was not. She was heading for hell, just like all of us who committed murder that day at the well.

Not you, said the Preacher, You are redeemed.

Polly saw Emily smile, asked her did she feel better.

Emily's eyes glazed as she turned to her sister.

He's here, she said.

Did she mean me? The Preacher? The devil? I wanted to ask her, but she died. All the women began to cry and shriek. I plunged into darkness.

* * *

Today Polly Adair surprises me by coming into the store. She isn't delicate like her sister was. She's grown up sturdy, with dark auburn hair and darker chestnut eyes. There is a fullness about her belly and her hips. I realize the likeness I have whittled of her is no likeness at all. I will have to start over.

She says she wants a ribbon.

I ask her what color.

I can see she's pretending to think about it. I admire her furrowed brow, the way she sits on her hip, a grown up version of her sister's brattiness. I have heard stories about Polly, about how men can't resist her.

Blue, like the summer sky, she says.

I find some blue satin ribbon, show it to her. She says the color is perfect.

I ask her how long a ribbon she might need.

Enough to go around my head, she says.

I eye her carefully, trying to determine the size of her head.

She appears uncomfortable.

She has a secret, the Preacher tells me, All secrets are sin.

I take my knife from my pocket.

Wouldn't scissors cut smoother, she asks.

No, I say, I keep this knife sharp. It will cut anything. Look.

I show Polly the likeness of Ellen Bridges I had been carving when she came in.

Why would you do that, she asks.

Whittle?

Make a play-pretty out of Miss Ellen.

I've carved all of us, I say, I could run over to the house and fetch them if you'd watch the store for a minute.

She turns as if to leave.

A bird squawks from the rafters. It must have followed her in.

I hate those damn birds, I say.

So do I, she says.

All the foul animals in our town, I say, Especially the birds.

The bird squawks as if to argue with me.

Especially the birds, she says, looking up at the ceiling.

Shall I cut this ribbon for you, I ask.

Without waiting for her answer, I cut the ribbon, hold it out to her.

She takes a small step forward, snatches it from my hand as if I might grab her if she isn't fast enough.

How much, she asks.

Take it, I say, A gift. From an old friend.

An unholy racket outside interrupts our argument. I come around the counter, and together we go to the door. When I brush against Polly, I can feel her secret sin, curled up and dark, growing inside of her.

The Preacher rejoices. There needs to be a sacrifice, he says.

Outside, a shabby, two-bit circus parade passes down the street, emaciated beasts painted on the side of the wagons. I am turning away when Polly says, They're setting up at Miss Ellen's.

How do you know that, I ask.

She tells me she saw them from the roof of the Fort; she tries to lie, says the soldiers let her go up there for the view. Now I know not only her sin, but how she came to commit it.

She's the one, says the Preacher.

Before I can say anything more, the parade marches off toward Miss Ellen's and Polly bids me goodbye as she steps out the door.

The crow in the rafters squawks. I find a slingshot, shoot it down, throw its limp body out the door.

See how easy it is, says the Preacher.

That was not a sacrifice, I say, chuckling.

I can feel the Preacher's anger at my lack of seriousness; it stabs behind my eyes so sharply I fear the onset of a seizure. To protect myself, I work for a while, not troubling him. When I sense he has calmed, I ask, Why a sacrifice?

To avenge my murder, he says. You can finally take my place. You will gain power of health and sanctity you have yet to imagine. Never again will you plunge into darkness. Never again will you be subject to mockery and disdain. You will make Sinking Springs a holy place, free of sin and witchcraft.

How, I ask.

Make the sacrifice first, he says, Tonight.

Where?

Follow the road to the circus, but wait behind the well. The rest will happen as it was meant to.

A Circus Performs on Cursed Land

The verdant smell of Spring combines with the musky scent of animals in the chill air. Delia and Carter arrive at dusk. As they step onto the property, neither of them mentions Ellen Bridges or the preacher.

On the path to the big top, they stop beneath the banners advertising the freaks.

What are they, asks Delia.

People, says Carter.

Maybe we should go on home, says Delia.

We don't have to, answers Carter, They're in a tent by themselves. There won't be any of 'em in the show.

Delia decides to rely on her trust for Carter, rather than her fear of the oddities painted on the banners. Still she hesitates before she follows him.

Carter buys their tickets at the ticket wagon, and they head for the main entrance. Together they approach the ticket taker, a large, bald pasty man wearing a shiny gold vest over a dirty shirt. Carter tries to give him the tickets, but he stares at Carter's hand as if it is empty. Then he squints at Delia.

I didn't know you small town folk had maids, he says, as he finally takes the tickets.

Carter opens his mouth, not sure what he will say, but Delia goes in ahead of him so he follows. They stop for a moment inside to examine the layout of the tent. A set of seats five levels high starts to the left of the entrance and circles around to the entertainer entrance directly across from them. To their right are the same type of seats, but they stop partway around the tent. This is the seating for White people. Beyond the right-hand seats, there is standing room wedged between the end of the seats and the entertainers' entrance. This is for anyone who doesn't look White.

Carter takes Delia by the hand and leads her toward the White seating, but the ticket taker suddenly appears beside them.

Those seats ain't for you, he says to Delia, You get on over there with your people where you belong.

Delia looks over at the standing room area. She sees people she knows, including Mrs. Ware, Elijah's mother, standing around chatting with one another.

We can leave, says Carter.

It's a waste of money if we go, Delia says, That's Elijah's mama, she adds, pointing toward Mrs. Ware.

Carter watches Delia walk away, cringing at his own cowardice. He should have stood up for her. For Delia's part, she's glad she doesn't have to take a seat and watch people she cares about stand.

To Carter's horror, a clown, a White man dressed up in petticoats with a beard drawn on with grease, swishes up behind Delia, imitating her walk while twirling his skirts. Carter's anger overcomes his cowardice; he starts toward Delia and the clown, not considering what he will do when he reaches them. Once more, however, he finds himself confronted by the ticket taker, who digs his fingers into Carter's arm, turning him around to face the stands where the White people sit.

Delia knows the clown is behind her. She knows the laughter in the tent is at her, but she doesn't let on. She sets herself in the direction of Mrs. Ware; it feels like an eternity before she reaches her.

Where's your brother, Mrs. Ware asks.

He took sick and died.

Mrs. Ware takes Delia's hand. Elijah will watch over him, she says.

I know he will, answers Delia.

Carter wrenches his arm from the grip of the ticket taker. Filled with shame, he sits on a bench directly in front of the ring, where he can see Delia across from him. He hopes she'll catch his eye, but she doesn't, not then, nor for the duration of the show.

* * *

Davis MacAllister can hardly contain his excitement about his night's mission. As he dresses, he pauses to calm himself several times, lest he fall into a seizure. He has just opened the door to leave the house when his uncle Asa appears, leaning on a cane as he shuffles toward Davis on wobbly legs. Davis can tell by the stiffness of Asa's walk that he has wrapped bandages around his legs to prevent the seeping of pus and blood from the still-oozing blisters through his trousers. Wrapped legs mean Asa intends to leave the house.

Seems we're going to a circus, boy, he says as he pockets his pistol.

Davis sighs. Asa will make it much more difficult to fulfill his mission. He considers seizing Asa's cane and knocking him unconscious. The idea would never work, of course, because by the time he came back home, Asa would be conscious and waiting at the door, pistol cocked. It passes through Davis's mind he could kill Asa, but he doesn't have time to murder him, get rid of his body, and concoct a story about how he died.

All right, says Davis.

He escorts his uncle through town toward the circus. As they slowly walk along the road, stopping with some frequency so Asa can rest, Polly Adair passes by, causing Davis's nerves to buzz.

Stay calm, says the Preacher.

I am calm, Davis says aloud.

Why would anyone care, remarks his uncle.

Davis explains to his uncle that he's just making sure he doesn't spoil the circus for them both with a fit.

Good idea, says Asa.

Once on the grounds, Asa does his best to hide his deformed gait. People still stare. There are many rumors about Asa Slacom's legs. Some say he gave his true legs to the devil in payment for surviving the insect plague; some say the devil comes to Asa on the full moon to drink from his sores as payment for staying alive; others say his aberration is punishment from God for his cruelty while in the Home Guard. Some believe there is nothing wrong with Asa Slacom, that he's biding time until he decides what evil he will bring next to Sinking Springs.

Both Davis and Asa ignore the stares. They also ignore the banners depicting the freaks. Davis buys the tickets, and they go inside the tent where Davis helps his uncle to the front bench where Carter Bridges sits. Always polite, Carter slides over to make room.

Asa sits down, but Davis does not.

I'll be back, he says to his uncle.

Without waiting for a response, Davis MacAllister turns on his heel and sets out to meet his destiny. He strides confidently to the well, where he sits down. While he waits to know what to do next, he whittles at his new figure of Polly Adair.

◦ ◦ ◦

As Polly Adair passes by Davis MacAllister and Asa Slacom, she does her best to behave as if she doesn't see them. Either one of them alone is discomfiting; together they make her queasy with anxiety and disgust.

On arriving at the circus grounds, Polly glances at the banners. Her eyes fix on the Fat Lady. That's one good reason why I'm not keeping this baby, she thinks. She buys her ticket and goes into the tent. As her eyes adjust to the dim light inside, she scans the seats for Peter Allan, his wife, and child.

There they are, sitting in the center of a row, high up in the last tier. Straightening her posture, Polly climbs the stairs to their row.

When she reaches them, Peter is speaking to his child, but sensing Polly's presence, he glances up. His eyes register shock, then anger. Almost imperceptibly, he shakes his head.

Polly smiles.

Excuse me, she says as she squeezes past him, then past his wife and son.

As she passes, she tousles the child's hair, smiles at Peter again. Once seated next to Peter's wife, Polly pulls out her flask and offers it to her. Tight lipped, the wife refuses the whiskey. Polly takes a deep drink.

* * *

When they step onto the land, Alva and her siblings are too enchanted by the tents to notice the well, or Davis MacAllister sitting there whittling. But the land does feel familiar to Alva. Her brother Edmond had taught her about this place, told her the story over and over again as she fell asleep at night; he had taught her to listen for the singing of Ellen Bridges, while remaining wary of the shadow cast by the preacher. She wishes Edmond were with her now.

She also wishes Johnny had come to get her like he promised. Alva had hoped to see him, but as she looks around at the growing crowd, there's no sign of him. Once inside the tent, a quick glance around tells her Johnny isn't in here, either. When a coldness descends on her, she tells herself it's just the sun setting. Shaking off her apprehension, Alva finds a bench with room for her family, and sits down, settling little Rose onto her lap.

* * *

As soon as he steps into the tent, Willie Reed's belly tightens; his heart beats double time, beads of sweat form on his forehead. He smells the sweat of everyone around him; he smells animal musk and dung, sawdust and sulfur. He smells expectation. All these odors he remembers from the war and the prison. Missing only are the smells of fear and death, though he can easily imagine them seeping under the tent, spreading mist-like across the ring.

Lucy smiles at him. Her smile distracts him from his ruminations. For the millionth time he admires her long blonde hair, her green green eyes. He needs to marry her. She is the only one who can save him. Why else could he choose to rise in the morning, toil through the day, go to sleep with the sun, except for a beautiful wife. How else could he break the curse of his father's death, but with a child of his own? He knew that with Lucy beside him in bed, he would no longer have nightmares of running through a forest littered with men blown to pieces, some with no legs, some just heads growing from the ground like mushrooms, all screaming for him to save them, and him still running.

Lucy leads Willie to the front row on the other end

from Carter Bridges and Asa Slacom. She is delighted by the tent, the ring, the crowd; but the tension of sitting next to Willie sucks at her joy, like he needs all she has to give just to stay seated among people. She had always dreamed of him needing only her, but now she remembers her mother's words. Things get broken, they stay broken. In this moment, Lucy realizes she could shine all the light of the sun on Willie, and he would yet need more. It breaks her heart. She decides she'll think about it later, after the circus. Who knows when she might see an entertainment again.

*   *   *

Finally, the last of the stragglers from the midway take their seats. The band strikes up, first a fiddle, then a bugle, followed by a drumroll. The ringmaster strides into the ring, his boots shining ebony in the red dirt. He wears a red, sparkling coat and a black top hat, lending him an air of sophistication. He raises his arms, silencing the tittering and murmuring of the crowd.

Ladies and gentlemen, he intones, his voice loud and low, like thunder rolling down the mountain.

Derisive snickers erupt from here and there in the stands.

Ain't no ladies and gentlemen here, someone calls out.

As if to prove the heckler's point, Johnny Harpe and his drunken friends stagger into the big top. Ignoring the ringmaster in the ring, they stumble up to the back row of seats on their right, tripping over people already in the stands, slapping people they know on the top of the head. The crowd boos and hisses as the drunks take their seats. No one notices that Johnny Harpe doesn't laugh along with his friends. His mood had turned sour when at the ticket wagon the cashier had pushed Johnny's money back at him.

You done gave up enough, she said, her voice dripping with pity.

I can pay like anybody else, he had said, forcing the money stolen from his mother back on her.

Inside the big top, Johnny notices Carter Bridges, who claimed to be Union, but as far as Johnny knows, did nothing but make pictures of those bound to die and those already dead. There's crippled Asa Slacom, but no sign of his epileptic nephew, Davis MacAllister. He remembers back to when he used to imitate Davis's fits. Johnny still doesn't like Davis, but he regrets taunting him now that he lives with an affliction of his own. Scanning the seats, he sees Polly Adair, whose father claimed to ride off to defend the Confederacy; Johnny had never seen nor heard tell of him, so assumes he kept riding north and was hiding up there like a rich, gutless cur. Polly slips a flask out of her dress, takes a manly swallow, making Johnny wish he himself had thought to bring a flask.

Across the ring, Johnny sees Alva with the children, looking so innocent. In his drunkenness, the sight of her fills him with contempt; like everyone's, her innocence is a lie. He can't help but spit, causing the woman in front of him to turn around and glare.

Hey, says Wade Butson, Ain't that your sister down there with that half-wit Yankee Willie Reed? Get down there and give him your best one-fisted fight.

Johnny stands up, intending to show his one fist to Butson's jawbone.

Ladies and Gentlemen, repeats the ringmaster. His voice now booms unnaturally, echoes around the tent, even shaking the seats. Johnny sits down.

The ringmaster continues: Welcome, from the great palaces of Egypt, Ali, the world's greatest juggler.

The juggler enters the ring, clad in a spangled leotard, only tights to cover his legs. His mustache is stupendous, bright red curling up and swirling against his cheeks: He wears a turban from which curly red hairs escapes. He gestures at two of the clowns, who scurry out of the ring, then scurry back carrying a trunk, while making a great fuss about its heaviness. The juggler takes white ceramic plates from the trunk; he rolls one across his arm behind his head, down his other arm, catches it, rolls it again, then adds a second, a third, a fourth.

From the shadows at the far side of the tent, the calliope grinds out notes, one at a time, forced, separate, until finally a melody arises. The juggler puts a plate on a stick, spins it, balances the stick on his head. He spins two more plates on his fingers. Amidst applause, he returns all but one of the plates to the trunk, retrieves a fork, an egg, and a turnip. These he juggles; he catches the fork in his mouth, tines up. He throws the turnip high into the air. It drops straight down on the fork, sticking fast to the tines, while he continues juggling both the plate and the egg.

The drummer beats on the drum, louder, faster. The juggler throws the plate and the egg higher and higher, fork with turnip still in his mouth. Suddenly, he flattens his hand, catches the plate. He throws the egg up even higher until it reaches the darkness near the top of the tent. As it falls, the crowd sucks in their breath. The juggler holds out the plate, catches the egg without breaking it.

While the audience applauds, three goats with monkeys on their backs run into the ring, chased by a clown. When the clown falls face down in the dirt, the monkeys jump up and down on the backs of the goats, seemingly pointing and mocking. The audience whistles and howls as the clown jumps up to chase the goats and monkeys from the tent. Even Willie Reed finds himself almost smiling.

Next, welcome from France, the family Bonjour, acrobats to the Emperor himself, intones the ringmaster.

A family steps into the ring: a mother, a father, and five children of varying sizes. The smallest toddles in behind the rest, as if she just learned to walk. All are dressed in black satin leotards; the children and the mother's costumes have ruffles at the neck and wrists. While the four bigger children sit on the ground, the mother picks up the baby as the father lies down on the ground, feet up. The crowd gasps as the mother throws the baby into the air.

Polly momentarily forgets Peter Allan as she watches the baby fly up further and further towards the top of the tent, then plummet towards the ground. Several women stand as if they would rush into the ring to save the poor child from her fate. But the baby lands on her tummy, square on her father's feet. He bends his knees, propels her back into the air where she spins onto her back, lands again on his feet. He pushes her into the air again and she turns back onto her belly. Father and baby keep on with this trick, faster and faster until with a final push he sends her high into the air. Another gasp from the crowd when the father stands up and turns as if to walk away. It seems certain the child will plunge to the ground, but her mother steps up, gracefully catching her.

The family brings in a seesaw and a wooden box nearly as tall as the father. The biggest child jumps from the box, sending a smaller child flying onto his father's shoulders. A larger boy does a handstand on his younger sister's back. Finally, the family stacks themselves into a pyramid, and a clown sets the baby on top, where she crawls around on her sister's back until she falls. The clown catches her and tosses her to her mother as the pyramid breaks up. With the baby clinging tight to her mother's neck, the acrobats all do backflips to the clapping, stomping and whistling of their audience.

As the acrobats scamper out of the tent, the gaslights go out. In the pitch dark, people whisper to one another. Alva's youngest sister Rose begins to cry. Alva holds her close; she doesn't like this much dark any more than her sister does.

Then, a flame. There stands the ringmaster, holding a torch. Another flame reveals a lean man stepping into the ring.

And now, for the first time, never seen on this continent, from the deserts of Arabia, Danto! pronounces the ringmaster.

The lean man holds the torch beneath his face. Some of the spectators scream as they recognize the red hue and horns of the devil.

All of Alva's siblings try to crawl into her lap.

I don't like this, Lucy says to Willie.

It ain't the real devil, he says.

Lucy wishes he'd take her hand. But Willie's eyes are fixed on the devil.

The devil tilts his head back, plunges the torch down his throat, spins in a circle; his eyes glitter; every person feels that his evil eye looks directly at them. All is silence. Until the devil pulls the torch from his mouth to spit fire.

The band launches into terrible music, all rumbles and flashes like a storm,

The lamps relight. Now the audience can see the devil clearly as he once again spits fire. His red arms bend at joints and elbows in two or three places. The scars piled on scars on the hand gripping the blackened torch create an evil map of burns and striations.

The fiddle and calliope let loose a series of screeching howls and dissonant notes. A premonition of terror grips Johnny by the throat. Carter thinks he hears his grand-mother sing a warning beneath the cacophony, but her song disperses and quickly fades away.

As the demon continues to crawl about breathing fire, a woman in corset and high-heeled boots struts into the ring. Two of the clowns try to sneak up behind her, but the ring-master snatches them by the backs of their billowing costumes and throws them out of the ring. The laughter is sparse. All eyes are on the woman. As she waves her skirt about, showing her boots and stockings, a few of the most upright of the town's citizens make a show of walking out, though some turn to look over their shoulders as they go. Delia would like to leave, but she doesn't want to bring attention to herself; it is one thing to be mocked by a clown, quite another to be tormented by the devil.

The strumpet taps the devil on the back, and he turns to dance with her. At first the band plays a waltz, but then the music turns lascivious, the notes of the horns sliding around the low, steady beat of the drum. The devil and the strumpet rub their bodies together, the devil spitting fire over the strumpet's shoulder. Just as the dance becomes too obscene for any person to watch, a clown runs into the ring, bucket in hand. He throws water over the devil and the strumpet, and the two separate with great shock and anger. The devil tries to spit fire, but instead a stream of water spills from his mouth. The tense laughter of the audience follows the soaking wet devil and strumpet as they chase the clown from the ring.

The ringmaster calls out, Now, in a death-defying

display of courage in the face of nature's fiercest animal, Great Southern Circus presents the courageous and dazzling Lucia-Marie, and, direct from the deepest jungles of wildest Africa, Leonardo, king of the beasts.

At these words, a lion, uncaged, lopes into the ring. Those standing near the entertainers' entrance back up. Delia takes Mrs. Ware's hand. People in the first rows touch their guns, while checking the distance to the exit. Their fear prevents them from seeing the beast's ribs protrude from beneath his thinning fur; his mane ragged and unkempt. He has no teeth. His roar, however, mightily recalls the jungle.

Carrying a torch and hoop, Lucia-Marie enters the ring, clad in a sparkling gold dress that clings to her body from neck to ankle. Barefoot, she pads into the center of the ring, lays the hoop on the ground where a clown rushes in to take it up. Lucia-Marie continues delicately, stealthily, toward the lion.

The crowd holds its breath.

She rests her hand on the lion's back,

With a terrible roar, Leonardo turns to lunge at her. She deftly swings the torch between herself and the beast, forcing the lion to rear up on its hind legs. She thrusts the fire toward it, waving flames in its face.

Lucia-Marie waves her free hand, beckoning the clown to bring the hoop. Reluctantly, he shuffles over. She gestures for the clown to hold the hoop in front of the lion. The clown's knees tremble elaborately; the hoop shakes in his hand. Lucia-Marie waves her torch at the clown until he forces his knees and hands to still. The hoop now steady, she turns her attention on the lion.

The sparkling lion tamer thrusts the torch at him, the flames nearly licking his mane. At first the lion rears up, once more swatting at the fire. But she parries with the torch until he drops to all fours. Holding the flame close enough to graze his body, Lucia-Marie positions herself behind the lion, where it appears she will set his tail alight as she herds him toward the hoop. The king of beasts trots toward it, keeping just ahead of the flame.

On the approach of the animal, the clown begins to tremble.

The ringmaster sneaks up with a whip, cracks it so suddenly that the clown snaps to attention just as Leonardo jumps lazily through the hoop.

The power of fire, ladies and gentlemen, cries the ringmaster as the band bursts into bright song. The golden Lucia-Marie uses her torch to herd her lion out of the tent, the clown following close behind with the hoop.

On their exit, a mule wearing britches enters, walking on its hind legs. He trips around the ring on the tips of his hooves, stopping every now and again to twirl around. Just before he leaves the ring he leaps, lands on his front hooves. He tiptoes out in his handstand amidst great admiration from the audience.

Immediately, a great whoop sounds throughout the tent, and ten Indians on ten horses ride into the ring. Johnny Harpe's friends cannot contain their mirth.

I guess even savages got to work, says Gantly Fletcher.

All of the Indians are White men wearing feather head dresses and war paint. Their horses are so fast, though, that the men's faces are a blur, and most audience members are convinced. The Indians ride bareback, gripping the horses' manes in one hand, wielding tomahawks in the other. As they gallop, the horses jump the perimeter of the ring. The Indians ride so close to the stands that the people in front have to pull their feet up on the seats.

Johnny watches closely, trying to determine the mood of the horses. He can see they are allowed to run as fast as they want, but he knows this is likely all the running they do: in circles, night after night. He considers sneaking back to the circus later to set them all free.

The Indians stand on the backs of the circling horses. Digging their toes in for balance, they raise their tomahawks in unison, emitting a high-pitched screech. One Indian throws his tomahawk. It sticks in the ground next to Asa Slacom's feet.

People glance at the exits, but the Indians ride so fast and constant around the ring, there is no escape. The tent rustles with the subtle shifting of weapons retrieved and hammers cocked.

The Indians shout and whoop. Another tomahawk flies, this one landing buried in the bench between Lucy and Willie. Lucy screams; Willie doesn't flinch.

More shouts and whoops herald the arrival of the Confederate cavalry. Falling into pace with the Indians, the soldiers stand up to place one foot on their own horse and one on an Indian's horse. Now the soldiers are outside the ring, the Indians on the inside, all the horses running neck and neck.

In a great show of victory, the Rebels raise their guns above their heads. The horses continue to gallop side by side, until an Indian horse pulls in front of the horse beside it. The soldier straddling the horses loses his footing and falls, while the Indian rides ahead. The horses behind them are unable to stop before they trample the soldier's body. No one in the audience moves or speaks.

Goddamn savages!

The voice belongs to Asa Slacom. He raises his pistol,

fires at the Indian on the horse that pulled ahead. The Indian falls.

Mrs. Ware tightens her hand on Delia's.

Let's go, she says, Ain't nothing good about to happen here.

They slip over to the side of the tent and wriggle underneath.

Carter sees Delia leave and makes his way to the exit.

Sobbing, Peter Allan's wife holds her child to her breast.

To Polly, who has nearly drained her flask, Mrs. Allan's behavior seems an obvious gambit for attention, to demonstrate how pretty she is, even while crying. Peter stands up; eyes on the ring, he squares his shoulders. He's about to act gallant, Polly thinks. To be a hero. It isn't fair. Before she can think enough to stop herself, Polly leaps up to shout into the silence of the horrorstruck crowd:

This Yankee put a baby in me! His northern wife isn't enough for him. He's got to ruin the virtue of southern women!

She has hardly finished her sentence when J. W. Caberness, a Confederate veteran sitting in front of the Allans, jumps onto his seat to throw a punch into Peter Allan's gut. The wife screams, and to Polly's satisfaction, does not look pretty at all.

A fight breaks out and quickly becomes a riot. Fists fly, break noses and jaws, knock the wind out of one man, make the ears of another ring. In the enthusiasm of the moment, no one cares whether the man he attacks hails from the North or the South. They've restrained their violence for a year; any man is a potential enemy. Men trip other men as they make their way down the stands, attempting to leap from seat to seat. Some just jump from the top of the stands, strangle whatever man they land upon. Some mistakenly punch women, who take advantage of the confusion to hit not only the culprit, but a few more men, just for the pleasure of it. Asa Slacom, who started it all, loses balance on his crippled legs. His cane falls and he disappears beneath the feet of the mob.

Polly Adair squeezes her way through the brawling bodies and leaves the tent, hoping Peter Allan will be knocked within an inch of his life.

With violence all around him, Willie Reed cannot move, no matter how much Lucy pulls at him. It is only when she tries to make her way out on her own that he comes to his senses. He runs to catch up with her, and once her hand is in his, he keeps on running, pushing men aside, dragging Lucy behind him until they escape the tent.

Alva watches Johnny and his friends fight their way through the riot, occasionally knocking a man down or taking knocks themselves. She picks Rose up as she hurries around behind the seats. Like Delia, Alva and the Calloway children slide out through the bottom of the tent. Outside, men burst from the exit, still fighting. Alva sees Johnny, his head bleeding, stagger toward The Hammer and the Axe.

What Was Meant to Be Comes to Pass

Davis MacAllister

Once I set Asa on the bench, I light out of the tent. Even if he figures out I'm not coming back, he won't have the energy or strength to search for me. I hope I can complete my mission and catch up to him before he makes it home. I'll tell him I was just out for some air, then I woke up on the ground, that I must have had one of my big fits.

I sit down by the well, lean against the stones, weave the story I'll tell Asa. That I had woken from the fit in the softest bed I've ever known. That at first there was no one else near, so I was able to look around at my leisure: small windows draped with red gauze, little tables with pearl tops, little statues of Greek gods and monsters. That while I gazed at these, a woman like a spirit came gliding into the room, long braided hair to her feet. When she bent over me, her braid brushed my face; her breath smelled like roses. I was so overwhelmed I went into the darkness again. The next time I woke, I was lying by the well, dizzy and sick. When I saw people passing by on the way back to town, I realized I had missed the whole circus, that he must be trying to make it home on his own; I had hurried as fast as I could to find him.

I run the story through my mind several times, until it feels true, especially the part about the exotic room and the woman with the braided hair.

Lightning flashes in the sky, but no storm clouds roll in yet. I consider whether I have time to go home for my umbrella.

Concentrate, says the Preacher.

I close my eyes. Imagine the bones at the bottom of the well, one crossed over another: the witch Ellen Bridges, the Preacher, my mother. I sense them waiting. They've been waiting for company, for me to send one of the murderers down to join them. Will Polly be dying for the sins of the others? Perhaps just to pay for the fact we survived the war?

Their fates are their own, says the Preacher, Tend to your own destiny. Destroy the girl's sin, she'll take yours with her. Then you'll be free, filled with power.

I try to imagine how I will lure Polly Adair to the well, how to make her go in. I take my knife from one pocket; from the other I take the new image of Polly I've been whittling since I saw her earlier today. I know it's superstitious, but I am certain holding her likeness in my hand will help me when the time comes. As soon as I think this thought I wait for the Preacher to lecture me on how superstitions lead to witchcraft.

Thankfully, he's silent. He must trust me. Of course he trusts me. He has entrusted me with this mission. Once fulfilled, finally free of my sickness, I will inherit the Preacher's work. And when I do, I will drive all evil from these mountains.

Music from the circus floats across the field. The sun sets to the thick notes of the calliope; a drum beats time to the moon's ascension. The somber spectacle in the heavens magnifies the importance of the coming ritual.

As the sky darkens, the full moon and stars don't give out enough light for me to carve the delicate features of the wooden Polly Adair. I pocket my knife and little Polly, lay my head against the chilling stone of the well. I watch the stars, listen to the music, wait.

I must have fallen asleep, because I'm awoken by a gunshot. Next I know, people come pouring out of the circus. Some of the men immediately attack other men; everywhere they roll on the ground, slamming their fists into one another. Women rush past me, dragging their children. I expect to see Asa come wobbling or even crawling along, but he doesn't. Maybe he's waiting for things to settle so he won't be knocked halfway to hell by the brawl.

The shouting, fighting, and stampeding feet shake the very air.

This is not what I had envisioned at all. My hand twitches. I swallow, swallow again, and again, and again, and again. I don't know how it went so wrong. The moon rose up as it should have. I sat exactly where I was supposed to sit.

My vision blurs, the air folds over itself.

Hold, says the Preacher, Look yonder.

To my amazement, I stop my seizure before it takes me. I blink to clear my eyes.

Then I see her. Walking. Not running or screaming. Walking slowly, like she knows the import of the night, and her part in it.

Polly Adair, I call out.

She stops, trying to discern who called her name.

Over here, I say, stepping a little distance from the well so Polly can see me in the moonlight.

What do you want, Davis MacAllister, she says.

Haven't you been curious about this place, I ask.

No, she says.

She makes as if to move on.

Suddenly, I have an inspiration. I cock my ear toward the well. My Lord, I exclaim. It can't be.

Polly hesitates.

I lean closer to the well.

It can't be, I say again.

Now she's curious. She takes a few steps toward me.

What is it, she says.

Come listen, I say, I swear I can hear Miss Ellen's banjo.

She stops again.

What tricks are you playing, Davis MacAllister? I'm not in the mood to listen to ghost stories, she says.

She turns away again, giving me only one choice. I moan, jerk my arms into unnatural positions, roll my eyes up into my head. Polly reaches me just as I throw myself at the ground. I'm surprised when she catches me; I wouldn't have guessed her to be that strong. I take several deep breaths as I regain my feet.

Thank you, I say, That felt like a big fit coming on. If you weren't here, I don't know what might have happened to me.

You're welcome, she says.

Since you're here now, you should listen at the well, I say, Tell me if you hear anything. I'm sure I heard Miss Ellen, but I do sometimes hallucinate sounds before things go dark.

Lucy Harpe

I ain't never been in a place so crowded as this circus. The whole town must be here; it feels like a celebration. It makes me think about everything I miss by never going nowhere but the river. Barn dances and the like. Now it's been a year since the war ended, there's more men than been in Sinking Springs for a long time. Looks like there's even some ain't maimed or drunk. If I could go places, I might even meet one of them. But how can I go any place? My brother would never escort me. Even if he did, I could count on him humiliating me like he done tonight, coming in drunk after the circus started. Ain't no one don't know who he is and how he is. He ain't even the only one-armed man around here, just the only one lost his arm after the war, and the only one trying to prove he's a man by getting in fights every chance he gets.

The first entertainment's a man who juggles things. I want to pay attention, but I can feel Willie's eyes on me instead of on the show. I don't know what there is to see that he needs to look so long and so hard at the side of my face. When an acrobat family comes in, Willie's still gazing at me, so I smile at him. He don't smile back. He stares right in my eyes, almost through them, like he's looking for something there. I laugh but it ain't a real laugh, it's the kind what's embarrassed and uncomfortable.

Willie, you see me every day, I say, We should look at the show.

He don't seem inclined to turn away from me.

Then the lights go out.

I think my eyes will get used to it but it's a darker darkness than even the woods at night. The dark presses on me 'til I think I can't stand it, but then fire bursts into the air, and that's worse. I have to stop myself from screaming when the ringmaster's face floats into the fire. I wonder if I'm having one of them nightmares filled with fire and faces and darkness, like I did in the war. I close my eyes until the ringmaster speaks. When I open them, I see he ain't just a floating head; it was just a trick of the fire. My sigh of relief ain't even full out of my mouth when that ringmaster shouts louder than cannon fire. He's yelling about how an Arabian's coming, then here comes another torch. It ain't no Arabian comes out, unless Arabian's another word for devil. I tell Willie I want to leave. To my complete surprise, he laughs.

That ain't no real devil, he says.

Willie keeps on watching that devil, and smiling a strange smile, like he knows him. Who would've thought that when at long last I see Willie Reed smile and laugh it'd send a shudder all over my skin.

The devil spits fire. If I could run out of this place without him taking notice of me, I would leave right now.

Thank the Lord, the lights come on. But now I can see the devil clear, his hideous red face, horns, hooves. Everything I always thought the devil to be. And I ain't the only one scared. All around me there's mothers covering their children's eyes. The children cry anyway. There's no hiding the devil, even if you don't look. Men hold their girls tight, let them hide their faces in their shoulders. Not Willie. He's just watching. I had wanted him to quit staring at me, but now I'd settle for a glance.

A woman comes out into the ring to join the devil. She's so pretty, it calms me some. Other women give her the evil eye. They know the very men who was just comforting them ain't thinking about them now. There ain't a single woman pretty as that in Sinking Springs. She's got no fear of that nasty old devil. Her not being scared finally convinces me it really ain't the real devil, and I feel stupid. Why would the real devil waste his time in a silly show in Sinking Springs Tennessee, nor in any circus at all. No wonder Willie made fun of me.

Now I know he ain't the real devil, I appreciate how graceful he is. I marvel at the way he spits fire. And, the two of them, him in his fancy devil suit and her in her gorgeous dress, they're so elegant. Now a clown runs out to throw a bucket of water over them. I'm as mad as the devil and the woman are about it. The crowd seems tickled. I think it's plain mean. To do such a thing and take pleasure in it. Them clowns, with their stupid costumes and fake red noses, I can tell they're just fat old ugly men who got nothing else to do but act mean and pretend it's funny. At least Willie ain't amused at this.

Next comes another beautiful woman, a poor sad lion with her. There's ladies behind me acting like that lion just came up behind them trying to bite their face off. Another reason to cling on to their menfolk. They must see the poor thing's toothless and flea bit. What I think, I think them ladies're scared because they want to be scared in a way that can't hurt them like the war and everything after it did, when they couldn't scream and there weren't no men to comfort them. That kind of comfort's something I'm finally coming to understand I don't have with Willie, real or pretend. A feeling rises up in me I ain't had before. Resolve. I know what I'm going to do, and where and when I'll do it.

After the show, I'll say I want to go to the river. The moon's full tonight. It'll be beautiful and he'll be calm. It's the best way to tell him. I can explain I'm still his friend like I always been. I'll explain that now I see we want different things from life. He'll accept it, I'm sure. He'll accept it quiet like he does everything he don't like.

My thoughts get interrupted by a bunch of fake Indians riding real horses, with real hooves that come too close as they gallop around. Being stomped is a real thing to be afraid of.

I try to tuck my feet under the bench. Dirt from their hooves still flies at my dress and face. And if that weren't enough, they got to throw an axe at us. It sticks right between Willie and me; I can't help but scream. Then, here come soldiers on horses chasing the Indians. Soon as they gallop in, I can feel every woman pull inside herself. Soldiers are also a real thing to fear. Not one of us wants to see them, real or fake, riding like that, making that wild noise like they do. Danger swirls around with the dirt kicked up by the horses. The danger's like a dizzy spell; anyone can see them horses're moving too fast for that small ring. The horses bunch up and one of the soldiers falls under all them stomping hooves.

Then crazy Asa Slacom shoots down one of the Indians. People stand up to see. The horses gallop slower and slower, but the soldier's body looks like a rag doll under their hooves that still keep stomping him. This is horror enough, but the danger's still rising.

There's more bad coming, I can feel it.

Just as the horses finally stop running, Polly Adair stands up and accuses a peacekeeper of putting a baby in her.

I don't even know how to describe what happens next. Seems every person in here's determined to knock down the person next to them. There's so much tumult that Willie takes my hand. I never knew he could move as fast as he does now. Head down, he crashes his shoulders into every man or woman in our way. We're out of that tent and down the path in no time, Willie still squeezing my hand so hard I fear it might break. He's pulling me toward the path to the river. Now I won't be able charm him by suggesting we go there. That's all right. He'll still start to calm soon's we get away from people and into the woods. We're nearly there.

But we have one more obstacle before we can get into the woods. Out of nowhere, there stands my brother Johnny, swaying like he's in a high wind.

Like as if he's been defending me my whole life, Johnny orders Willie to get away from me.

Willie laughs for the second time in one night.

Then Johnny tries to accuse Willie of walking out with Alva Calloway, giving me my turn to laugh.

The laughter infuriates Johnny so much that instead of punching Willie like he seemed about to do, he turns away to stagger toward The Hammer and the Axe.

Finally, Willie lets loose my hand. Finally we're going toward the river, where I can put all of this to rest. I ain't never before wanted so much to get back home to my own bed to sleep.

Polly Adair

Once I sit down next to Peter Allan's wife I am satisfied with my trip to the circus. I offer her a drink from my flask, assuring her continued discomfort, and much more important, Peter Allan's discomfort.

I toast every act, drink extravagantly. When the whore comes out to dance with the devil, I once again offer my flask to Mrs. Allan. She's so prim in her refusal, pursing her lips until they nearly disappear. I smile my biggest, most charming smile at her. Then I lean over her and her child to offer the flask to Peter. He waves his hand dismissively, puts his arm around his wife, whispers in her ear, kisses her cheek. I'm impressed at how convincing he is. Anyone would think he'd never seen me before. I drink to him and his wife both.

The circus goes by in a blur of fire and animals. When Indians and soldiers come out to gallop around in circles, my head begins to spin. Finally, after six years of trying, I am drunk. Finally I know how those lucky men who stagger out of The Hammer and the Axe feel. I almost think I'm hallucinating when a soldier falls under the horses. The spinning in my head slows. The crowd sits so still you'd think everyone's drunk as me. I'm having so much trouble containing my laughter. Then Asa Slacom stands up on his infected legs, calls the performers savages, and shoots one of them.

Inspired, I stand up. Disregard the savages, I yell. We are still besieged by the northern aggressors. This one—I point at Peter Allan—snuck into my rooms to take my innocence and fill me with his bastard. Yet here he sits, with his wife and child!

The mayhem is immediate. Mrs. Allan manages to slap her husband before the reconstituted Rebel army descends upon him.

I stroll out. It seems to me the fighting men and women part for me like the red sea. I emerge from the tent unharmed, make my way to the quiet path toward home. The full moon and twinkling stars add to my sense of justice done.

To my annoyance, someone calls my name.

I look around. And there, almost shimmering in the moonlight, is the old well. Standing next to it, Davis MacAllister.

Alva Calloway

I never thought a circus was so long. Rose fell asleep on my lap. The others can barely keep their eyes open. Even Robbie's lost his enthusiasm. I'm thinking about gathering the children and slipping out when Asa Slacom shoots the Indian and Polly Adair accuses a man of getting her with child. The violence what follows terrifies us all. When I look over toward the entrance, all I can see's a jumble of limbs and rage. I stand up with Rose, take Nathan's hand, he takes Robbie's, and Robbie takes Sara's. We carefully snake our way to the tent wall. We're gon' go under, I say, Robbie, you go first so I can slide Rose to you.

Robbie wriggles under and out. Rose cries when I push her out, but Robbie quiets her soon's he picks her up. Next I send Sara.

Nathan's excited to crawl through; for him it's an adventure.

I'm just about to go under when two men come flying toward me, intent on pummeling each other to death. They knock me down, fall on my legs. I manage to get my head and shoulders out of the tent.

Robbie, I call out, Give Rose to Nathan. Pull me out.

He has to yank hard on my arms, but he frees me.

When we start down the path my legs hurt, but I can walk. I let Nathan keep carrying Rose. We're almost to the path that turns off to our place when I see Johnny arguing with his sister and Willie Reed. I'm afraid there'll be more fighting but Johnny walks away toward The Hammer and the Axe.

Robbie, I say, Will you take the others home, check on Ma when you get there?

I love my brother for saying yes without no questions. He's like his older brother Edmond was, wise and kind beyond his years.

I have never done a thing that feels so selfish as this before. In my heart, though, I know that if I save this love, I save my family. I can't believe Johnny'd be mad with me just on account of Willie Reed bringing me wood.

Maybe he thinks 'cause of his one arm I wouldn't want him. Maybe it shamed him to see Willie carry that wood what he cut hisself. I don't know how Johnny could think I'd of let him have me without it being on my mind to marry.

Delia Boyd

When I see them pictures of creatures hanging there on big flags for everyone to see, then Carter says they're people, then I see a man taking money to go in to stare at them for real, I should turn around and go right back home. I don't want to hurt Carter's feelings, though. I let him buy our tickets.

Right at the gate we run into trouble when a big ugly White man digs his fingers in my arm, pulls me away from Carter, then pushes me so hard I trip over my own feet. I gain my balance before I fall, but not before a nasty clown with his mouth painted huge and wearing a too-small hat that makes his head look ungodly big notices me. When he follows me, it's worse than any nightmare I've had. His panting hot breath dampens my neck, and his dead rotting animal smell fills my nostrils.

Ahead of me I see Elijah's mama standing among some other folks from the village. She puts her finger to her eye. I focus there, right on her eyes, keep walking, the clown behind me, White people having fun at my expense. I keep on looking right at Mrs. Ware's eyes, take one step, then another, another, another, nearly forever, before at long last I reach her. Immediately, she clasps my hand in hers. I want to throw myself into her arms. I want to cry and have her hold me the way my mama used to do. Of course, I don't. Not in a place like this.

The clown goes on to the other side of the tent. Thankfully, everyone forgets about me. I'm shaken though. When the music starts up, I don't feel no better. Some of it sounds like a dream of being underwater, some of it sounds like a scream. All of it crashes around inside my head.

In the ring, there's sparkles, things fly through the air: vegetables, plates, even babies. The air becomes fire, the devil dances before our eyes making Mrs. Ware and me hold hands again, grip tight to one another. I know it ain't the real devil, but still I say a prayer lest this trifling with the devil brings the real one on. After the devil dances with a lady showing her stockings, a clown and a barefoot woman torment a poor sick animal.

The music pounds in my ears 'til it's joined by the pound of horse's hooves. Everything pounds until a gun fires. Everyone screams, then Polly Adair shouts something and all the White people start to fighting each other. It looks like an explosion of fists and boots. It spreads into the ring, spills out.

Mrs. Ware pulls at my hand.

Nothing good coming out of this, she says.

We crawl under the tent, out into the cool of the night. We can still hear the fighting, so we move fast to get away from the tent.

Elijah's mama asks me like she done so many times since my parents died, why don't I just come home with her. I appreciate her concern, and I know I ain't necessarily safe out home all by my lonesome. But I can still feel my family there. I'm scared if I leave, I'd lose the feeling of the presence of them I love. And if I lose that feeling, how will I know how to stand on this earth? I tell Mrs. Ware I'll think on it.

As I take my leave of her, there comes Carter Bridges. I'd hoped he'd left without me.

I'll walk you home, he says.

I know my way home, I say.

Carter insists he wants my company. That's when I

realize I want his too. These last days, though I've been sad, I've been glad to have someone to talk to. And to tell the truth, after seeing all those White folks looking for violence, I ain't completely comfortable walking through the woods alone. In spite of my misgivings, I make myself to not think about the circus, the clown, and the way Carter hadn't stood by me.

I tell him all right, he can walk with me.

We continue on together toward my home.

I saw Davis MacAllister and Polly Adair at the well, he says.

Those two always did like trouble, I say.

Looked like they had some kind of fire burning up out of it, he says.

You sure that part's real, I ask.

I don't know, he answers.

He takes my hand as we walk into the woods. It makes me think of all them hands took mine before: Mrs. Ware, just tonight when I was scared and humiliated; my papa when we went to town; Elijah who loved me so much; Promise when I didn't want him to run off. I'm so filled with the sadness of missing so many. I'm glad when I see my home up ahead.

Carter stops, making me worry he sees fire again. I hope he don't got a vision of it on my cabin. But he's not looking at my cabin, he's looking at me. He takes my face in his hands and kisses me.

I kiss back.

In the touch of our lips I feel all the need, all the loneliness in us both. So different from the tender love and hope for the future between me and Elijah.

I'm the one breaks the kiss. I tell Carter I'm unsure

about what we're doing. I tell him I'll watch out for fire, and water too. I tell him I can make the rest of the way home by myself.

Willie Reed

Ain't no surprise at all this whole mess they call a entertainment turns violent. Every part of it twists up real life someways, making fun out of cruelty. Them clowns, that lion, them Indians. If Lucy wasn't so excited about it, I would of walked out long before Asa Slacom shot a man and Polly Adair made men to think they're at war again.

So here I am trying to get Lucy out safe. It's the first time I hold her hand since we're children and the only concern I got is am I holding her tight enough she can't get drug away by the current of the fight.

When we get outside I let go my breath, gulp more air in. I don't even know how long I weren't breathing.

I tell her I got something to say can we go to the river, I say it humble, full of love so she'll say yes, and she does.

I shouldn't be surprised when before we can even gain the path her drunken hateful brother come staggering up, pushes me, tells me get my filthy hands off his sister.

Your sister's with me of her own free will, I tell him.

She know you sneak around days with Alva Calloway?

Lucy, she defends me, says I would do no such thing.

Harpe cackles, drunk and ugly.

We two, Lucy and me, we just step around him; we don't look back. We don't have to. We both know he's stumbling on back to The Hammer and the Axe.

Side by side we walk the path, among the trees, to the call of the river, to the river itself. Once we're away from the crowds and her brother, I can feel how tonight's special. I don't make her stand on the bank watching me throw sticks. We walk along the river to where the big rock rises up near the middle, with smaller rocks leading out to it. I help Lucy along so she don't slip and fall.

We sit down side by side on the big rock. This is how we'll see the rest of our lives, I think. Side by side. I can work at the quarry where my pa died, fill that work with love, the love that made me not a coward no more. I pick up a small, smooth stone.

When I toss it, it skips along the water.

I'm getting work, I say.

I wait for her delight but it don't come. She asks what work.

The quarry, I say.

She says but your pa died there. She says her ma told her that quarry's part of the curse on both our families.

We can break the curse, I say, The things that happened in the war made me stronger. You made me stronger. I ain't afraid to work in that quarry, ain't afraid to take care of my wife.

You know that ain't our only curse she says. She says we got curse piled on curse, she says there ain't no reason for us to think there won't be more.

Polly Adair

Davis MacAllister calls out, says he hears music coming from the well. I have had enough excitement for one night. I just want to go home and think about Peter Allen's bleak future. I suppose I've forfeited the money he was going to give me, but tonight was worth the price.

Not tonight, Davis, I call back.

He sticks nearly his whole head into the well, intending to convince me, I suppose.

Really, Polly, he says as he stands up, Just come and listen.

Some other time, Davis, I say.

I don't get two steps away when from the corner of my eye I see him twitching. No, I say to myself, Someone else will help him. People limp around me, some carrying others over their shoulders, everyone occupied with their own emergencies. No one even glances in that direction. Davis's whole body jerks. I have no choice. He's right next to that old stone well; if he falls on it, he could smash his head open again.

I run to help him, cursing myself for stopping to answer him in the first place. I catch him as he collapses. It takes all my strength to shove him up on his feet. One of his little carved people falls out of his pocket. I don't mention it, he might want to show it to me.

Hold on to the well, I say, It will steady you.

He puts both hands on the well.

You're all right now, I say, to him, I need to get home before my mother worries.

Wait, Polly, he says. You're here now, you should listen. See if it doesn't sound just like Miss Ellen's banjo.

I know he will go on and on about it unless I listen. The sooner I stick my head in that well, the sooner I can go home.

I lean over the well.

I don't hear anything, I say.

I feel a tug at my hair ribbon.

Before I know what's happening, Davis has my ribbon around my neck and he's pulling it tight. I can barely breathe enough to register my shock that he is killing me. The baby inside of me is suffocating too. My stomach cramps as we both run out of breath. In the darkness of the night all around us, there's another darkness that comes from Davis himself. No one will save me from it.

I remember that little wooden figure on the ground. If he has that, he likely has his knife. A strange noise escapes from my throat. Something's wrapped around my middle just as tight as the ribbon wrapped around my neck. They both squeeze so tight I can feel my consciousness slipping. If I faint, I'll die.

I reach back to find his pocket, find the knife, grip it tight. Quick as I can, I stab him in the thigh. He loosens his hold on the ribbon, and I turn to face him. I stab him in the throat and leave the knife there. He falls forward, still holding my ribbon. Gasping for air, I step aside. He falls over the side of the well, but he doesn't fall in. He hangs there, like he's listening again for Miss Ellen's banjo. All I have to do is lift his legs to send him down there with the preacher and Miss Ellen.

A cramp knocks me to my knees. I reach for my flask to dull the pain, but I drank all my whiskey at the circus. I'll rest here a minute before I try to get up. I can get more whiskey once I get home.

Lucy Harpe

When we reach the river we walk alongside it.

Let's go sit on the rocks, says Willie.

One of the rocks looks like a shadowy mountain rising up from the black of the river. Water rushes around it, bubbles glint in the moonlight. For the second time tonight, Willie takes me by the hand. This time his tenderness for me comes through.

It's shallow, he says as he helps me across smaller rocks to the big one. The top of the rock is smooth and flat. We sit down.

Willie reaches into the water, lifts out a stone, let's me feel it, small and sleek. He tosses it. The stone splashes across the water, once, twice, three times. Then quiet when it sinks to the bottom of the river, where likely it will stay. Should we want to wade out, we could probably find it again, so different from Willie's sticks, what make a single splash, then float on to places we don't know.

For the first time, I ask myself, what if I was to leave this place. Would I be the same Lucy? Would I have the same thoughts and feelings? Loves and worries? Or would I be free to make up a new self, one feeling, one decision, one action at a time, until I build a Lucy who walks a whole different way in this world. One thing I do know. I can't build any kind of self with Willie. He's got a picture in his mind of the Lucy he wants, and she ain't me.

Before I can tell him my thoughts, Willie asks me to marry him. Straightforward, just like that. The last thing I thought he'd do. I'm so surprised I forget all my carefully planned words.

I say, Don't be silly, you got no money for a family.

I regret the words as soon as they're out my mouth. Willie's eyes turn black with the hurt I'm causing him.

He picks another stone out of the water, throws it. It plunks into the water in the distance of the dark.

I touch his arm, try to control the flutter of pity in my heart.

Don't be mad, I say, I haven't minded walking with you, or even the way you moon. But marriage, that's different. That's a time to be practical, Willie.

I can get me some work, he says.

What kind of work?

At the quarry. It ain't much. Enough for the two of us. My pa took care of my ma on that work.

But he died there, I say, My ma says it's a curse on your family. You can't work there, Willie.

We can break the curse, he says.

How?

He says if he's brave enough to work in the quarry, the curse will break.

I can't imagine how he came to this idea. I try to tell him that ain't the way of curses. Even if you could break that one, I say, we still got the one the preacher laid on us and the one the war laid on us. We're drowning in curses, Willie.

He's come up with some fantastical idea that all us children left alive from that day at the well have to love each other, and we'll break the curse.

It's our destiny; why else did we survive that war, he says.

Johnny and Alva are already in love. He goes as far as to say Carter Bridges loves Delia Boyd, and I know that ain't true 'cause she's a Negro. The more he goes on, the more I understand I have to speak plain with him.

Willie, I don't want to marry you, I say.

That ain't true, he says.

I thought I could, I tell him, I thought if we love each other, then good wins. But it ain't enough, Willie. You fought for those that killed my brothers. My sisters died because the Union had to come down here where we didn't need them or want them. And even if that weren't so, I don't want to live poor, Willie, eating soup like your ma. I don't want to spend my whole life between a shack and the river.

We can't live if we don't marry, he says.

He picks out another rock from the water, this onbigger than his hand.

Carter Bridges

Delia lets me walk the path to her home with her, and somewhere in the midst of the woods, she takes my hand. Her hand is stronger than mine, and rougher. I'm ashamed knowing how hard she works to stay alive, while I live a life of ease. I've always told myself I have a right to have it easy. I lost my parents; I lost my grandmother. I live with the burden of my visions. I tell myself my pictures do something other people can't do: they take a moment in time, of life, of a person, and hold it still. I put moments out into the world where anyone can experience them, even if they've never seen that place, that person, that event. But I know in my heart it's also a way to keep myself apart from life; there's always the camera between me and everybody else.

I kiss Delia before I think of all the reasons I shouldn't.

She kisses me back. We stand there kissing, only the trees for witnesses.

Too soon, she breaks the kiss, tells me she don't understand what's happening between us.

I say I don't either.

She says she'll keep a watch out for fire, she says maybe the fish I saw around her mean she should keep water nearby. She says goodnight.

Wait, I say.

What, she says, not turning all the way around.

I let the words rush from my mouth:

I do know how Elijah died.

She retraces her steps back to me.

I was there, I say.

She stands in front of me, waiting.

Maybe you don't want to know, I say.

Tell me.

I take a breath, and I tell her.

＊ ＊ ＊

I was at Nashville in December of 1864. It was freezing and snowing. There was both black and White soldiers there, all of them tired and cold. They was eager to fight, but they couldn't because of weather, so all of 'em huddled around fires, eating what little food they had left. I sat around the fire with White officers or hid from the biting winds in my wagon. One day I decided to take a walk, and my path took me past the Colored troops. That's when Elijah spied me. He came to join me, asked if I was making pictures of the war.

Yes, I answered.

Why, he asked me.

Because people don't know what it looks like, I told him.

I ain't seen it stand still none, he said.

Some of it does, I said, The lines. Men around a fire.

The dead, he added.

Them too, I said, And those who want their portraits made for folks back home. I could make yours, send it back to Delia.

She's already got that one you made before.

She might like to know you're alive.

I don't want to stand still and look at a camera, he said. He said he moved through the war fast as he could, just to stay alive, to rush the war along, get it done with, so he could start a new life with you.

I was about to answer him when I had a vision: a train, speeding through snow like as if it had no need for tracks, snow blowing up on both sides of it. That train ran right up behind Elijah, cast a cold white haze all around him. For the first time since we was young, I saw Elkanah with him.

He could tell when I had a vision, so he asked what I saw.

A train. Stay away from the tracks, I warned him.

I got no reason to go near any tracks, he said.

I told him his brother's here, but he weren't surprised.

He been watching over me, he said, It's why I ain't as lonely as I could be.

Then Elijah went his way and I went mine. I wished I could of invited him to warm up in my wagon, but I knew it wouldn't look right.

For the next few days I continued making pictures of officers when I wasn't wrapped in a blanket in my wagon. I didn't see Elijah at all.

At long last came the day the ground thawed some and no snow fell. When I heard they gave orders for the Colored regiment to head out, I packed up to follow them. There was other photographers out with the armies, but none was taking pictures of the Colored troops. I was determined to be the first to show the world the war life of Negroes.

The troops marched and just kept marching. It didn't feel right. But the White colonel said keep marching, so they did, with nothing but the silent cold all around. When they stopped, I had lagged behind them on a ridge. I could clearly see the cut in front of the regiment. I could also clearly see the Rebels come up in force both behind them and in front of them across the cut. I set up my camera.

Some of the soldiers turned to fight, more jumped down on the train tracks, where they became easy targets for the Secesh. Most all of the Colored regiment died, including Elijah. I come down and made pictures of the scene afterwards. I saw Elijah dead, Elkanah standing over him. I waited for Elijah's spirit to rise up to join his brother.

* * *

Tears run down Delia's cheeks.

I should stop, I say.

Tell me, she says.

I waited for Elijah's spirit to rise up to join his brother, but that ain't what happened. Instead, Elkanah faded into the air like breath in the cold.

Did you bury Elijah, she asks.

No, I say.

Why not?

I don't know.

I'm too ashamed to tell her it was because I was traveling with White officers and didn't want to face their judgment.

You ain't no friend to me, Carter Bridges, she says.

But I am, I say.

You ain't, she insists.

I watch her leave.

I know can't nothing be gained by following her, so I make my way back toward the boarding house. For a moment, I think I smell smoke, but I don't see nothing, so I blame it on my imagination.

Walking home, I listen for my gran, wish for at least a few strands of melody on the breeze, but the night's just crickets and owls. Down the road at The Hammer and the Axe, I imagine the men who've drunk away the awfulness of tonight. From inside come faint refrains of a bawdy tune my gran would of surely disapproved of.

When I get home I go straight to bed, but I can't sleep. I

wish I had found a way to explain to Delia. How it was to be out there taking pictures, not knowing was it more important to show the world the truth, or to enter into the fight. Seemed to me there was enough doing the fighting. And folks in every town was thinking their own soldiers was heroes. I wanted to show them what men endure to become heroes. Without pictures, the whole war would become a story, told one way by the winners and another by the losers without anyone seeing the faces of them that died on the battlefield, what it looked like when bodies was strewn across the fields, along the sides of the roads, and in cuts where they was tricked into jumping. I had recorded all of it. I had done right by history and truth, I was sure of it.

I get out of bed. I take up the pictures of the war, the ones I've been avoiding, lay them down one by one across my bed. As I examine each face, remember setting up my camera among the dead, doubts come creeping in, plaguing me with questions. Was there any of these men I could of saved? Elijah among them? Should I have hidden him in my wagon? Then what would of become of both of us? Anyways, he wasn't the sort of man to hide. Should I have jumped into that cut to save my friend, or to bury him, when surely I'd of been shot to death too? What would of been the purpose of that? I was so sure of the importance of the pictures when I made them. Now what use are they? Will they convince men in the future, when they start rallying to a cause, getting swept up in the force of violence, that carnage is the truth of war? Will it even repel them? If I gave one of these pictures to every man born in the future, would it give him pause before he signed up to kill and die?

Or in the end, am I just a coward, and worse, a man who used other men's deeds to make his own name? And how long did that fame last? Some pictures shown at Nashville and at Knoxville when the war first ended. Crowds gawking at pictures of the dead. Some there to see if their own kin might be in a picture. Then the pictures was took down, and life went on.

Early in the morning, the bells of the Fort and the church interrupt my thoughts. I go to my window, where I can see a fire, a real one, already ravaging the mountain. I go and tell Nora she needs to get her boarders out and go on up to the Harpe farm. Fire's unlikely to make it up there. They'd all be safe.

Once Nora goes to gather the boarders, all I can think of is Delia. I leave the boarding house, start toward Delia's place, but I'm barely at the edge of town when I see her walking towards Elijah's mother, who must of also thought to go get her. I finally understand. Delia won't forgive me. There ain't nothing she needs from me.

I go back to the boarding house for my camera. The place is empty; I go upstairs. I don't have a wagon no more, so I can't take much. Likely a camera, plates, and a few pictures.

I don't know which pictures to take with me. I never realized how many I made. I don't need none that was posed. I did them for money, and aside from those I left with Delia, ain't none I care about. I sort through the war pictures. There's some of roads, of lines of soldiers on the march, of men at their mess, of boots left behind after mud pulled them clear off a man's feet. This was the day-to-day of the war. These were the long, dull days what wore men down like rain works at a boulder, a little at a time. I should of taken more pictures like this. I should of thought it through, tried to show what war does to men over time. I didn't know then. I was bored like the rest of them. I was itching for battle. I wanted to be among the first to show the real war, and by that I meant death on the battlefield.

When I come out of the boarding house, the fire's jumped the river and the first of it's lighting the trees into torches one by one, each closer to town than the last. Outside people run everywhere, men for water, women and children up the north mountain. I put down my things so I can go and help with the water.

Then I hear the fire, like a thousand marching feet, coming right for us. Now I remember the excitement I felt during the war. I'm overpowered by the need to capture the fire, hold it, show its spectacular devastation to the world. I pick up my camera and plates, follow the women and children up the mountain behind town. Midway up the mountain, I stop to set up my camera. Through the lens I watch the blaze roar through the town.

Johnny Harpe

The tavern's full of men with black eyes and bloody lips. I see the ones I was with earlier, but I don't feel friendly just now. I order a whiskey, then find a corner where I can be left alone to drink. I can't let go of how this day started with dreams I hadn't dared dream coming true. Then it got ruined by that low living snake Willie Reed slithering around the nicest, most innocent woman. I blame Edmond for making Alva so unknowing and trusting.

As if I conjured her just by thinking on her, I look up to find Alva standing over me. I do love her face. But the sight of her now, knowing she looks on others with the same softness in her eyes, that same sweetness on her mouth, brings a fury on me. Even now, she's looking around at the other men in the room. I shout at her to go away. The men nearby stop talking to watch us. I expect her to run away, but she holds her ground.

I can't leave, she says.

The men around her laugh.

Sanders mimics her, I can't leave, he says in a high voice he thinks sounds like a girl.

Look at Harpe, says Handon, Little girls got to come take him out of the tavern. He ain't man enough to stay out late by hisself.

Alva begs me to come outside with her.

Now for sure I have to send her out. Everyone in here already doubts I'm a man.

But I got to live among men, do business with men. One day Pa's farm will be mine. I'm already at a disadvantage for getting any respect, I can't have her take what little I got of it away. No, I tell her.

Tears come up in her eyes. I'm the only one she's

looking at now, and I'd have to lie to myself to say I can't see love there. Why did she have to let Reed bring her that wood? Why did she have to come in here humiliating me in front of other men? I could of taken her to the circus. I might be laying beside her right now. A voice in my head says if you didn't kill her brother, and my rage doubles. That was his fault, just like this is her fault. I stand up. Get out, I yell.

She runs, the men laughing behind her.

At least you got the gumption to know when to let a woman know who's boss, says Fletcher.

Someone buys me a drink. I hate everyone in here, but I drink it, and the rest that's put in front of me after.

As I drink, my hate for Willie Reed rises like a flood inside me. On my way here, I seen him with my sister. It made my blood boil. I walked on up to them both, told him he should get away from her.

Lucy answered for him, pathetic as he is, can't speak for hisself. She accused me of starting trouble just because of being drunk. I couldn't make her understand how I hate that bastard, drunk or sober. The sight of his mournful eyes makes me want to put a bullet through his head.

I tried to explain to her, he's like a wild pig, rooting around, but instead of mushrooms he's trying to root up whatever woman might take pity on him.

Blind as she is to his faults, it didn't surprise me when she called me ridiculous, said she seen him every night so he couldn't of been out with no other girl.

What about the days, I said. This pile of manure don't work. Ask him what he did today.

Before Lucy could speak, Reed answered for his own damn self. He went all hangdog-like, admitted he was out to

Alva's, that he used the excuse of bringing her some firewood.

I thought Lucy would see right through him, but she didn't. She turned on me, told me I should be ashamed of myself. Told me don't I know them folks out there's poor, that they need all the help they can get.

Then Reed speaks up and tells Lucy to ask me how I know he was there. He tells her to ask me what I been doing with Alva Calloway.

I hit him for that, and sure enough he showed his true colors. He come at me like an animal, knocked me to the ground, sat on my belly growling like a rabid dog. I believe he would of bit me if Lucy didn't yell out his name.

Willie stopped, stared at me like he ain't never seen me before, then slowly stood up, staring at me, muttering under his breath as Lucy, damn her soul, made things worse by rushing to help me up. Now you seen his true self, I said.

You come home strange as him, she answered.

Would a man who loves you try to kill your brother?

Why'd you go to Alva's? Did you take that horse out there?

That ain't your business.

You better not be taking advantage of that poor girl.

I walked away from them then, left them to their own sins.

I did not take advantage of Alva. I couldn't of. I loved her since we was children. Of a sudden, all the mean goes out of me. I feel tired. I just want to find the place where me and Edmond and Alva played and sit down to rest awhile. Think on things. I make my way through the men, ignoring those who try to make me stay and drink more. Outside, it don't matter how drunk I am. My feet take me where I want to go.

Before long I smell the river, and soon I can hear it. Then I see the river roses glowing like flames and I think it must be the drink. They've always been unnatural red, but now they're like lanterns guiding me. This is the spot. I walk toward the water, my heart pounding. For some reason the light in these flowers makes me anxious. When I get close, my heart quits pounding, squeezes so tight I can hardly breathe. Though my heart has already told me what's there, I'm unprepared for my eyes and my mind to understand. Right there where Edmond and me and Alva used to play dead girl, Alva lies face down in the water.

I know that stillness, I seen it so many times. I kneel down beside her, watch her black hair float in the current. When I roll her over, her eyes is open. Though I know I should close them, I look into them, hoping to see the last thing she felt. Did she fall or was she killed.

It don't matter. She's dead. She's dead and she wouldn't be if I didn't yell at her. If I had been a man and walked her home. If I had trusted her instead of letting my addled brain and my jealousy take hold of me.

Willie Reed

You got to marry me I say to her. Lucy, I say. I say her name so she knows it's true. I say it to her face, so laughing, so pretty so hurtful.

No, Willie, she says, That ain't my future.

She touches me I must be her future. She don't want me to be mad she don't mind the way I moon. She loves me. I tell her now I got courage I can work in the quarry, she says no. She says the quarry's cursed, she talks about my pa.

That weren't no curse on him, I say, It was an accident he died. Turned out it cursed Ma and me. But if you was my wife, Lucy, I can work there, I can work there and not die. That's how a curse gets lifted.

She says no. She says we got curse piled on curse we ain't ever gon' lift ourselves out of 'em all.

I say we can because of love. All I seen and done what shattered me, I still love. There's others do too. Love lifts curses I say, If it don't then what we living for?

Lucy, she looks straight at me, eyes like green jewels and just as hard.

I don't love you, she says.

That ain't true, I say.

She says she don't love me; she wants more than poverty and soup. She says she don't love the river. It's just water. It moves because that's its nature. Nothing special about it.

I see her now. She ain't mine, she can't be mine on this tainted earth. I need to send her on. Later I'll join her. We can be together in heaven where there ain't no murders, where there ain't no wars. After she's gone, I can make myself worthy to join her. I'll walk through the water to purify my body, walk through the fire to purify my soul.

She'll leave first, by my loving hand, I'll leave after, by water and by fire.

When I plunge my hand into the water, my fingers find the edges of the rock I need. I only need to work it a little with my fingers for it to come up. When I slam it into my beautiful Lucy's head, my arm aches like her pain's coming up through it, like her pain might grow inside me 'til my own skin opens up.

She bleeds but she don't fall. I have to hit her again. She's suffering. That weren't what I wanted but it's how love is. We suffer for it and from it. We die for it. I raise the rock again. She says my name before she falls.

I watch the daylight coming close. I smell the fire of the sun like the end of the world, scorching bushes, trees, animals. The sun rises through the trees, splashing the purple-black river with yellow-white light. Lucy's hair, Lucy's skin glow with the morning, all the beauty hurts me down to my bones. Her long blonde curls. After all this time I touch them. I hold them curls tenderly in my hand. They's soft as I always imagined. Gently, tenderly, I roll her into the river. She floats just like I knew she would.

Delia Boyd

As I try to walk away after that kiss, Carter catches my hand.

I have things to tell you, Delia, he says.

Can't they wait 'til tomorrow?

No, he says. I best tell you now.

I been having a dream, he says. About those we know floating down the river. He names Johnny and Lucy Harpe. Edmond and Alva Calloway. He names Elijah. Edmond and Elijah's dead. But the rest is still alive. He don't name me, but that don't mean he didn't see me. Then he tells me all them he dreamed burst into flames.

I look to the sky, imagine I smell smoke.

What do you think it means, I ask?

I don't know, he says. But it's most of us in that dream. Me?

There's another thing I have to tell you, he says.

Then Carter Bridges, the man I let kiss my lips, he tells me the story of how he watched my Elijah die. How he saw him, how he spoke to him, how he had a vision, but didn't warn him. He tells me how the Colored regiment was sacrificed. How he watched the slaughter, then made a picture of it.

Somewhere in his home, right this minute, Carter Bridges got a picture of my love, his old friend, Elijah Ware, dead in a pile of twisted, murdered men. My mind and heart fill with rage. My body fills with sickness.

How will I ever rub off the poison of your kiss, I ask him.

As I walk away, I hear him beg forgiveness. I keep on.

Fire's coming, he calls out, Let me help you.

I keep on 'til I can't hear him no more.

I realize now too, I wasn't imagining the smell of smoke in the air. Sure enough there's fire somewhere up that mountain. If it comes down and jumps the river, it'll burn my cabin and everything around it. I think of my baby brother buried here in the ground. Do things what's buried burn? I suppose it don't matter. His spirit's flown already.

I go into my cabin, stand still, admiring each piece of furniture, each pot, pan, dish. Each quilt made by my mama, the broom I made myself. The worn rug on the floor where I learned to crawl, and Promise did too. All that's left of them I loved. That and the pile of pictures on the table.

I must of fallen asleep because I wake early to the sharp smell of fire as it eats up everything on the mountain. Though I never had a knowing like my mama, nor visions like Carter, suddenly I know this fire will jump the river. I could do no more than sit right here, and soon enough I'd be with my family and Elijah. I go outside to stand over my brother. This wasn't my fault, I tell myself. He wouldn't of got better. How long was I supposed to watch a little baby die? Feel his fever rise 'til he's too hot to touch? See him shake like the devil hisself got hold of him. I had feared that the devil really was in our cabin. I am grown enough to fight the darkness, but Promise, he didn't even know what it was. I always thought he'd be safe. He was a light unto himself. I loved him like my own soul, and when I kilt him with my pillow, I kilt part of my own self.

When Elijah's family offered to take me and Promise in, I shouldn't of said no. I was sure that by myself I could raise my little brother to fight for what was rightfully his in this world. That I could keep him safe. That there weren't no more reason to trouble us out here. I never thought God could be so cruel as to make me take my own baby brother's life.

I go back inside to sit at the table. I recall the fish Carter seen. Maybe I'm meant to walk into the water. I've heard it's a pretty way to die. If the fish is the colors Carter saw, I could walk in among them, let go all my breath. Blue and purple and green fish would be the last I see of this life. Then I'd go on to heaven to see my loved ones. I know God forgives me for Promise, because I took away his pain. And for the past, he'd never blame us little children. We didn't even know what dead is when we pushed that preacher into the well. What a thing it would be to go to heaven. To have all my pain just washed away.

Exactly when I have them thoughts, the broom in the corner falls, bringing me to my senses.

Is drowning what my mama and papa would want for me? What Elijah would want? What do I want for myself? I'm the only one left alive of us to fight. I find myself on my feet, examining the room again. What should I take? What would help me hold onto the love of them I lost.

My eyes land on Carter's pictures. I pick them up. Here we all are, the way he saw us through his camera. I look more closely at the pictures than I ever did before.

Papa, rigid, staring straight at the camera. That wasn't him. He was stern and fun by turns, but never this still, this guarded as he is in this picture. And Mama. None of her intelligence got captured here. She didn't want her picture made, and she's looking to the side, when in life she could look anyone, Black or White, man or woman, straight in the eye without flinching.

Elijah. I look into this picture and I see the way he trusted Carter. His smile. He saved it only for those he loved. He didn't know he was looking at the person who could and would betray him. I can't bring myself to look at the picture of me.

None of these is how I remember them I loved. I leave the pictures to burn. I leave everything, walk toward the village.

As I near Elijah's family home, the town bells ring. The fire's about to jump the river. People pour out of their houses. Men run toward the new well or to the river below the falls, returning with buckets of useless water. Women and children run up the mountain on the other side of town.

Elijah's mama sees me.

Delia, she says, Thank the Lord. Come with me. The men'll save what they can.

I walk toward her. I fully intend to join her, to escape up the north mountain 'til it's safe, then come back to help rebuild the village. Maybe later head north to study teaching.

As I get close to Mrs. Ware, I see in her eyes that like everybody else, she has her own idea of who I am and what I should do. If I head north, them White abolitionists already decided what I would be as a Negro teacher, how they'd gain honor for themselves by giving me their knowledge.

I can't stay, I say.

Fire's coming, Delia, she says.

I'm headed west, I say.

Before she can protest, I turn away. I go on through the village, out of Sinking Springs. I know I got to avoid Nashville, I got to get out of Tennessee, out of Kentucky. The West is wild, I've heard. I'll find a place where no one's already decided what I can be. With every step my fears drop away. My heart fills with the music of the unknown.

Johnny Harpe

I can't leave Alva lying here. I can't take her into town neither; I'd surely be accused of her murder, and though it's my fault, it ain't no one's business to hang me but my own. I can't take her home for those little children to see neither. Better they think she just run off. I lift her from the river.

Water pours off her, back into the river, onto the bank, and into my clothes as I put her over my shoulder. I'm not even thinking where I'm going. I carry her 'til we come to the bridge the Yankees built during the war. Somehow no one thought to burn it.

We cross the bridge, climb.

We climb up the mountain 'til we reach the place, high up, where Miss Ellen told us an avalanche of snow once came down to bury her family.

I lower Alva onto the ground. I think to leave her here to nature, but it comes to me some animal, a panther or a bear could find her and tear her to pieces. And vultures, what I hate to this day, would finish off what was left of her. It would be dawn before I could get to a shovel and come back to bury her.

I take out the lighter I got off the man who took my arm and set my beautiful Alva on fire. As I leave, I say our prayer, and this time I remember it all:

*Round and round
Round in the ground
Round up to the sky
Round down to the river.
In the sap. In the roots.
Raising in the fires. Raising in the earth.
Blown down by the winds.
It lives. It dies. It rises. God.*

It comes to me Alva's fire will spread down the mountain.

Good then, I say to myself. Let it.

The voice of the preacher whispers inside my head: Those what belong in hell going to feel hell on earth.

I don't intend to burn in no earthly hell; I seen enough hell in life. If the only reason I survived is to die on my own terms, I accept that gift.

When I come up the path into my yard, Out of the Fog stands outside the barn door ready to help me. We go together into the darkness of the barn. Dust rises from our footsteps into the shadows as I search out the rope. It's a struggle to make a noose with one hand, but I do it, serviceable enough for its purpose. I throw it over the rafters. Then I climb on my horse, hope he'll obey, be willing to let me go. For a moment I sit there, feeling the rough rope around my neck, Out of the Fog's spine beneath me, his breathing against my legs. I close my eyes.

I remember the river, the birds, the grass, the flowers, the rain. I remember Alva. I remember Edmond. I touch my heart one last time to feel it beat. I kick my horse's flanks; he walks out from under me.

A song echoes through the barn:

Time moves forever.
All is forgiven.

Alva Calloway

I hear music as I walk toward where Johnny is. I know it's the spirit of Miss Ellen singing to me 'cause of Edmond teaching me to listen for it. It makes me feel blessed, makes me believe I'll find him. But this time the music don't stay a sweet melody like usual. It's more like them circus horns, all blasts and sharp edges. It builds in my ears 'til it hurts. It grows up like a wall of noise, and the closer I get to The Hammer and the Axe the harder it is to walk against it.

At the door, the music stops. My ears ring with the silence inside my head. Then there's the sound of men shouting at each other from inside, too loud, not joyful. A coldness and a darkness hover round about the building. I close my eyes, sing a prayer under my breath:

> *No cold can claim my heart*
> *No evil gathers in my soul*
> *I fill my hands with light*
> *Hold it gently, gently, gently*
> *Send evil back to its source.*

I see Johnny soon's I open the door. Sitting alone, his eyes focused on his drink. I go toward him, through the smells of sweat, dirt, and spilled whiskey. The men's voices rumble around me. Johnny don't look up 'til I'm standing directly in front of him. Go away Alva he says.

I can't, I say, 'Cause you're mad with me.

The men nearest me laugh. Their laughter mixes with the sour air.

Johnny, please won't you come outside, I say.

He tells me he's drinking. He tells me again to go away.

I try to touch him, but he jerks away like I'm poison.

The men laugh louder; I hear my words all 'round the room, a filthy echo: pleasepleaseplease.

I keep my eyes set on Johnny, I make my ears to only know his voice. Will you meet with me tomorrow I say. I'm praying with all my heart: Yesyesyestomorrow.

Get out, he shouts, Get out!

My heart pierced by his words, I run from the tavern. I run into the woods, toward the river. I jump over roots, push through laurel. I run until I am nearly at the place where Johnny, me, and Edmond made ceremonies. The flowers down here still glow in the moonlight like it's a fire inside them. Their high, lovely voices call to me. I run closer to them like they could actually warm me. My foot strikes a rock. Then I'm flying. I close my eyes.

When I open my eyes, water surrounds me, rays from the moon bending in the current. I can't find my voice. The water's so cold.

One by one, burning flowers fall onto my back. Their fires die as they absorb the cold of me.

The freezing water seeps into my skin. I understand now this river will kill me. Seems I've known all my life how I'd die. Me and Johnny and Edmond, we practiced my death in this very place so many times. I hold Johnny's name in my heart; I know my love makes the flower bushes above me burn red against the moon. I hold the red behind my eyelids as long as I can, but it don't take long for it to fade away. Then it's all darkness. I wonder where God is. Then I remember God is earth and air and bird: I have to wait to become them. I never thought I'd have my senses to feel it happen.

It don't hurt none.

I'd be glad to become part of this river what I've lived my whole life near to. To sink into the mud of its banks, let some pieces of me get drunk up by plants, some small pieces like tiny stars slip into the gills of fish. Give some parts to the crawdads, let some of me soak into rocks 'til I'm part of them, bright and hard, let part of me become the moss, too, soft and cool.

I'm growing into this new way to be when I sense something new. Sorrow. Mine? No. No, it's Johnny, finally come to find me. I can't feel him touch me, though I know he does. His pain and regret fill me. He wants forgiveness. Of course I forgive him. I wish I could feel my hand to reach out to comfort him.

Once again, I'm flying, Away from the river. High up the mountain, carried by the one I love most.

Johnny's sorrow hovers over me, hiding the moon and stars. It hurts him, but he lights the fire that will set me free. I rise through the flames and above them. I scatter into the sky and across the land. I float on the music of the river.

Now I understand what Edmond always known: we ain't nothing 'til we're earth, water, air, stars. 'Til we're all people, friend and enemy. 'Til we're bear, rabbit, fish, bird. 'Til we soar into the universe.

The Ballad of Ellen Bridge

Heather Jones

In the town of Sinking Springs
In the state of Tennessee
There lived a witch named Ellen Bridge
All hidden in the trees, O
All hidden in the trees

She lived in a cabin in the woods
Her eyes were icy blue
They say her singing could break hearts
And make the flowers grow, O
She made the flowers grow

But with all her magic ways
She spent her days alone
So she lured the children from town
She sang a haunted song, O
She sang a haunted song

She led them deep into the woods
Bewitching them to stay
They laughed and danced like never before
Thus passed a year and a day, O
Thus passed a year and a day

Then one night a preacher come
He rode to Tennessee
To catch that witch named Ellen Bridge
And set the children free, O
Set the children free

He rode atop a humble mule
He knew what he would do
He promised he would save the children
He swore his pledge was true, O
He swore his pledge was true

He rode into the mountains high
He rode so tall and fine
He found Witch Ellen deep in the woods
Dancing 'neath the pines, O
Dancing 'neath the pines

The preacher fell on bended knee
Told her he loved her eyes
He said her singing called him there
He said she smelled like roses, O
He said she smelled so sweet

Witch Ellen Bridge, she was beguiled
She believed the preacher's words
She pledged to him her lily hand
She thought his heart was true, O
She opened her cold heart

The preacher found the children then
He told them of the magic
Witch Ellen used to make them dance,
And told them they were tragic, O
They were lost and tragic

He told them of their parents' tears
He told them she was evil
Witch Ellen Bridge would steal their souls
Just like she stole their wills, O
She had stole their wills

The children thought the preacher lied
About their dear Miss Ellen
They swore she'd know about his false heart
They'd tell her in the morning, O
They'd tell her in the morning

Wait, O wait, the preacher cried
Until the full moon shines
You will see the truth of her
Right here 'neath the pines, O
Here beneath the pines

The children waited up that night
They hid amidst the trees
That's how they saw witch Ellen Bridge
Rise up in the sky, O
She rose up in the sky

Now they knew her for a witch
They joined up with the preacher
They bent their knees they said their prayers
They told him he should kill her, O
He should kill Witch Ellen

He told them he was here to help
But the spell was cast on them
They had to kill her by themselves
The preacher had a plan, O
The preacher had a plan

Now Miss Ellen loves me true
I'll lure her to the well
While she's waiting for a kiss
You push her in the well, O
Push her in the well

The preacher went to Ellen's door
He begged her sneak away
Let's go to the well beyond the woods
Just let the children play, O
Let the children play

She said yes because she thought
Her spell would hold them there
She went with the preacher trustingly
While combing her black hair, O
Combing her black hair

The children followed through the woods
Witch Ellen didn't see
She was blinded by the preacher's lies
She was happy as can be, O
Happy as can be

Heather Jones

With her back against the well
her rosy lips on his
There the preacher held her fast
Although he feared her kiss, O
The poison of her kiss

The children burst out from the woods
They rushed o'er to the well
They took Witch Ellen by surprise
They pushed her and she fell, O
She fell into the well

Before she died Witch Ellen Bridge
She cast an evil spell
To take the preacher down with her
Down into the well, O
He plunged into the well

From the darkness Ellen Bridge
She spoke her final curse
That when they found their own true loves
Their tender hearts would burst, O
Their loving hearts would hurt

That when they had all lost their loves
Their curse would bring a fire
All across the mountain top
Burning tree and briar, O
Burning tree and briar

The fire would rage through Sinking Springs
Burn every house and home
Then Sinking Springs would disappear
Their story would be done, O
Their story would be done

By the preacher's sacrifice
Witch Ellen Bridge was gone
So they ran to Sinking Springs
Were welcomed in their homes, O
The children all ran home

They all forgot Witch Ellen Bridge
Forgot they had been cursed
Each of them found their true love
And all their loves were fierce, O
The way they loved was fierce

As soon as they gave their hearts
The terrible days began
One killed his love by the riverside
To prove himself a man, O
To prove he was a man

He picked a rock up off the ground
He smashed it in her head
She begged of him to spare her life
I cannot stop he cried, O
I have to take your life

Another lover took his knife
And cut his lover's throat
And as she bled and died in tears
He gave up all his hope, O
He gave up all his hope

Another lover found a stick
Beat his true love to the ground
Then he fell upon her breast
His sobs were heard miles round, O
His sobs heard miles around

One had supper with her love
She fed him poisoned fish
While he watched he sicked and died
She cursed that wretched witch, O
She cursed that wretched witch

The last one shot her lover dead
With her father's gun
She went with him to walk one night
She shot him 'neath the moon, O
He died 'neath the full moon

And as these murderous lovers cried
About the crimes they'd done
The mountainside burst into flames
The curse was almost done,
O The fire had begun.

Selected Works Consulted

Adams, Michael C. *Living Hell: The Dark Side of the Civil War.* Johns Hopkins University Press; Baltimore, 2016.

Andersonville: Giving Up the Ghost: A Collection of Prisoners' Diaries, Letters, & Memoirs. Eds. William Styple et al. Belle Grove Publishing Company; Kearney, NJ, 1996.

Ballard, Byron. *Staubs and Ditchwater: A Friendly and Useful Introduction to Hillfolks' Hoodoo.* Silver Ring Press, 2012.

Berry, Stephen, Ed. *Weirding the War: Stories from the Civil War's Ragged Edges.* The University of Georgia Press; Athens, Georgia, 2011.

Campbell, Carlos C., Robert W. Hutson, William F. Hutson, Aaron J. Sharp. *Great Smoky Mountain Wildflowers: When and Where to Find Them,* 5th ed. Windy Pines Publishing LLC; Northbrook, IL, 1995.

Catte, Elizabeth. *What You are Getting Wrong about Appalachia.* Belt Publishing; Cleveland, Ohio, 2018.

Child, Francis James. *English and Scottish Ballads.* Little, Brown & Company; Boston, 1857.

Drake, Brian Allen, Ed. *The Blue, The Gray, and The Green: Toward an Environmental History of the Civil War.* The University of Georgia Press; Athens, Georgia, 2015.

Dunaway, Wilma A. *Slavery in The American Mountain South.* Cambridge University Press; Cambridge, United Kingdom, 2003.

Faust, Drew Gilpin. *This Republic of Suffering: Death and the American Civil War.* Vintage Books; New York, 2009.

Groce, W. Todd. *Mountain Rebels: East Tennessee Confederates and the Civil War, 1860-1870.* The University of Tennessee Press; Knoxville, 1999.

Manning, Chandra. *What This Cruel Was Over: Soldiers, Slavery, and the Civil War.* Vintage; New York, 2007.

McCutcheon, Marc. *Everyday Life in the 1800s: A Guide for Writers, Students & Historians.* Writers Digest Books; Cincinnati, Ohio, 1993.

McKenzie, Robert Tracy. *Lincolnites and Rebels: A Divided Town in the American Civil War.* Oxford University Press; New York, 2006.

McPherson, James M. *The Negro's Civil War: How American Blacks Felt and Acted During the War for The Union.* Vintage; New York, 2003.

Miller, Brian Craig. *Empty Sleeves: Amputation in the Civil War South.* The University of Georgia Press; Athens, Georgia, 2015.

Nelson, Megan Kate. *RuinNation: Destruction and the American Civil War.* *The University of Georgia Press*; Athens, Georgia, 2012.

Porcher, Francis Peyer and Confederate States OF America Surgeon General's Office. *Resources of the Southern Fields and Forests, Medical, Economical, And Agricultural.* N.P; N.D.

Ritchie, Fiona, & Doug Orr. *Wayfaring Strangers: The Musical Voyage from Scotland and Ulster to Appalachia.* The University of North Carolina Press; Chapel Hill, 2014.

Robertson, James. *The Untold Civil War: Exploring the Human Side of War.* Neil Kagan, ed. National Geographic; Washington, DC, N.D

Rutkow, Ira M. *Bleeding Blue and Gray: Civil War Surgery and the Evolution of Medicine.* Random House; New York, 2005.

Shields, A. Randolph. *The Cades Cove Story.* Great Smoky Mountains Association; Gatlinberg, TN, 1981.

Slap, Andrew L. *Reconstruction Appalachia: The Civil War's Aftermath.* The University Press of Kentucky; Lexington, Kentucky, 2010.

Smith, Mark M. *The Smell of Battle, The Taste of Siege: A Sensory History of The Civil War.* Oxford University Press; New York, 2015.

Zeller, Bob. *The Blue and Gray in Black and White: A History of Civil War Photography.* Praeger; Westport, Connecticut, 2005

About the Author

Heather Jones grew up listening to her father sing murder ballads. She raised her own children in Western North Carolina, and regularly returns to visit.

Heather's plays include "The Hoarder's Child," which won the award for "Most Inspirational Work" at the Asheville Fringe Festival, and *My Unspeakable Confessions, Gala Dali Declines to Explain Herself*, which has recurrent productions at The Dali Museum in St Petersburg, Florida. Her plays, fiction, and poetry have been published in literary magazines including *The Louisville Review*, *Cartagena Journal*, *Cleaver*, and *Sawgrass*.

Heather holds a B.A. in Literature from University of North Carolina at Asheville, and an MFA in Writing from the Naslund- Mann Graduate School of Writing at Spalding University, Louisville, KY.

She currently teaches writing at University of South Florida.

Learn more about Heather at Unfoldedwriting.com